The Hidden Depths of Love

By

A. L. Smith

MAPLE
PUBLISHERS

The Hidden Depths of Love

Author: A. L. Smith

Copyright © A. L. Smith (2021)

The right of A. L. Smith to be identified as author of this work has been asserted by the author in accordance with section 77 and 78 of the Copyright, Designs and Patents Act 1988.

First Published in 2021

ISBN 978-1-914366-65-9 (Paperback)
     978-1-914366-66-6 (Ebook)

Book layout & Cover Designed by:
    White Magic Studios
    www.whitemagicstudios.co.uk

Published by:
    Maple Publishers
    1 Brunel Way,
    Slough,
    SL1 1FQ, UK
    www.maplepublishers.com

A CIP catalogue record for this title is available from the British Library.

The views expressed in this work are solely those of the author and do not necessarily reflect the views of the publisher, and the publisher hereby disclaims any responsibility for them.

Acknowledgments

The acknowledgements go to my family, especially my mum and Bob dad who have spent many hours proof-reading, editing, taking my phone calls and the raw end of my stress but taking enjoyment of this journey with me. I couldn't have done it without you both. Here's to the next novel!

I would also like to thank Dale for being so supportive at the start of this journey, the endless takeaways and enduring my hours of sitting at the laptop.

I'd also like to thank my friends for reading the manuscript and for giving their honest feedback, you know who you are.

Lastly, to my incredible daughter, who has been patient and understanding throughout journey. Mummy loves you Bella.

Biography

I was a girl who detested school and didn't particularly enjoy reading. It seems incredible that I have now entered the world of writing. Having not picked up a book until I was eighteen, I began reading romance novels, and thoroughly enjoyed them. After all, who doesn't enjoy a love story!

After several years of enjoying this genre, I decided to give writing a go, initially it was just a hobby and I didn't really see it going anywhere. Thankfully with the encouragement of my family and friends they pushed me into taking my novel further.

My life is quite ordinary, I am a hairdresser by trade and a single working mother. I started this novel several years ago and decided to pick it back up again after the second lockdown began. When I started writing this novel, it was in the traditional form of pen and paper. I only ever invested in a laptop for my daughter's home schooling. It was the use of a laptop that sparked completing the novel. I hope you enjoy reading my novel as much as I have writing it.

Prologue

Ava blindly runs down the stairs at high speed, breathless and panting. She can hear the words coming from behind her.

"Don't you dare run from me Ava May!" He shouts from the top of the stairs. Ava stands at the kitchen worktop and runs the tap, rinsing her face with ice cold water, trying to calm her anxiety. He thuds down the stairs and storms through to the kitchen with a red angry face.

"I said don't dare try and run from me Ava!"

"I don't have anything to say to you," she whispers, staring out of the kitchen window at the dull drizzly day. The tears are falling from her eyes and a pain is rising in her chest.

"You, Ava, you won't make *me* feel guilty, we are married and as *my* wife we share *all* our assets!" stepping forward to invade her personal space to intimidate her.

"You!" Ava spins round to face his fierce eyes.

"You stole from me! You took *my* bank card and made a withdrawal of *my* money, without asking me, *again*!" she screams at him.

"Yeah, I did! And what the hell are *you* going to do about it, Ava?"

"Screw you, Richard!" as she tries to get past him, he pulls her by her hair and pins her against the wall. He pushes his face within inches of hers and she can see the hatred burning in his eyes as he says without feeling.

"You *DO NOT* tell me what I can and cannot do. Do you hear me?" as he shoves her small body against the wall even harder. Ava turns her face away from his large, blackened pupils, she can feel a real fear within her whole body for the very first time. Ava is scared of the man she is married to and she is scared for her life!

Richard removes his powerful hold of her and makes for the exit, leaving her alone slamming the door behind him with great force. She is left not knowing when he will return again. Richard can be gone for days at a time. Ava is left shaking and pacing the house. What is she to do?

"Harry, bring the car and come get me, please?" Ava asks on the phone. She hangs up.

Chapter One

Ava's stomach is doing somersaults. Is it fear or anticipation as the Bentley pulls into the drop off point at the airport? She is positive that she has everything from her dollar bills to her favourite pyjamas. Making sure she has picked up her passport and tickets off the passenger's seat and placing them in her handbag, she is ready.

"Would you please wait here while I see her right in, Harry?" says her mother in a firm but kind manner. Ava hugs Harry and says her goodbyes.

"Good luck Ava and take care, my darlin." Harry whispers in her ear whilst hugging her back.

It is dark and it is hard for Ava to take in her mother's beauty. The choking feeling in her throat is getting stronger now, as she grabs her suitcase from the Bentley. Harry shuts the boot and sits back in the car to wait. Her mother Florence is so calm, and Ava admires her mother for that trait, only it wasn't one she had inherited.

"Okay, young lady are you ready?" Florence asks as she takes her daughter's case and makes her way towards the Departure's entrance.

The bright yellow signs are glowing which, when seeing them, normally heightens Ava's excitement in the pit of her stomach, usually knowing she's off on her holidays. On this occasion, however, Ava doesn't feel excited but nervous as this wasn't a holiday, it is far more than that for her. Her big brown eyes look more fearful than excited as they step through the automatic doors.

"Ava, darling, don't look so worried, sweetheart. This is going to be the best time of your life!" Her mother tries to say as enthusiastically as she can.

Ava can really see her mother's beauty in the bright, almost clinical, artificial lights. Her long dark hair looks slightly unbrushed, when usually her hair is well kept and neat. Her big, chocolate button eyes were clearly filled with so much love. Her olive skin looks slightly aged, but she has the biggest, warmest smile. Ava hugs her petite mother as tightly as she can.

"Love you mum," she says through the hidden tears.

Ava is taller than her mother and of a bigger build too. She carries many of her mother's looks, but she has her father's button nose. Brushing the hair off of Ava's face, Florence looks saddened by her daughter's departure. This isn't a holiday. Ava is off to America, to start a new life.

Hugging one for another longer than usual, Ava shuts her eyes tight ignoring the tannoy announcements and the bustling noise of her busy surroundings. She enjoys her mother's affections and embeds the smell of her mother's perfume into her memory. Ava knows this would be the last time she would see her mother for a long while.

"I love you too baby girl. Now go, enjoy, be free and live your life! This Ava is all about you. You truly deserve this. I'm so proud of you. Now what do the Yanks say? Call me when you get to your apartment?" She slides back into an English voice, from her attempt at an American accent. "Now on this occasion you can talk to strangers, well, apart from weird ones, or the homeless or the ones who hang out at the subways or -" Ava interrupts abruptly. "Okay, mum, I get it. Don't talk to random looking men, predominantly who look like they could murder someone or worse, me!" Ava is beyond sarcastic now, her arms flying all over the place as she becomes exasperated, by her mother's vivid imagination beyond their little hometown in Suffolk.

Without any further hesitation, Ava steps onto the escalator as it ascends up to the main floor of the airport. This is it. She is doing it, starting her new life, on her own without the support of her immediate family.

Florence watches as her daughter is moving further and further away. Ava stares back at her mother and waves, then turns and faces towards her new future. Florence wipes the tears away from her cheeks, takes a deep breath and turns away abruptly, pulling her shoulders back and walks towards the exit. Her thirty-year-old daughter is heading for adulthood for the first time.

The cold air hits her face with a sting as she heads back to the Bentley. January weather is never pleasant in the UK, but the last week has been colder than she remembers in a long time. As Florence opens the door of the car she looks back at the automatic doors once more in the hope that Ava has changed her mind. Florence sighs, climbs in and shuts the door.

"Thank you Harry." she whispers.

"That's okay, Flo. Did she get off okay? Not too emotional for you both, I hope?" He pauses, "You know if Geoff were 'ere, he'd be so proud of her. Well, of all the girls he always knew she was destined for more than just little ole Suffolk. My Mable always said it too!" Florence stares out of the window at the cold night as they pull away.

"I know he did," she whispers under her breath with a pang of pain in the memory of her beloved Geoff.

"How is dear Mable? I hope she is well?" Florence asks.

"She is indeed, thank ya for askin."

Harry is the loyal and long-term family chauffeur of the Turner family, and has been for over forty years. After Geoff's passing a few years earlier, he remains close to Florence and her four daughters, Clare, Katelyn, Ava and Lydia. After all, he had been employed by Geoff and still plays a massive part in all their lives.

As the escalator comes to its end, Ava steps off and wheels her suitcase off behind her. Then she takes the deepest breath. She's standing bewildered at her large, open and busy surroundings and hears the tannoys announcing that 'any unaccompanied luggage will be removed and destroyed'. Ava listens to the people around her talking, laughing, children screaming and playing. There she stands taking it all in. Finally, she looks at all the check in desks. Air India, KLM, Emirates, and finally with a rather large queue is British Airways flight number EWR014. Ava goes to the front pouch of her Mulberry handbag and grabs her ticket. There it sits, in big bold writing EWR014. The anxiety rising like a wave in the pit of her stomach and her heart beats faster. Is it excitement, she isn't sure. This is her queue. She gets in line with the rest of the passengers. It is a tedious task waiting for your turn to check in your luggage, especially when you are alone.

After a long wait Ava steps forward to the desk not feeling her most radiant. She had to start this journey by waking in the middle of the night, not shy of 1 a.m. to be exact, and travelled 150 miles. Comfort is more important than style for her travels. So it is grey jogging bottoms, a baggy cream woollen jumper and stylish trainers. Her hair is freshly washed but tied up in a top bun and not a scrap of makeup. She stands before a well-groomed, pristine check in assistant called Dulcie with a porcelain dolly look, wearing an ecstatic expression on her face making Ava feel incredibly inadequate. Handing over her passport and ticket to the assistant, she is asked in a harsh Essex accent to put her suitcase on the weighing scales. Now, she must make her way through the security checkpoint, so she takes a big, deep breath preparing herself for the next stage of her journey.

⸺◈⸺

Chapter Two

I t is half-way through the flight and Ava is starting to feel rather exhausted. She had the money to go First Class but thought going economy would be okay. How wrong she feels now!

On one side of her is an overweight man. He is American, whose bald head is sweating with beads running down his forehead. He is using both the armrests on either side, one being Ava's, and laughing loudly at whatever he is watching. Every time Ava drops off into a light sleep his bellowing laugh startles her, making her feel even more irritated. On the other side of her is a charming enough older lady, but she is talkative, too talkative for Ava at this time of the day after a lack of sleep.

The lady is in her mid to late sixties and is tall and slender. It is obvious that she loves the latest fashion by her personal appearance. She proceeds to tell Ava her life story. Pamela is an American woman who has grown up in Fort Montgomery, New York. Her husband has passed away and she was visiting her daughter, Evelyn, in the UK. Evelyn has married a British man who is in fact a doctor.

Ava has the sudden need to stretch her legs as she is starting to get cabin fever. Having never been keen on flying, she interrupts Pamela's book reading.

'Sorry, would you mind if I squeezed past, please?" Ava questions.

"Oh! Of course, sure, let me get out of your way!" Pamela says grabbing her bag and steps into the aisle to let Ava out.

Ava makes her way up the aisle, all too relieved to be out of that confined space. She reaches the toilet cubicle, and it is already in use. Ava stands daydreaming, almost in disbelief of her own actions. In the genuine disbelief that she is on a Boeing 747 aircraft by herself and she can hear the cabin crew rattling around behind the curtain preparing the refreshments and snack trolleys. Ava is alarmed by the door swinging open right into her, causing her to stumble. She is confronted by a handsome, blonde, clean shaven man.

"Well, fancy standing right in front of the door, m'am!" he says rather sarcastically. His eyes as blue as the ocean glare at her.

"Well, I'm sorry, there isn't exactly much room on this Boeing 747!" Ava retaliates, trying not to get lost in his eyes.

"I'm sorry, m'am, I was trying to be funny," he replies and searches for eye contact.

The hostess steps out from the curtain, "everything okay, Madam? Sir?"

"Fine!" Ava admits, "just, fine!" She steps into the toilet shutting the door in a temper!

The blonde man has unsettled her, uncoiled her insides and those eyes have disarmed her. Ava thinks to herself, "Who does he think he is? He doesn't know me. We're stuck in an aircraft at 30,000 feet, for goodness sake!" She flushes the toilet, washes her hands and she carefully opens the door. Looking back at the mirror she says to her reflection, "Bloody m'am!" Her head down she makes her way back to her seat.

"Sorry Pamela, it's me again," Ava interrupts.

The overweight guy is still laughing at his screen. Ava's fury builds at this again.

"Hi, can I have my arm rest, please?" Ava says curtly.

The fat American replies, "Yeah, sure, why not?" Continuing to stare at his screen and Ava rolls her eyes at him in irritation.

A voice announces over the tannoy "Ladies and gentlemen, this is your captain speaking, if you could put your seatbelts on until further notice. We have hit some turbulence. Thank you." And then the seatbelt sign pings on above their heads.

"Great!" Ava huffs.

"I get the impression you don't like flying?" Pamela notices, while flicking through her magazine.

"You know, Pamela, you're right, I don't, and I haven't flown in years, and even when I did I flew with my husband."

"Oh, you're married?" Pamela asks.

"I was married. I'm not anymore," Ava settles back into her seat and as she starts to drift off she thinks of the last time she had been on holiday. It was four years ago and that was with Richard. They went to Athens, Greece. Ava had hated the amount of homeless people that lived on the streets. She vividly remembers seeing a homeless heroin addict jacking up in a shop doorway and it had haunted her afterwards for days. Richard, on the other hand hadn't seemed bothered by the ordeal and couldn't understand why Ava was so affected by it. She finally falls asleep.

Ava wakes with a startle. It is 3:30 a.m. Ava sits up and checks his side of the bed. It is empty and the house is silent. Ava stumbles out of bed half asleep and grabs her dressing gown off the back of the bedroom door. She creeps downstairs, into the hall and slowly tiptoes towards the office.

He's not there.

The office is crammed with novels and geography books and there is a large desk filled with paperwork and a laptop. There is a small green desk lamp giving a very soft lighting. She walks over to the laptop to see if he has been working late again but it's off.

Where is he?

Ava walks down a long hallway to the kitchen. The kitchen light is off but there is a cool summer night breeze coming from the patio doors and she strolls towards the garden. As she strides out onto the large wilderness at the back of the garden he spots her.

"Ava baby, what are you doing up?" He slurs.

"Richard, what are you doing out here?" she asks gently.

"Having a whiskey, come and join me?" swirling the rich golden liquid around in his glass tumbler.

"It's 3:30 a.m. Rich, come to bed?" She pleads.

"Oh come on Ava, join me we can watch the sunrise and have a drink together?" Richard tries to persuade.

"I don't want to, Richard, I'm going back to bed." she looks down and wraps herself tighter in her dressing gown.

"Don't forget to lock up," and she turns back towards the house.

"Don't be so boring, Ava! You always look at me in such disgust!" He hisses, back in retaliation.

Ava mutters under her breath, "Because you repulse me when you drink!"

Clenching her fists either side of her as she traces her steps back to their bedroom. She climbs back into bed and lays there for a while. A tear rolls down her face. She is sexually attracted to her husband. She knows that much, but is it love? She isn't sure anymore.

Richard is a very attractive man. He has rich dark hair, with darkest lashes to match and the bluest of eyes, those that should belong to a husky dog. He is a well-built muscular man with broad shoulders and he has the whitest smile and manly hands. Short stubble on his face meant he was too busy to shave.

Ava is finally asleep when Richard retires to bed. She faces one way and he faces the other. Ava and Richard have been married a long six years but been together for nine. Some very good times and some not so good. The question is, can their marriage be saved? Or is it going to get worse? Only time will tell.

Ava stirs from her dream, her eyes are heavy as she lifts her eyelids.

Pamela soothes, "We're about to land, I didn't mean to make ya jump."

Ava sits up and goes to put her seatbelt on, but it's still on from earlier. She realises she has been asleep for a long while. She rubs her eyes trying to wake herself up. She dreamt of him. She kicks herself internally.

"I've been asleep for a long while. I hope I didn't snore?" she giggles to Pamela.

After the aircraft lands, and she has gone through passport control, Ava waits for her luggage. It's 9 a.m. Eastern Time. There is a sea of people swarming around like bees, occupied with their own activities. Arriving from their trips away or now leaving for their holidays, families travelling or those going alone. Ava is so transfixed on people-watching that she hasn't noticed that the man from the toilet scenario was standing right next to her. Leaning forward to collect her suitcase from the continuously circling conveyor belt, they brush shoulders.

"Oh gosh, sorry...I'm so sorry!" Exclaims Ava.

Both make their apologies to one another at the same time. With a nervous laugh, Ava stares into the man's eyes as she is attracted by the colour of them, so much so, that all the anger subsides from their earlier incident. She refocuses her thoughts, shakes her head knowing that her face is flushing like it's sunburnt.

"I must be going. I have somebody waiting for me," she runs on and in the blink of an eye Ava has gone, disappearing into the crowd like a turtle into the sea.

"It's okay," he pauses, "no need to worry!" He says so quietly, taken aback by her brisk exit.

Ava makes her way through the JFK airport. She is overwhelmed by the size of it, and how much quieter it gets as she approaches the arrivals exit.

The exhaustion suddenly hits her from her travelling from GMT time to Eastern Time.

Ava mutters to herself, "Okay, right Ava, don't panic. Look for a black Ultra Sudan. The man will be holding a board with your name on it!" She begins to stroll down the con-course looking at the parked vehicles and those driving past. She sees a black vehicle ahead of her, and a chauffeur standing with a board.

"Ava Turner?" The man calls.

"That's me! My uncle James has this car arranged for me!" she confirms.

"That's right, Miss Turner. Let me take your case for you?"

Ava clambers into the back of the sleek car, shutting the door and puts her seatbelt on. Ava feels all too relieved to have a helping hand to get to her new apartment. It is a forty-minute drive to where she needs to be, so she can relax and enjoy the journey.

The driver is smartly dressed. White crisp shirt, black suit, and shiny footwear. He is in his early fifties, with short salt and pepper hair, dark eyes, and fairly tall and slim.

The driver makes general small talk. 'What brings you to the States? How long are you staying?' Ava gives only short answers. She's beyond small talk and making friends. She needs food and sleep. Before anything else a shower is required, or better still - a long soak in the bath, if there is one.

Ava had never flown for more than four hours and has never experienced jetlag. It has come as a short, sharp shock. Settling in the back to enjoy the rest of her journey.

The sedan pulls to a halt on 34th Street in front of a tall glass high-rise building. The driver gets out of the car and walks round to let Ava out. She steps out and looks up at the towering building and gasps.

"This is just how I imagined. It's just like in the films." She beams at the driver.

"Make your way up Miss Turner, and I'll bring your luggage," as he opens the boot of the car.

Ava walks up to the entrance. It has its own doorman, who opens the door to her. It is all too much, stunning in fact. A pristine building standing in its own elegance, the reflection of the clouds in the sky gliding across the glass.

As she walks inside the lobby she sees that it has a double-height ceiling. It's enormous with white marble walls and floors, and it's incredibly spacious. The chandelier, again, is elegant, beautiful and breath-taking. The whole feel of the lobby is contemporary, and it subsides all of Ava's anxiety. The seating area is filled with four, white-backed directors' chairs. An immaculate white and chrome coffee table sits in the middle of the waiting area, ready to be used.

A flower display stands in the corner, fresh and outstandingly displayed. Ava can see white Japanese lilies, her favourite.

She walks over to the reception desk. The whole lobby is empty except for one man who stands before her.

The man is in his late forties, not the most attractive, but his charcoal suit is very stylish, and extremely well-fitted around his shoulders and chest.

"Good morning. Welcome to the city New York, Miss Turner. I'm Mr Truman and I'm head of security here, at Pedro House," remaining stiff and professional, he does not gain eye contact but instead keeps a steady eye on the screen in front of him. He swivels on his heels to a locked cupboard behind him. It has the keys to all of the apartments in Pedro House, there are hundreds. He peels back the several layers of panels in the cabinet like pages of a book. He finally reaches Ava's floor, grabs a set of keys, shuts the key cabinet, locking it and turns to face her again.

"These are your keys, you're on the eleventh floor, room 1107."

Ava stands there, completely shell-shocked. How does the head of security know who she is? He hasn't given her a chance to speak and he is now handing her a set of keys without asking for any identification.

Ava composes herself to ask what she feels could be a ridiculous question.

· "I'm sorry, Mr Truman? Did you say...?" She pauses, "How did you know that I am Miss Turner?" He cuts her off, "Miss Turner," gaining her eye contact "I am the head of security. You look exhausted and '*your driver*' is Mr James Turner's personal chauffeur. He is outside talking to our doorman carrying '*your*' case. This is Mr Turner's building and my job is to be vigilant on who comes and goes from this building and it's also my job to make every person my business," he says powerfully.

Ava's jaw drops. She goes to reply and thinks it wise to just take the keys and say nothing else. She can feel her face reddening from embarrassment.

"If you would follow me please, Miss Turner?" He says swiftly.

"Of course," she nods, saying nothing more.

Never being good with her words and not knowing when to be quiet has always been Ava's flaw. She was forever getting herself into trouble at school for always speaking out of turn, and as she has grown into an adult she has learnt when enough is enough. She remembers a memory of telling her dad when she had misbehaved as a teenager and playing up in class. He had been furious with her childish behaviour, and had banished Ava to her room along with Lydia who too found the story funny.

Walking from behind the desk, Ava notices that Mr Truman is actually more well-built than she first thought. He has a stern aura about him and a man not to argue with. She follows him quickly and quietly to the lifts across the lobby. Mr Truman presses the 'call' button. Still looking ahead, he declares, "Pedro House offers a host of amenities to its residents. We have a commercial lounge, gym, two outdoor oases, an urban garden, and a rooftop deck with, I must say, a stunning city view. You have access to all of these. Any questions?"

They step into the lift and turn to face the closing door. Ava is feeling quite foolish. She looks at all the floor digits in the lift, watching Mr Truman press the '11' button.

"So have you worked for my uncle for long?" She asks, trying to make conversation with the mysterious man. There is a deathly silence as the lift ascends upwards.

After what seems a lifetime, they arrive on Ava's floor. They walk along a clean, bright, fresh hallway until they approach a door numbered 1107. Mr Truman opens the door with the key and holds it open to Ava.

She strolls through and is instantly drawn to the full glass fronted view of New York City.

The view is astonishing, of high-rise buildings, each with unique architecture, something Ava has never seen before. It truly takes her breath away. The skyline looks incredible yet Ava can see each individual building standing out. Every structure is different. Some are oblique, some completely tower over others. She can see the spires vividly, the materials used on each building are different yet they come together harmoniously. The bold and noble buildings stand alongside the classical original buildings, fitting together like a glove to a hand. The view looks like a canvas or a photo.

"Will there be anything else Miss Turner?"

Although Ava was accustomed to this lifestyle as a child, she rebelled against her wealthy background as soon as she hit her teenage years. She passed her driving test at seventeen and purchased her own car with the money she earned babysitting and working at an American style restaurant in a neighbouring town. She turned her back on the wealth and all that came with it. The treatment she had received from her estranged uncle was alien to her.

"No. No, Thank you, Mr Truman. You've been most helpful." He makes his way to the exit. "The driver will be up with your belongings shortly," he turns back to inform Ava.

The room is breathtaking. Outside the windows, the sky is beginning to clear off the fluffy clouds and a bright blue is beginning to appear. Ava slides the glass door across to reveal the bitterly cold New York air. She takes in the deepest breath and shuts her eyes. Is this what freedom feels like? Ava is enjoying her balcony view, but a knock at the door interrupts her trail of thought. She returns to her apartment and slides the door shut. She makes her way across the apartment when the door sounds. She opens it to be greeted by the driver, and her uncle James.

It has been many years since she has seen her uncle. He strides in and grasps Ava in his arms, and gives her a bear hug.

"Ava! Welcome to New York City! How was your journey? You must be exhausted. I hope you like the apartment?" Her uncle fires so many questions, Ava doesn't have a chance to answer the first before he fires the next.

"Uncle James! Hi! Yeah, exhausted, journey was okay. Mum and Harry took me to the airport, I must tell her I've arrived, actually," she reminds herself.

"No need, I've made your mother aware of your arrival, now you must rest. The fridge is full of food, and I made sure the heating was on for your arrival." He steps towards her again, and holds the top of her arms gently, kisses her forehead, and turns to the driver and asks him to leave the case.

"Very well," the driver concurs, and he leaves, shutting the door behind him.

James turns his attention back to Ava, "Now, is there anything else I can get you my darling?" he asks.

"No thank you, I need to get some rest. The travelling has taken it out of me!"

Ava sees her uncle out, thanks him again for all he has done and shuts the door.

She returns to the view of the open plan apartment, where the bright white furniture in the grey room sets a relaxing ambience, and there is a glass coffee table that stands on a deep tread, dark grey rug which is between the television and the grey cotton velvet couch. She stands for a moment and begins to laugh to herself. She's in New York City. Cupping her face, she realises that she has made the biggest decision of her life - leaving the UK and starting afresh. Ava puts the television on for some background noise. The channel Fox News is broadcasting the daily news updates. The kitchen area is lit with numerous bright spotlights that are set into the ceiling. She opens the gleaming white cupboards to be greeted with American snacks, crisps and candy bars. She turns to the American style graphite fridge and opens it. Yoghurts, apple juice, fruit as well as other perishables and wine are staring at her. She decides she isn't hungry.

The bathroom is a large space. The walls are Napoli stone resin with a roll top tub standing in the centre of the room. There is a white buff vanity cabinet with a light glowing underneath it. There are candles scattered around the room. Looking in all the cabinets, there is everything she needs. She starts to draw a bath. The smell of lavender fills the bathroom air, and the steam wafts around her as the tub fills. She sits on the edge and stirs it every now and then, making sure the temperature is right for her.

After a long soak, Ava climbs into the king-sized bed and nestles down for a well-deserved rest. It may well only be 12:30 p.m. but she feels exhausted. Her eyes grow heavy and Ava drifts into a deep sleep.

"You have got to stop this, Rich!" she yells as he lays paralytic on the bathroom floor.

"Ava Burton, if you were any kind of wife, you'd give me what I want!" he hisses, as he is unable to control his limbs.

"Richard, you are out of control!" Ava says, in a raised voice. She leaves him sprawled on the floor, drifting in and out of consciousness. Flying down the stairs, and grabbing her coat and the car keys from the sideboard, she heads out of the door.

Ava arrives at her sister's house, frantically knocking at the door in tears. Clare opens the door, and Ava thrusts herself in her sister's arms, crying hysterically.

They sit in the kitchen drinking coffee, it's 2:30 a.m. Ava wipes her tears with the sleeve of her pyjamas.

"You can't keep living like this, Ava!" Clare protests. "He is going to be the death of you, sis!" shaking her head at her younger sister, whilst pouring more coffee.

Ava cries some more. Her cheeks are flushed and soaked from all the crying she has been doing.

"I know Clare, I'm trying my best, I can't just leave!!" she mutters.

"WHY, WHY CAN'T YOU!" Clare shouts!

"Because, I'm," she pauses, "weak and feeble, Clare." Ava whispers whilst trying to hold back the tears.

They sit in silence. Clare walks around the island in the large kitchen and holds her sister tight while she sobs. Clare's husband appears at the door shrugging his shoulders. She shakes her head and nods for him to go back to bed mouthing "Don't."

This isn't the first time Ava has banged down the door to her sister's enormous house out in the sticks. It's become more and more regular over the last six months. The more Richard drinks, the more Ava flees the marital home.

"You can kip on the couch Ava," Clare says, staring at her sister's broken expression.

Ava lies on the large brown leather studded chesterfield sofa and shuts her eyes.

Ava bolts upright from her sleep. She is sodden with sweat from her dream. Why is she dreaming of Richard? Is it guilt from her change of life? Is this punishment for wanting to be free, for wanting a new beginning? Leaping out of bed she runs through the living area of her apartment. She is disorientated from her dream. It is dark. She checks the clock on the oven, 5 p.m. The sunset was at 4:30 p.m. She already misses the daylight.

Ava walks to the kitchen, flings open a cupboard, and slides a glass out of the cupboard and runs the tap. A cold glass of water is a necessity. She sits on the sofa and flicks the widescreen TV on. Ava is trying to decipher her dream, she sits blankly staring at the screen. It was no good, she couldn't shake the cold feeling her dreams had left her with. She picks up the phone from the glass coffee table. She flicks through to a name, clicks on it and it dials. "Hello, Ava, is that you? How are you?" they pause, "Is everything okay? Why are you calling me?" the voice says. She hangs up.

Chapter Three

"Thank you so much for your time," Michael says appreciatively, shaking the manager's hand.

"You're welcome Mr Johnson, we look forward to seeing you start here 'At the Deli'." Mario replies. Having landed himself a job so quickly on his return to New York, he goes to leave.

'At the Deli' is a family run business, and Mario is the nephew of the Mexican boss. It's a popular place for New York workers to choose. One side of the deli is a sit in service and on the other side is a take-out option. They offer a wide range of foods like cakes made by Camilia, the wife of the owner, and of course, there are also wraps, sandwiches, and soups on a winter's day.

One counter is full of cheesecakes, caramel sponge cakes and rich chocolate cakes. The aroma of freshly made coffee lingers in the air. There are bags of fresh coffee beans sitting in hessian bags by the door and the tables are laid out for four diners with a menu sitting in the centre of each. Before Michael exits, he looks back at the hustle and bustle behind the counter and smiles.

As Michael walks up 34th West, the crazy English woman from the flight crosses his mind. Why did she intrigue him so much? Michael has been single for such a short time after his long-term relationship ended, back in England.

Michael was born and bred in New York with Albany being his hometown. His mother and grandparents still live there, but he has decided to crash on his friend's couch in Queens until he has saved enough to get back on his feet. He enjoys the energy of the city itself, and rarely sees the same face twice. Michael hasn't had it easy being a failed architect back in the UK, and it's come hard to him, returning to the US.

As Michael walks, the icy air hits his face with a sting as he strolls along, through the blocks of New York, reminiscing over his life of the past ten years. The way of life in England was familiar because Cambridge had become his home. It feels strange for Michael to be back in the States, he feels he has changed, but New York hasn't. He wraps his scarf around his neck tighter and stuffs his hands in his pockets.

As Michael turns the corner, he flags a yellow cab down.

"Queens Main street, please?"

"Yeah sure, jump in!" the driver replies in a harsh local dialect. The cab has a grey interior and it is an older car. The seats are worn from the hundreds of fares it has carried over its time in service. Michael stares out of the window as the taxi pulls out into the busy daytime city traffic. He is sure he spotted the lady from the flight, walking down the street. He swings round to look out the back window and watches her from a distance. He is convinced it is her. He shakes his head in irony. How is this possible? Manhattan is massive and yet at this moment, he happens to see her. He smiles to himself.

'She was crazy.' he mouths, shaking his head.

After twenty minutes, the cab draws up to Michael's destination.

"That's thirty five bucks," the driver says, turning around to address Michael. He hands over the $40 and leaves a five dollar tip, scrambles out of the cab, and shuts the door. He walks one block, turns the corner, and arrives at his temporary address.

Michael enters the apartment block. It is dark and gloomy in the hall. There are no carpets on the stairs and the railings are painted black. He climbs two stairs at a time around the winding staircase and ascends three flights until he arrives at his floor. As he approaches the door, he fumbles for his keys in his tan long coat, his fingers still stiff from the cold. As he puts the key in the lock and turns, he pushes the door open, and is greeted by his friend Mia.

The apartment is on a small scale, but it is Mia's. The kitchen area is only along one wall with the units painted purple and a wooden worktop. The black and chrome breakfast bar is free-standing and only caters for two people at any one time. The couch is immediately behind the breakfast bar. It is old and worn, tan in colour but incredibly comfy. The table that stands in front of the sofa is a unique piece of furniture, Mia had acquired it at a market. It is a reclaimed Indian Sheesham wheelie table. She designed the apartment, and even though nothing particularly matches, somehow she has made it work. Her furniture is from all over the world - from intricately carved African pieces to old British antiques. She has modern lamps from Macy's and old lamps she inherited from her grandparents, which means they have travelled from Mexico.

"Hey Mike, how'd it go?" Mia asks, turning to look at him.

"You know I got the job, right? Thanks for organising that for me, Mia," Michael says, while hanging his coat on the peg.

"It was a sure thing, and you're welcome!" Mia exclaims giggling.

"It's cold out today. You want coffee?" Michael asks. He turns the coffee machine on and places a chipped navy blue mug underneath the dispenser. He rubs his hands together, trying to warm them up whilst the machine gurgles away.

Mia is sitting up at the breakfast bar, working on her laptop. She continues looking at her screen while handing her mug to him, without saying a word. He takes her cup and places it under the machine again, letting it do its magic.

"Work busy today, huh?" He enquires placing her coffee down next to her.

"Sure is! Practising law as a student, comes at a price, Mike!" Mia mutters while her fingers tap frantically at the keyboard.

Michael perches on the stool on the opposite side of the breakfast bar, and takes a sip of his warm frothy coffee.

"Look at you Mia, making it in life," he pauses, and takes a long sigh, "and here I am, back here, with a failed career, a failed relationship, taking a job in a coffee house!"

"You mean deli," Mia teases.

"Okay, deli, you know what I mean," running his hands through his blonde messy hair.

Mia pauses, looks up from the screen and stares at him for a long moment.

"Mike, you can either obsess at the past, or you can call it a lucky escape. Okay, so your career is on hold and so what if your relationship is failed?" she says sternly, thrusting her hands into the air while Michael continues to stare at his now half empty coffee cup.

"You could be stuck in a job you hate, in a relationship or worse, a marriage where you can't stand your wife and in a country where you don't belong." She stares back at her screen and continues with her work.

"I know Mia, but I had it all, and it seems overnight it's gone," he says mournfully.

"Okay, less of that. I need a break, let's eat?" She stands up from her stool and stretches her body that's been slumped at a computer most of the morning.

Mia is half Mexican. Her family moved to New York from Georgia when she was seven. Her father, Epifanio is Mexican and had moved to Georgia when he was just ten. Her grandparents and father fled Mexico because of the crime, and the Cartel taking over the streets of their small town Guerrero. Michael and she became friends in sixth grade and have remained best friends ever since. They both came from similar backgrounds - parents divorced, lots of siblings, with their grandparents living just a few blocks away.

Michael's parents divorced when he was twelve and that came harder to him than his siblings. Given that Mia had already been through it, she supported him through that emotional time of his life. Her parents divorced a short while after they moved to Albany, and this is the basis of their close friendship.

They were both well liked in middle and junior high and got plenty of attention for their ravishing looks but neither was interested in dating throughout their high school life.

There were three of them who hung out in high school, Joey being the third, but he now lives on Staten Island with his wife and two children. He had matured quicker than both Michael and Mia. He settled at twenty five, and now works in an office block doing insurance. Both Mia and Michael tease him for his *great* life choices.

Mia and Michael slob on the tired looking couch in their comfys, watch a mindless series on television, talk, eat snacks, and laugh into the late evening. Mia moans that she needs to start her essay and study. She kisses Michael on the cheek and says goodnight. Michael sits for a moment and switches the TV off. He grabs his laptop from under the couch, lifts the lid and fires up the machine. Going to the search bar he researches architectural job vacancies. There aren't any so he flips the lid back down and makes up his bed on the couch.

He wakes up the next morning to the bang of the purple rustic painted kitchen cupboard doors.

"Come on senor, wakey wakey," Mia calls as she is preparing a bowl of cereal for her breakfast. Michael is chilly as he is only wearing his pants. He stretches all his limbs to awaken his body. Throwing himself out of the blankets and off the sofa, he makes his way to the bathroom.

"Mike, it's a shame I don't find you attractive in any way," she teases. Michael hysterically laughs himself to the bathroom to get showered. Although Mia and Michael appreciate each other's beauty, they have never had a thing for one another. It is strictly platonic between them, though there has always been speculation from outsiders of their friendship.

Today is Michael's first day at 'At the Deli'. He hates the uniform he has to wear which is an olive green T-shirt with a matching cap and black trousers. Before leaving for the day, he grabs his long cream coat and black scarf off a peg and throws them on. Mia hands him his phone as they make their way out of the apartment together. Mia slams the door behind them making sure the Yale lock is triggered.

'Michael's father would love for him to work at the family company, if only he knew that he was here!' Mia thinks to herself.

Michael and his father, George, have a strained relationship. When he moved to England his father wasn't happy with the decision, and Michael feels continuously judged for his life choices. George wanted his son to work under him but Michael couldn't handle being under that scrutiny. His father is just as stubborn as him and they don't see eye to eye. Mia knows that Michael is a stubborn character and has always wanted to stand on his own feet. Neither of his parents know that he is back in New York, yet Mia wants and feels the need to help try and rebuild his relationships with his mother and father.

Mia knows all too well what it's like to have strained relationships because she barely talks to her mother. She is much closer to her father, who has funded her ambition of going back to university to study law at the age of thirty two. Mia had had a series of unfulfilling jobs and it was Michael's mother, Cora who encouraged her to chase a dream of studying law. The street crime by drug gangs in Guerrero had left a lasting scar on her father. The family had fled Mexico after she was held at gunpoint as a child. As an adult, Mia would like to make a difference by helping to clear the streets of New York of the same crimes.

Mia is motherly over Michael as she can see that her best friend is having an internal battle with himself since he's back. She has never liked Michael's long-term girlfriend and could see through her *'perfectly kind'* act. The *'perfectly kind'* ex-girlfriend is called Olivia, who comes from a wealthy family that isn't a broken one, and she has only one sibling, Donny. Donny is arrogant, but incredibly good looking and attracts every woman he comes in contact with, and this includes Mia. She spends her time thinking about a man she knows she can't stand and even more, his rotten to the core sister, who has broken her best friend's heart.

They stand outside 'At the Deli'. The street is very crowded.

"Okay, so... good luck today, you'll do great. Are we meeting later to eat?" Mia asks.

The city workers are weaving past the two as they talk, all trying to get to their destinations in one of the busiest cities in the world. Michael steps closer to the edge of the sidewalk, making more room for the pedestrians to get past.

"You're kidding me, right? It's working behind a food counter and serving the New Yorkers coffee and food. It can't be that hard," he laughs, "and yeah, we'll eat together tonight."

"Yeah, that's true," Mia retorts, "but Mike, you asked me to get you a quick fix job. I called in a favour with my uncle. You're here on the quiet. You had the choice to go and work for your father but you didn't want to."

Michael doesn't have a reply.

"So I need to head off and get to the DA's Office for my work placement. We're working on a really big case right now. So, shall we say around 8 p.m., when we've both finished? I'll meet you outside here?"

"You got it boss! See you tonight!" Michael says kissing her on the cheek quickly before entering his new place of work.

After spending the morning learning the ropes of how 'At the Deli' is run, Michael is thrust behind the counter and shown by Mario how to work the till. All the food is freshly prepared by the staff who work behind the counter in the kitchen and the tables are to be wiped down regularly too.

Michael is fully aware that this work is below his pay grade, but he knows he has to start at the bottom in order to save enough money to restart his life in New York and get his own apartment.

Serving a rather jolly gentleman his coffee and wrap, he hands the man his change and brown paper bag. He glances at the self-service section. There she is again! The *'crazy lady'* from the flight. He can feel himself getting rather flustered and tries to get someone else to take over. Then she looks in his direction.

'Oh my God, you gotta be kiddin' me!' he thinks to himself. He gives the dullest wave with a half-hearted smile that stops her in her tracks. She looks at him astonished.

She approaches the counter with her mozzarella, tomato and pesto wrap and asks for a black coffee. Michael is busy tapping at the digits on the till when she interrupts him.

"Hi again," she smiles, "I just want to apologise for what happened on the flight,"

"I'm Ava, Ava Turner." she smiles. He can't believe that it is his first day and she comes in here, seeing him like this, working here of all places. He can feel his embarrassment swallowing him up.

"Look it's okay, it's done. That was a while ago now, and it really doesn't matter. I'm sorry if I offended you. By the way I'm Michael, Michael Johnson," he smiles, whilst bagging up her purchase and passing the black coffee.

"Well, Michael," she pauses, "it's nice to meet you properly, and now I know where to avoid," she laughs. He stares back awkwardly not knowing what to say.

"Anyway," she gestures to the door.

"I best get going. I have to get back to work, and just because my uncle is my boss doesn't mean he goes easy on me!" she chuckles awkwardly.

Michael tells Ava to take care, and she slips out the door. He stands staring after her as she crosses the busy road. His insides flip at her absence while serving the next customer.

The day drifts away and Michael's first day 'At the Deli' finally comes to an end. He helps to put the chairs on the tables whilst one of his co workers mops the floor. Outside the door Mia is waiting for him. Michael explains the ins and outs of his day as they walk to the subway to return home to Queens.

Mia and Michael sit down to a Mexican that Mia had prepared for them both.

"Mike, you've had a look on your face since I met you from work," she remarks.

"Have I?" Taking a mouthful of his black bean and corn nacho which fills the air with a spicy aroma.

"You so have. What happened at work today?" She smirks, waving her empty fork around.

"Well," he says, chewing another mouthful. "Where do I start? When I was flying back from the UK there was a woman I ran into on the flight," he pauses, "and well," he pauses again to take a sip of his beer.

"Well... what?"

"Well... she came into 'At the Deli' this afternoon," he grins broadly.

"That's it?! She came into the deli, and that causes you to smile like *that*?"

"I know it sounds crazy, Mia. But there is something about her. She completely took me by surprise! I thought I saw her the other day coming back from 34th Street after my interview. It made me feel strange. *She* makes me feel strange," Michael explains, looking puzzled.

"Michael Johnson. Are you crushing on this mysterious flight woman?" Mia is smirking.

"Laugh all you want, Miss Garcia. But on that flight she completely disarmed me. I wasn't prepared for such rawness and she made me feel alive, again!"

Mia nods, taking in what he is saying and she pats his hand with affection.

They finish up their spicy Mexican dinner. Mia washes the dishes and Michael dries up. She announces that she is meeting a friend for a drink locally in Queens. She grabs her coat and bag then kisses him on the cheek. "I have my cell if you need me for anything. Okay?" Michael nods a reply as he is focused on CNN news. She makes her way to the door and stares back at him. She wants the best for her dear friend. Mia leaves shutting the door behind her.

Michael spends the evening with his large sketch pad in hand, creating drawings of different architectures. He knows even though he isn't in that line of work currently, it doesn't matter. He needs to keep his mind in the zone of creating all types of designs and drawings. He can feel the fury building within him, and he slams the lead pencil and pad down.

"Don't be crazy, Mike, the deli counter is where you work at the minute!" He mutters to himself.

Ava crosses his mind again, and he grabs the laptop from beside him on the sofa. He clicks on a social media page, curiosity gets the better of him. He types her name in, not expecting to find her. There in big bold writing - Ava May Turner, and as quick as that, her face is on the screen. He clicks on her profile and begins scanning. There is next to nothing on her page so he decides to look through her pictures instead.

He can't get over her beauty. He continues to click through and comes across a picture of her and a man next to her. They look intimate. He zooms in on her photo. She has a wedding ring on. *Hang on!* Is this woman he is fascinated by married?

He thinks back to today and their encounter, and tries to remember if she had a ring on.

"She had gloves on!" reminding himself. He runs his hands through his hair and rubs his smooth tanned face.

"What am I doing?!" Michael hollers. He throws his head against the back of the sofa and shuts the laptop, deciding sleep is the best thing for him. As he lays there trying to sleep he tosses and turns all night, he can't settle. What has this Ava done to him?

Chapter Four

Ava is rushing around trying to find her other heel, with toast hanging from her mouth. This would be the second day she was late to the office in a week.

"Come on Ava, this is not good enough!" She says to herself out loud.

"Ah there you are you little bugger!" As she scrambles and grabs the shoe from under the unmade king size bed. Her phone rings and she answers. "Mum, I don't have time to talk right now, I am late, *again!*" she says annoyed with herself.

"Good morning Ava May Turner. You haven't rang in a few days... I was worried!" Florence runs on.

"Look Mum, I'll call after my meal tonight," Ava explains.

"Oh darling, who are you dining with this evening? A man, oh please tell me it's a man?" She appeals excitedly.

"No mother, it's not a man but uncle James. I've barely seen him at the office as he is always tied up in meetings all the time. I have had a few business lunches to attend as well, so it's been difficult and I'd really like to get to know him again." Ava grabs her coat and bag and heads for the door still on the phone.

"Oh... I see, well send my love to James, won't you?"

"Of course I will. Now I really must go as I've got to take the stairs. I've missed the lift and I'm honestly really late!" Ava replies in a real fluster.

"Of course, speak soon, Ava darling," and the call ends.

Ava arrives at her office in a sweaty unorganised mess and the phone rings. She dumps her coat and bag on the desk and answers, all flustered.

"Ava Turner's office."

"Good Morning Ava, uncle James here," she cringes at the sound of his voice. "Would you mind dropping by my office when you get the chance, please?"

Ava rubs her forehead, worried. If her father is anything to go by, she knows her uncle runs a tight ship too.

Ava had worked under her father back in the UK and he was always strict when it came to work and completely different to how he was as a father.

"Yeah, of course uncle James. What time is best for you?

"Shall we say an hour? Is your schedule clear?"

"I'll see you on the hour," and the line goes dead.

"Oh dear God, I am in trouble." She mutters under her breath as she takes a seat at her grand white desk.

Her office is large, extremely bright, and well lit. The floor is tiled with white marble and the walls are painted a brilliant white, very clean and very clinical. Her uncle certainly has a theme throughout all of his buildings. She also has a view of Manhattan's skyline out of her window.

She has a table where the architectural models sit and also get created. Ava is currently working on one, and it is calling for her attention. She picks up her materials and sets to work.

Ava rushes to her uncle's office close to 10 a.m. James sees her approaching the fully glazed door. He gets up from his desk to greet her.

"Ava May, come in, come in. Take a seat," he gestures to a cream leather chair, shuts the door for privacy. He walks around the desk to take his seat back at his throne.

"How are you finding it here at 'TAC'?" He asks, crossing his legs and leaning back into his black leather chair. He fiddles with a pen on his desk, not taking his eyes off her.

"Yes it's great," she smiles, "The people here are very kind and help me where they can, and I go out for lunch most days."

He interrupts, "Ava..." he pauses, uncrosses his legs and sits upright, and places his red tie straight. "I run a tight ship here, very much like your father did. I can't keep having you arrive late, I put my neck on the line to bring you over here and the other corporate owners are moaning," Ava puts up her hand in defeat.

"Of course uncle James. This is a professional business and I understand my duties. I won't let you down again." she reassures him.

"Good. Ava. You are an incredible architect and I want to see you do well here," he stands up and gestures to the door. Ava rises from the chair and understands that she is to get on with her job.

"Ava, are we still on for tonight?" He asks, holding the door open for her, as she leaves.

"Of course we are," she smiles brightly.

"Excellent. My car will collect you at eight,"

"Oh and Ava?"

She glances back, "Yes?" turning to look at him.

"Don't be late!" He smiles and winks, Ava grins then she makes her way back to her own office.

Lunchtime arrives. Ava thought she could work through it, but she is just too hungry. Loving the Deli she had stumbled across before, she decides to pop in heading straight for the wraps and ciabattas, picking up a mozzarella, tomato, and pesto wrap which had been so delicious before. Standing in line to pay she can see Michael behind the counter. She can't help thinking he really is handsome. Finally at the counter, Michael gives her the biggest smile.

"I thought you said you knew where to avoid now?" he laughs.

"Well given that the wraps are so good, I had to come back!"

He doesn't say anything else and just smiles.

"That $8, please."

Ava hands over $10 and tells him to keep the change. She walks back to the office with a broad smile on her face.

The day is passing by in a flash and Ava has been working on a drawing and a model for the majority of the time, but now it's time to wrap up her work and head home.

Ava approaches the receptionist who is sitting at her enormous marble desk.

"I'm heading home now, Hannah. Any messages for me before I leave?"

"Ah, yes actually, Miss Turner, someone called Lydia? She didn't leave a message. She just said you'd know who she was?" Shrugging her shoulders, "And, that's it," she says, checking her notes and staring back at Ava.

"Lydia called the office, and didn't leave a message?" she looks confused. "That's strange. Okay, well thank you. I'll call her from my mobile on the way home. I'll see you tomorrow?" Ava asks.

"No, not tomorrow Miss Turner, it's my day off, but Betty will be in."

"Oh okay, well, you enjoy your long weekend. Night." Ava runs her hand along the solid marble desktop and walks away.

Ava flags a yellow cab and returns to her apartment block. Her feet are in agony after a long day, and she can feel them throbbing with pain. Going to dinner with her uncle was the last thing she wanted to be doing, but some bonding time is needed. Ava gets her phone from her handbag but the battery is dead.

Ava arrives at her apartment block and pays her fare. She enters the building. Mr Truman is in his usual position behind the desk. Ava calls for the lift and looks in his direction and catches his eye.

"Good evening, Mr Truman."

"Miss Turner," he stares at her and then looks back at his screen.

Arriving on her floor, she has half an hour to get changed and meet her uncle's driver outside. Ava approaches the door and fumbles in her handbag for her keys. The bag is full of junk. She begins to panic. Grabbing handfuls of items from the bottomless pit of the bag, she tosses them on the floor.

"Oh no, for goodness sake. Where are my keys?" She exclaims, running her hands through her tassel dark hair. Scooping up the items off the floor and chucking them back in her bag, she turns to call the lift again.

In comparison to her sisters, Ava has always been the least organised. It has always been a joke amongst the Turner family, that Ava was never given important tasks to complete. The only time Ava has ever been organised is at work.

Entering the lobby, she proceeds towards the desk.

"Excuse me Mr Truman, I seem to have misplaced my keys. Do you have a spare I could use, please?" She says flustered.

He continues looking at his screen, "You have misplaced your keys, or you've lost them completely?"

"Erm, well I'm not entirely sure until I check the apartment," Ava replies bashfully.

He looks up and turns to the key safe.

"Luckily for you, we keep a spare for each apartment. You must keep me informed as to whether you find your key, Miss Turner." She feels incredibly small from his answer, like she has been a naughty school girl. He hands the key over and huffs. Checking her watch she has fifteen minutes to get ready. Retracing all her movements she is finally in her apartment, and there are her keys sitting on a ledge..

"Phew!" She says to herself.

Shutting the door and leaning against it she takes a breath. Running through to her glamorous grey bedroom, she slings her clothes off in a hurry and quickly looks in her white Chester wardrobe.

"A dress, I'll wear a dress!" she says as she whips one off the hanger and slips it on, replaces the black patent heels she's had on all day, applies a rich red lipstick which is sitting lonely on her makeup table and grips her brown locks up with a black crocodile clip. She looks in the mirror, running her hands down her dress and decides she is more than respectful to go to dinner.

Running through the hall in a rush, she yells to Mr Truman.

"I have my keys!" and throws the spare to Mr Truman who catches it without hesitation. She continues towards the exit, where the doorman swings the door open for her. The black sedan is waiting at the bottom of the steps. The driver steps out of the car and opens the door for her as she approaches. She slides in, all too relieved.

'What a drama', she thinks to herself.

The sedan comes to a halt outside Le Bernardin. Ava's door is opened by the driver. She glances over at the restaurant and feels completely unprepared for this meal. She strolls past the enormous plant pots, with the most gorgeous flowers that smell glorious. It's an arrangement of tulips, Iris germanica and lilies. She takes in a deep breath and opens the doors.

Ava is greeted by a waiter who leads her to a table. Her uncle is already waiting and stands to greet her. He leans over to give a brisk kiss on the cheek and they take a seat.

"So... this place is nice," Ava says as she stares around.

"I'm glad you approve, my darling," James nods. Another waiter appears at the table to take their drinks order.

"We'll have a bottle of your finest white," he orders and Ava nods in agreement. This experience feels strange to her as it has been many years since she has had the company of her uncle.

The restaurant has the most exquisite dark oak wood walls and a sparkling light display in the centre of the dining area. The tables are laid with fancy folded napkins and glistening crystal glasses. Not a smear mark is present on the silver cutlery. Ava leans forward to take the menu. The waiter dressed all in white returns quickly to take their order.

"I'll have the entrecote steak, with new potatoes, asparagus, and mine with vine tomatoes please, and Ava you'll have the same?" He glances in her direction.

"No, thank you Uncle James I'll have the fish platter, please."

They are in conversation about work when their food arrives.

They move their napkins and place them on their laps delicately so the food can be laid in front of them.

Picking up his knife and fork Uncle James gets into a deeper and meaningful conversation, as he cuts into his deliciously succulent smelling steak.

"So... Ava. You're here and I haven't really been able to catch up with you, properly, since you got to the city," he pauses as he goes to take a mouthful of his steak. "How are you? I know these last couple of years have been full on for you?" He pauses again, awaiting Ava's response.

"Well, you know, it's been hard," She grabs her glass of white and takes the biggest gulp. Having this conversation with an uncle she hasn't seen in years feels odd and uncomfortable, she places the glass back on the table.

"I know if your father was here, to have witnessed what you have been through, he most definitely would've been furious, but also the kindest, and would have seen you through it," he says warmly.

"I know," she sighs, "I could have really done with my father around for strength *and* his wisdom," She says in a whisper, and takes a mouthful of her swordfish.

"Ava, I know your father and I, we didn't always see eye to eye in the last few years, hence I am here. But I always respected his wisdom. Us not talking when he passed will always stay with me," he says solemnly.

Ava looks at her uncle endearingly.

"At the time I was so wrapped in being newlywed that I never really knew the ins and outs of your fall out, Uncle James."

James looks up astonished by her comment.

"You didn't?" He takes a sip of his wine and places it back on the table. Turning his attention back to her, "Your mother never told you after he passed away?"

"No, she didn't. Why should she have?" Ava questions, placing her knife down.

The atmosphere is quiet, intimate yet intense. She knows an argument won't happen, but she is now nervous of what is about to come.

"Well, we had a row, as I wanted to expand our business, the *joint* business here in the States and your father wouldn't have it. So I took my share of equity and left. I came here and started again, and as you can see I've made a real success of myself. That wound your father up even more. So when I called, he'd hang up, and I wrote but he never replied," he pauses. "And, then he died and I couldn't make it right. It was too late. Then when your mother called out of the blue and said you needed a fresh start and a new beginning after Richard, I felt it was making things right with your father," he leans back in his chair, links his fingers, ready for the questions.

Ava's father had passed away suddenly. Geoff was away on a mini break and felt unwell, he had an aortic aneurysm and died in hospital the same day. Her mother had to travel back alone, broken and shocked by the passing of her husband and had to tell her daughters.

After his death, Florence inherited Geoff's half of the business and remained a silent partner. Ava had worked under her father after she had gone to University at Oxford Brookes for three years. She was always the closest to him and wanted to follow in her father's footsteps. Ava took his death incredibly badly and wanted to take control of his business but the investor/partner proceeded to make this incredibly hard. Ava didn't find it difficult to decide to leave and go to New York.

"I had a feeling, it was something along those lines. You know what my father was like, stubborn, and in his wisdom he always thought his way was the right way, uncle James," she replies. Pausing, she places her fork down on her plate.

"I don't blame you for your decision. You did what you felt was right at the time, and with all due respect my father hated to be proven wrong. So there we are. And I do know mum has said he really did miss your wisdom within the business, too." She pats her mouth with her napkin and goes for her glass.

"You shouldn't carry that burden anymore, it is done and several years have now passed," she finishes, leaning forward, folding her fingers under her chin.

"Ava, my darling, thank you. It really does mean a lot to hear you say that."

They continue with their meal, discussing work, general life, and not mentioning Richard or her father.

After a lovely evening, Ava returns to the apartment. Her uncle got the bill, and she is grateful for the night away from the four walls of her plush apartment. She plugs her phone in, switches it on, letting it charge.

She heads to the bathroom to brush her teeth when her phone pings. Heading back to the lounge with toothpaste around her mouth and clutching the brush with her teeth, she finds a message from Lydia.

'Call me ASAP, Ava!! It's IMPORTANT! Love Lyds xxx'

Ava rolls her eyes and turns the screen off.

Lydia is the dramatic one of the four girls. There was always a drama and she hadn't made the best life choices. Lydia dropped out of university at nineteen for a boyfriend. They travelled around Thailand for a year, and when he cheated on her, Lydia returned home. Of course he eventually chased after her when he had realised what side his bread was buttered. She had this boyfriend who was a waste of space in Ava's eyes and they were always on and off. Lydia couldn't hold down a job either and went from one to another frequently.

She strolls back to the bathroom to carry on brushing her teeth. Spitting in the sink, wiping her face and looking in the mirror, she says to her reflection. "I can't be dealing with that drama tonight." She heads to her room and turns all the lights out on the way.

Folding back the crisp white sheets, she climbs onto the bed and switches the side lamp off. Ava lies there for a while. It was a lovely meal with her uncle and she is glad to be reconnected with him after so many years.

As a young child her uncle was around a lot, but after the falling out and losing touch for several years, she still didn't feel ready to discuss Richard with him. She wasn't sure how much her mother had told him, but she wasn't ready for it to come from *her* yet.

"Firstly I'd like to thank my beautiful wife Ava, for saying yes and giving me the opportunity to make her my wife." Ava looks up at Richard in complete awe. She has married the man of her dreams. Two years of planning, and it's their wedding day. They are surrounded by everyone who loves them together and individually.

"Ava, I chased you for six months. I harassed you until you agreed to go on a date with me and it has been the best three years. I am extremely excited and honoured to start our future as husband and wife. I can't wait to see you become the mother to our children and to spend the rest of our lives together. So I would like to raise a glass to the new Mrs Ava Burton." There is a massive cheer from all the breakfast guests and a round of applause. Richard bends down and kisses Ava on the lips. The new Mr and Mrs Burton.

◆◄▶◆

Chapter Five

"**M**ichael! You're back in New York, and you didn't think you needed to tell me?" Says the stern voice down the phone.

Finding himself pacing around the kitchen, fiddling with anything in sight, he finally replies, "Mom, hey, look I've been meaning to call."

She cuts him off, "Michael I don't wish to hear your excuses right now. I'd like to see you, so perhaps you could come for lunch, today?" She hangs up.

Michael knows his mother is furious with him.

Michael doesn't work Saturdays so he grabs his laptop to check train times. It's 9 a.m. Mia walks from her bedroom to the kitchen.

"Si, Papa, Te amo, adios." She says hanging up.

"Epifanio?"

"Yeah, our weekly catch up, you know how it is. You okay? I thought I heard you talking?" Mia says, placing her phone down on the counter to make coffee.

"Yeah, my mom called. She knows I'm back in town and I have to have lunch with her today, so just checking train times," he stares at his screen. "The thing is," he pauses, "I don't know how she knows I'm back."

Mia pauses, winces and turns to him then sighs.

"It was me Mike, I had lunch with her last week and I said you were staying with me."

"Mia, why? I hadn't spoken to her for a reason," he snaps.

"Well how am I supposed to know? You haven't even mentioned her. She had the right to know you're back Mike. She's your mom and she loves you, and you're in a delicate place right now. You need everyone around you who loves you."

"Mia, that wasn't your decision! It was mine and you went behind my back! I'm gonna go shower," he stands up and stomps to the bathroom.

"Mike, please don't be mad... Mike?" Mia begs. "Maldita sea!" slamming her hand on the breakfast table.

Before Mike gets in the shower he sends a text, *'I'll be at the station for 2:37 mom. Meet me there?'*

He clicks send.

His phone pings.

'I'll see you there, Michael. Mom'

After getting out the shower and throwing some clothes on, the realisation hits him. Mia only ever does these things because she cares. He swings open the bathroom door and calls for Mia, but she isn't there, she has left. Time is running out and he needs to get to the station.

The train journey from Queens to Albany is three and a half hours, that gives Mike enough time to prepare for his lunch date with his mother. He stares out of the window mindlessly as the train departs. He shuts his eyes for a short while, and takes a deep breath. The relationship between him and his mother is strained, but he still loves her all the same.

Coming to a halt in Albany station, he steps off the train. His mother is standing there waiting for him. Cora is an elegant woman, with a short blonde bob, and piercing blue eyes that you can see from a mile. She is wrapped in a grey long jacket and black scarf, gloves and knee length boots on. Michael's heart is thumping.

"*Here goes,*" he mutters, walking towards her.

"Michael James!" She says, holding her arms out for a longing hug.

"Mom" he replies, returning the gesture. They hug tightly for a second or two, and they head towards her Silver Chevrolet Impala.

They climb in and drive back to her house.

In Hollywood Avenue, they pull up to a cream timber house, with grey concrete steps. The front of the house is lawned and sprinkled in snow. Michael hasn't been home in eight years and he feels strange being back.

He slides out of the car, heading towards the front steps, then waits for his mother to unlock the front door.

As it opens he is greeted with a familiar odour. It smells like home. The fragrance of freshly baked cookies and scented candles hits his nose. It feels warm and cosy so he removes his coat and scarf and hangs them on the stand near the door. His mother heads straight for the kitchen and turns on the coffee machine.

Michael stares to the left of him. The lounge has been newly decorated. The couch is navy blue and the furniture is light oak. The curtains are a cream fabric and there is the fluffiest throw scrawled across the arm of the couch. He can see a warm glow coming from the fire. Straight ahead are the stairs, painted a bright white and a dark oak finish on the steps. The kitchen and dining room are joined to the left of the stairs. The walls are olive green with units of a high gloss cream colour, and spotlights create a bright ambience. He strides towards his mother who is waiting by the coffee machine.

"You decorated?"

"Yeah I did. About a year ago. It needed updating," she says fumbling about in the cutlery drawer, to find a spoon to stir the coffees.

"I like it. It's modern for you, mom."

"Michael, you haven't come to talk about interiors with me. You've been back for over a month and I had to hear it from Mia," she accuses him.

"What are you doing hooking up with Mia, anyway, mom?"

"We meet once a month, for a catch up and lunch, Michael."

"To talk about me you mean?"

"Oh Michael," she says exasperated, "no... not to talk about you. Mia and I have a close relationship. You know that, but now you've brought it up."

After Michael had moved to England, Cora and Mia became very close. Mia kept in close contact with his mother because she had taken his relocation across the ocean incredibly badly.

"Mom, I'm not getting into this," Michael says pacing around the kitchen,

"What?" She begins. "Because you know I never approved of Olivia. You were never good enough for her, Michael. There was always an excuse. Wait until your promotion, wait until we can get a bigger house," she pauses, "and then, you lose the contract and in her eyes are a failed architect so she ends your eleven year long relationship," she holds out her arms, shaking her head frustrated.

"It wasn't like that, mom," he retaliates.

Cora has never liked Olivia and although Michael is her eldest son she always takes great care in looking out for him. Of her three sons and one daughter, Michael had a rough start to life. He was born five weeks early and she wasn't ready for him. He was whisked away from her for the first few days of his life and she has spent the rest of it making it up to him and mothered him too much.

"Then how is it, Michael?" she blurts out, "Because from where I'm standing, that's exactly how it looks. All too ashamed of how it ended, so you hide at Mia's and don't tell a soul you're here?" Cora leans against the counter and folds her arms.

Michael runs his hands through his blonde locks and places his hand on the oak counter for support.

"Look I'm here now. It's been a long time. Let's not fight over her, she has taken enough of my time." he sighs.

"Does your father know you're here?" She questions.

"No he doesn't, I am not prepared for that right now."

"Look Michael, don't think we don't care, when we very much do, probably too much, but I'm your mother and it's my job to look out for you. I do it because I love you. You're my son and I just want to see you happy," she says fondly.

"You may feel like that. But dad, he'll want me to go work for him and I want to make it on my own," Michael says, raising his eyebrows.

"I know. You know what your father is like. Do the twins and Chloe know you're here?"

"Like I said, no one knows I'm back, not even Joey," he replies.

Cora and Michael enjoy a heart-warming pot roast and homemade cookies. She gives a tour of the rest of the house and they come to his old bedroom. Michael's room has been stripped of all his personal memorabilia, the photos of beach babes in their bikinis which smothered his walls and his trophies from his school football career were now put away to storage. Now the room has a double bed dressed with cushions of different shades of blue. It was no longer a 'boys room' but now ready for guests when they stay. It has changed from how he ever remembered it and didn't feel like his bedroom anymore. However, on the sideboard was a blue folder with all of his early architectural drawings.

"You kept these?" He turns to ask her as she leans on the door frame with her arms crossed.

"Sure I did. You never know when you might need them," she says walking towards him, as he holds the folder. They flick through the drawings remarking on the good ones. The drawings are from when he studied at Harvard University in Cambridge, Massachusetts for five long years. His parents and his wife, then girlfriend, had visited him regularly.

"They're pretty incredible. You should take them with you. It's some of your best work," she says, stroking her son's arm affectionately.

"I think I will, mom. Thanks for keeping hold of them," he says, shutting the folder with a snap. She rubs his shoulder and makes her way for the stairs. Michael is left staring at his folder confused about what to do next.

It's eight p.m. They are heading back for the station and Cora is feeling emotional. As they arrive she gets out of the car to say her goodbyes.

"Don't be a stranger, Michael. Come back to see me," she pleads.

"I will mom, don't worry. I'm only three hours away, now," he says searching for her eyes.

She flings her arms around his neck and gives him the longest motherly hug. She has truly missed her eldest but forever baby son.

"Okay. You best be off or you'll miss your train. Perhaps I can meet you in the city in the week?" Cupping his face.

"Yeah sure. I'll ask Mia if you can stop by for dinner one night?" he replies holding her hands on his face.

"Sounds perfect," sliding her hands off his face onto his chest where she pats him.

Michael joins the moving parade of travellers making their way to the train. As he steps on, he pauses looking back at his mother and blows her a kiss. She blows a kiss back and waves frantically. He finds an empty seat, sits down, throws his head back against the headrest and sighs.

His phone pings. Mia.

'I hope you have forgiven me and had a lovely time with your mom. Let me know what time you are back. Te amo Mimi x x'

He replies.

'I can never stay angry with you for too long. The train is now departing. I should be back in Queens at nearly 1 a.m. Love you too. X x'

The train departs and Michael is feeling exhausted. He flicks through his architectural folder for a while. He shuts his eyes and dozes contentedly for the remaining part of the journey. Arriving back at the apartment an hour and a half past midnight. He turns the key slowly and quietly opens the door to find Mia.

"You waited up? It's late," Michael says, shutting the door.

"Of course I did. I wanted to make sure you got back okay. Do you forgive me?" approaching him.

"Of course I do. It wasn't that bad after all."

"I didn't want to undermine you, but I thought you need her right now, Mike."

"I know, I know. Let's just forget about it. I'm gonna head for a shower I feel dirty after travelling." Michael trundles towards the bathroom and Mia calls. "You want a hot chocolate?"

"Yeah sure!" Michael replies from the bathroom.

They settle down and sip their hot chocolate and wrap themselves under the woollen blanket.

"So, how did it go with your mom?" Mia asks.

"Yeah okay, she lectured me about Olivia, obviously. But she kept this," Michael waves the portfolio folder.

"No way she kept this?" as Mia takes the folder and flicks through the drawings.

"I know right. Crazy! I can't believe after all these years she still has them."

"You're so talented, Mike," she says, turning the pages one at a time.

"You should definitely send these drawings out to all of the architectural offices in New York. Now you're back to stay you could seriously open your horizons here," Mia encourages.

"Yeah, but after what happened in England, I'm not sure I can be classed as reputable anymore, Mia," staring at her regrettably.

"You'll never know until you try. Mike... what happened in the UK wasn't your fault. The project manager was a crook!" Mia says in a raised voice, placing the folder down and stands authoritatively in front of him.

"Crook or not I hired that guy, and he spent the money on other projects. That job was meant to be the turning point in my career instead it got my ass fired. I lost everything, Mia, I'm just not sure I'm prepared to take that risk again."

"Well, that's your choice," she pauses, "It's just that I know you are worth so much more and, you need to work at bettering yourself now that you're home."

"I don't know," he sighs deeply. "Anyway, it's late and I'm so exhausted," he says, as he rubs his face.

"Okay, you're right, it's like 2:30 in the morning, I'll let you get some rest." Mia bends down, kisses him on the cheek and heads to her room.

After Mia turns all the lights off, Michael settles down on the couch. He throws the blanket over him and puffs the Mexican embroidered pillow with his fists. He nestles in getting comfortable and finally rolls onto his back.

He lays there thinking over the last few years and he knows that deep down what his mother said about *her* was right. Olivia had a manipulative way of always putting off the engagement and marrying him. She always moved the goal post. When he first asked her, they lived in New York. She put it off and said, *'Let's wait until we get to England. A new move is a lot of stress, so let's wait until we have settled and we can really enjoy planning our wedding.'* That was exactly what he did. He gave Olivia every inch of him yet he always felt he was chasing his tail.

They both moved to Cambridge and got themselves the sweetest mid-terraced house and a BMW. She had got herself a job in a clothing store and he was working on a fairly good project at the time. When he asked her, he was so convinced that it was the right time but she declined. So he waited until he got a better job, but that wasn't the right time either. They then moved after they had saved for a mortgage, and he asked her again but Olivia said she was struggling with the move from New York and it wasn't the right time. But whenever she had spoken to her family she always painted their life in England to be magnificent. She told her father that it was just perfect and at the time Michael believed her too. He hung on her every word.

The relationship turned stale when Olivia finally had a break in the fashion industry. She was always working late or was off to Europe for some fashion show, or meeting some designer with her boss. Ah yes, the boss, Franko. Franko was an extremely handsome man and Michael knew it. Christ, even he fancied him. If a man could have a man crush, Franko was it. He was Italian with jet black hair, the darkest olive skin, pearliest white teeth and the biggest, greenest eyes. Michael was a good looking man, and even he felt threatened by the way Franko looked, and with that Italian accent he spoke frequently, he had every woman at his feet, including Olivia, and Michael knew it. It made him anxious every time Olivia went away on a trip with him. Michael was always insecure that there was something more to Olivia and Franko but never dared look into it or question the nature of their relationship.

He closes his eyes and tries to settle down for some sleep.

Chapter Six

"Good morning Betty, how are you today?" Ava asks as she approaches the reception desk. Ava is suited and booted for the working day. Her tailored black dress clings to her beautifully and close toed black heels frame her feet with perfect class.

"Good Morning, Miss Turner. Can I grab you a coffee?" she replies.

Betty is outstandingly beautiful. She has the longest legs and gorgeously long blonde hair that is never out of place. She has rather large breasts that always seem to be a little on show. They clearly do the job as she is the favourite receptionist here at TAC. All the men have a soft spot for the twenty-two year old and Ava can see why. She is incredibly efficient too.

"I'll have a mocha this morning please, Betty. Could you bring it to my office? Thank you," and Ava turns to head towards her office clutching her heavier than usual black leather carry case.

She hears a voice she recognises and turns to where it is coming from to see who it is.

"Ah... Good Morning! I have an appointment with Mr Turner," the voice says leaning over the desk. He is standing in a navy blue suit with tan brogues, his blonde hair is brushed back from his face and touches the top of his ears, but looks tidier than usual.

"Of course. What was the name?" Betty replies then stares back at her computer.

"Michael," he pauses, "Michael Johnson," standing himself up straight. He is carrying a folder in one of his hands.

As he waits, Michael realises that if all goes well today, he could be handing in his notice and potentially be starting in a week. Mario should be more than understanding because the job at the Deli was always viewed as a temporary one until he found something more substantial.

Ava watches him curiously.

"Of course, Mr Turner is waiting for you. Would you follow me, please?" Betty says coming away from her desk.

Ava is shocked to see him, and addresses him.

"Michael, I'm surprised to see you here?" Ava says walking alongside him in the direction of her office.

"I could say the same thing?" he scoffs.

"This is where I work. This is my uncle's business."

"Well, I'm here to see Mr Turner."

"Here is Mr Turner's office," Betty interrupts before Ava gets the chance to say anything else.

"Well, I'll be seeing you," Ava says perplexed and she heads into her own office.

She walks in and shuts the heavy duty glass door, leaning against it and sighing, she says to herself '*I'll be seeing you. Why did you say that Ava? How embarrassing!*" Ava runs her hands lightly over her face to remove loose strands of hair, and strides to her desk. Betty brings her mocha shortly after. Ava is sitting at her computer. She pauses.

"Betty, do you know why Mr Johnson is here, seeing my uncle?" Betty places the coffee on her desk.

"Um, no I don't, but, I *have* to say he is *hot* with a cute *ass.*" she laughs.

"I can't say I looked but the face is handsome, I have to agree."

"Will that be all, Miss Turner?" Betty is sprucing up her hair.

"Yes. Thank you Betty." Ava gives a broad smile. She can sense that Betty is taming her hair for Mr Johnson. Betty leaves the office in a sexy walk swaying her hips. Ava grabs her bag from under her desk and gets out her mirror to check her own face and hair.

The morning goes by reasonably quickly for Ava, with phone calls and completing drawings for clients. She never saw Michael leave but the curiosity has got the better of her, and she needs to find out why he was there. Pushing herself away from her desk on her wheeled chair, she goes to her office door with purpose and swings it open.

She trots in her stiletto heels across the hall to her uncle's office and without thinking she bursts in. He is on the phone, so she pauses and holds her hand up but waits at the door.

"Of course, I understand, uh-huh, okay," he nods, "I'll speak to you soon, take care". He hangs up from the call and resting his elbows on the top of his desk, stares at Ava.

"Sorry to disturb you, uncle James," Ava says awkwardly, "that gentleman you had in here earlier, Michael Johnson. Why was he here?" She is now enthusiastically leaning over his desk.

James seems to be in a daze.

"Uhh, I'm opening up a position here at the company. He brought a portfolio in with him and... he has some good work and has some *serious* experience too."

"So... he's an architect?" She asks, intrigued, then staring at her uncle realises that he looks somewhat distracted.

"Is everything okay?"

"Ava," he pauses, rising from his office chair, "I think you had better sit down."

He walks over to his thick glass door and shuts it. She turns to face him.

"What's going on?"

"I understand that Lydia has been trying to get in touch with you, darling?" he replies, walking towards her.

"Oh she has for weeks in fact, and that woman lives an *eventful* life. To be honest, I can't be dealing with her or her drama, so I have avoided her calls at all costs. Why do you ask?"

"Ava. That was your mother on the phone," he says in a clipped voice.

"That sounds ominous. What did she want? I didn't know you and my mother speak so regularly?" she giggles, not taking this seriously.

"Ava, I don't know how to tell you this," he pauses.

"Is it Lydia?" The panic begins to grow in the pit of her stomach and she starts to take his tone more seriously.

"No it isn't Lydia," he pauses again, "she has been trying to get hold of you for good reason. Your mother is somewhat angry about the situation, and also with Lydia so she intercepted and called me."

"Okay, so what is it? You're worrying me now, what's wrong?"

"It's Richard, Ava," he pauses.

"What about Richard? Why would my mother be calling you about Richard?" she snorts, "I don't understand," as her confusion grows.

James strides to his drinks cabinet in the corner.

"Can I get you a drink?" Ava shakes her hand to say no, patiently waiting for what she is about to be told. James pours and swallows his bourbon in one, then returns to sit behind his desk.

He stares at her attentively. "Ava," he pauses for a moment, "I'm unaware of all the details. Only that he fell ill a few weeks ago and Lydia was trying to call you to tell you. But last night he passed away."

Ava sits completely frozen, numb, emotionless and unable to move a single limb.

"You must be mistaken. Of course he isn't dead, he's thirty five years old. Lydia must be confused or she has her wires crossed. This can't be right?"

She takes a moment "It can't be," A few more seconds pass. "You're wrong. This is so wrong. You've been misinformed!" Ava is panicking now and close to hysteria..

"Ava. I'm going to put you on compassionate leave with immediate effect. You are in shock. Understandably. Take your time, get your head straight and do what you need to do."

He stands and walks around to the corner of his desk and perches there. He rests his hand on her shoulder. "Ava, I'm so sorry." He says quietly.

Memories of Richard come flooding back. She can smell his aftershave and hear his whispers when he'd stir her in the dead of night, wanting a chat. Ava can even remember him whistling when he was shaving in the mornings before work. She can recollect him now more than ever.

"I need to go back to England tonight. Can you sort me a flight for as soon as possible Uncle James? But business or first class. I can't sit next to another fat American that sweats and laughs obtrusively." She says staring into space completely senseless.

"Of course, anything you need, I'll sort it for you, my chauffeur will take you to the airport," James tells her as she sits in silence totally immobilized.

"Ava. Can I get you anything?" He asks helplessly.

"Yes... do you have any scotch?" She stares up at him.

Harry the family chauffeur meets Ava in Arrivals at Gatwick airport at 5 p.m. as dusk is falling. After a long journey the car finally turns into an entrance with a long gravel driveway that leads to a large country house. Ava is arriving home at her mother's having had little or no sleep after the tragic news. There is a warm glow coming from the windows because no curtains are drawn and Ava can see her mother standing at one, patiently waiting for her arrival. It is not quite 8 p.m. GMT but it has been dark for two hours. Harry and Ava have barely spoken a word since meeting. When he met her, the only thing he did was hug her tightly, take her luggage and escort her to the Bentley.

As Ava gets out of the car, the cold air hits her like a shard of ice and she knows she is utterly exhausted. Florence opens the door and throws her arms out to Ava running towards her. She hugs her mother tightly.

"Is Lydia here?" she mutters.

"Yes she is in her room, Ava. Why?" Ava releases herself from her mother's embrace.

"Excuse me a moment please, mum." She races up the large cream carpeted staircase to the upstairs hallway. It is light and airy and there is a sideboard with a cream lamp that gives a soft lighting. The walls are covered in photos of the girls growing up. Graduation photos, playing in paddling pools, gymnastic poses and ballet show poses. Today however, she does not notice them. She storms down the hall, arrives at Lydia's door and swings it open. Lydia is laying on her cream king size bed with the side light on. She is reading. She looks towards the door, shocked by Ava's entrance.

"Ava, you're home?" She says startled, sitting up and putting her book face down on the bed.

"WHY? WHY Lydia? I go to America, I try," she pauses, "I try *so* hard to restart my life and *you* are relentless at trying to keep me there, in that place with him."

Florence runs up the stairs as she hears Ava's raised voice. "Ava, darling. Come on now."

Ava throws her arm out, to create an invisible barrier. "NO mum. No!" Florence stands there watching, cupping her face with her hands rubbing the loose hairs from her cheeks.

"She *will* listen to what I have to say!" Ava turns her attention back to Lydia.

"Why? Why did you think I needed to know? Do you have any idea what it is like to leave a man that you love? Knowing you can't save him. I left him because I had no choice, Lydia, I was just beginning to piece my life back together and now here I am again." Ava's eyes begin to fill with tears, her voice breaks and a lump forms in her throat. Tears run down her reddened face.

"Here I am. Broken, I AM *BROKEN, LYDIA, BROKEN!*" She drops to the floor and completely breaks down. She is hysterical. Florence bends down and sits on the floor with her daughter and cradles her in her arms.

"Shhh... Shhh... Shhhh, come on now sweetheart, let it out, let it out." She rocks her daughter back and forth stroking her hair. Ava rests her head on her mother's lap, the tears continuing to flow.

Looking at Lydia, Florence hisses, "You still think it was a good idea, telling her, Lydia?"

Lydia scrambles from her crumpled bed sheets, tears rolling down her face too.

"I did what I thought was best," she hesitates, "I thought she had the right to know." she whispers looking to the ground.

Florence supports Ava to her old bedroom. Ava has finally stopped crying. She moves her body like a walking empty shell. Her mother talks to her but she doesn't get a reply. She puts her exhausted daughter to bed, Florence flicks the bedside lamp on and creeps towards the door. She leaves the door open and is greeted with a voice.

"Where's Ava?" Clare tries to whisper.

"She's laying down, darling." Ava hears her mother reply. She lays on the bed, listening.

"Lydia, go downstairs. You have done enough, I know... I know you were doing what you thought best but now you need to give her some space. Mum, go with her. I'll be down in a bit."

Clare creeps into the bedroom, crawls across the bed and lays behind Ava and says nothing, but instead she wraps her arm around her sister. Ava says nothing. She tries to hold her breath to stop the tears. Instead her whole body trembles trying to cry silently. She hears Clare whimpering behind her. They both say nothing, but instead cry until they fall asleep.

As Ava heads down the stairs there is a letter hanging from the letterbox. She withdraws it from the flap. It's addressed to Richard. She flips the letter over. It says 'private'. At that moment she feels the need to open it, so she does. She heads into the kitchen and flicks the kettle onto boil and hangs the seal of the letter over the steam to melt the glue. She grabs a butter knife from the cutlery drawer and slices through the glued seal.

It's to do with his overseas account. He has withdrawn a substantial amount of money. Why wouldn't he tell her if he has made a massive investment, she thinks to herself. She can feel the worry growing in her stomach, she refolds the letter and places it back in the envelope; her hands are trembling. She sweeps her fingers along the seal tightly to smooth it down and places it on the worktop, as if it hadn't been tampered with. She makes herself a cup of coffee, and then decides that she needs to investigate his office. She has half an hour until she needs to leave for work.

Going through the first drawer of the dark oak desk she starts to rifle through the mountains of letters. There isn't anything of interest so she goes to the next one and does the same, there isn't anything there either. Finally she goes to the bottom drawer of the three and it is locked! The drawers are never locked! Now she knows he is hiding something, but what is it? Ava checks her watch and realises that she is going to be late. She goes to the shoe cupboard and grabs a pair of black heels.

She runs back through to the kitchen and swipes her technical drawings case off of the dining table and scrapes her keys off the worktop in the kitchen. Her coffee stands there completely untouched. She runs out the door on her way to work.

Ava's eyes flick open, and the blood drains from her body. It is still dark. She tries to sit up and her body is weak. She looks to the side of her and sees the silhouette of Clare. She can feel the whirlwind of emotions building inside of her body. The realisation that she is home and that Richard really has gone hits her.

She weakly pulls herself off the bed and tiptoes to the door, so she doesn't wake Clare. She creeps through the door and the whole house is in darkness, shuffling down the hall on her feet and feeling the tears rebuilding in her eyes she makes her way to the stairs.

Her mother's home was her childhood home so she knows the house like the back of her hand and she can make her way in complete darkness to the kitchen. She pauses and decides she needs a cigarette to go with her coffee. She quit twelve years ago, but after the last thirty six hours she has had, she believes this is what she needs.

Knowing Harry smokes from time to time Ava heads for the front door and turns the lock. She walks to the Bentley in the hope that he has a stash in there. The car is locked. She makes her way back into the house. There is a key box to the left of the door so she goes to it. Swinging the little door wide she sees the spare key hanging there. Pulling the key off the peg she heads back to the car again. She presses the button, the car lights up indicating it's unlocked.

She opens the door and noses through the driver's side and under the driver's seat there is a packet of twenty Mayfair.

"Bingo!" She exclaims.

The relief that she has found them rushes over her. Quietly shutting the door and relocking it, she walks over the gravel as quietly as she can to the front door, places the keys back and shuts the key cupboard door. Now to find a lighter.

'Ah mum has a candle drawer in the kitchen and there is bound to be a lighter in there!' she thinks to herself.

Deep down Ava knows this is all a distraction. She shivers. The blue tiles in the hall are cold and Ava spots a pair of fluffy slippers near the stairs. She slides them on and flip flops towards the kitchen door.

The kitchen is incredibly warm because the Aga is burning hot. Ava removes the whistle kettle off the stove and fills it at the tap above the butler sink. Placing the lid back on and putting it back on the Aga she starts to rummage through the drawers. Her mother is a very meticulous woman so it doesn't take her long to find the neatly organised candle drawer and there is a lighter staring at her. She takes the lighter out and hugs it tightly against her chest. After having made her coffee, she sneaks to the back door which leads out to a courtyard area and a glass greenhouse. She can see the white picket fence glowing in the moonlight.

Ava remembers the distant childhood memories of helping to plant seeds, and then when they were ready, she'd re-pot the seedlings. She spent hours in that greenhouse with her mother and sisters. Ava has never been afraid of the garden, but in the dead of tonight she is nervous. Coffee in one hand, cigarettes and lighter in the other, she briskly crosses the lawn to a stone building, trying not to spill her coffee. Concrete steps led her up into the games room. It is in complete darkness and extremely chilly.

Entering through the door, her father's garden jacket still hangs on a peg to the right. She grasps the jacket and drapes it around her still holding the hot coffee in one hand. She flicks the light on, but the brightness is still gloomy because half of the bulbs have blown. There is a pool table and a mahogany bar with stools at the far end of the room. She perches on one of the stools. On the bar is an old ashtray sitting there. Her father only ever smoked socially and this was the only place he was allowed to do it, when he entertained his friends.

As a child, Ava would often find her father out here in the dead of the night, shooting balls on this very pool table. If he couldn't sleep he'd come here to unwind. Now Ava is here doing the very same thing. This was his space. There was also a dart board. His darts sat on the bar just as they always did. She strokes her hand over the brown leather case where the darts always lived. Ava stares around the room and shivers. Turning back to the cigarettes she takes one from the packet and places it in her mouth and lights it. She inhales and breathes a sigh of relief. This was just what she needed. She has no idea of what the time is but if she was to guess she'd say about 3 a.m.

She takes a sip of her warm steamy coffee and another drag of her cigarette. Rubbing her eyes she tries to remove the stinging feeling from the little sleep she has had and lets out the biggest, deepest sigh. Her chest feels tight and that isn't from the cigarette. It was the anxiety taking her hostage.

She sits mindlessly, trying to process everything and there is a touch on her shoulder. "Oh my God! You scared me!" She is completely startled by the touch. It is Harry. "Sorry Miss, ya can't sleep either?" He asks.

"No, I had a dream and it woke me."

"You found my stash, 'eh?" He says gesturing towards the cigarette in her hand.

"Oh yeah... I hope you don't mind?"

"No, course not, Christ with the shock of Richard, I'm not surprised you wa'ted a sneaky fag."

He turns and looks towards the pool table, "Fancy a game?"

Ava has her back to the table and is facing the bar. She swivels around on her stool to see where he is looking. She turns back, takes one last drag of the cigarette, blows the smoke from her lips and stubs it out in the ashtray.

"You know Harry, that's a great idea," she slides off the stool and picks a pool cue from the wall rack. Harry sets the red and yellow balls in the triangle rack. She chalks up and grabs the cue ball, placing it on the table. Getting into position with her cue in between her fingers she breaks. They play the game in silence.

Harry always knew when to talk and when not to when it came to the girls. Ava bends down and leans over the table to take another shot. "I'm surprised Peppi and Lola didn't wake." Ava finally fills the silence after taking her shot. Harry re-chalks his cue.

"You know what them two are like. They aren't exactly guard dogs." he chuckles.

"No, they are not. They are lazy girls." Ava laughs then stops herself. It's her shot but she pauses and looks at Harry.

"Our marriage wasn't the same after my father passed away. I wasn't the same, I changed, I was less," she pauses, "tolerant. The drinking wasn't a problem in the beginning, I knew he liked a drink... but it increased." She moves towards the pool table again to take her shot.

"He got hooked on the stuff?" Harry finishes her sentence watching her play her move.

Ava glances up from her eyeline over the table and nods. Harry then steps forward focusing on the balls. He walks around the table to take his go and he pots another yellow.

"Yes... exactly. But there was way more to it than that, Harry... it was the lies... it was the secrets," Ava admits.

"I hope you dun't mind my sayin' Miss Ava, but this in't your fault. None of it is your fault," he says sympathetically to her.

"That's where you are wrong. I should have stayed, I should have helped him," she looks directly up at him, "and please Harry just call me Ava." Her eyes begin to fill with tears again.

"Ava that weren't your responsibility. He was a grown man and he had to do it for 'imself. You left cos you had to save yaself, we saw ya change, we saw what the marriage was doin to ya, even if ya din't ever say the words."

"Harry I called him one night when I was in America. He knew it was me, I don't know how, he just did. I never spoke, I just hung up, but... what if... what if *that* phone call is what did it? What if that phone call is what finished him off?" Ava bursts into tears.

Harry rests his cue against the pool table and walks towards her and embraces her. She grasps him back tightly, crying hysterically.

"Ava, that in't what finished him off. He drank himself senseless. He abused his body and his organs failed, ya can't, and shun't bloody blame yaself for that." He whispers to her while still hugging her.

Ava lets go of his fatherly embrace and steps back staring at him.

"It wasn't just drinking Harry, he started doing cocaine too," she says, staring him right in his concerned eyes. He says nothing just embraces her again, silently, tightly. It was more severe than the family had ever realised.

'*No wonder she left the way she did!*' Harry thinks to himself.

Ava returns to her bed. She needs to try and rest if she is going to face the days ahead. She hasn't eaten for nearly two days and she is running low on energy because of sheer exhaustion.

Florence is sitting in the kitchen, up at the table with a coffee in front of her. Lydia walks through the back door, with the two King Charles spaniel dogs, Peppi and Lola.

"You're up early Lydia. Did you take them across the fields?" She asks.

"Yes. I couldn't sleep, I needed some fresh air. We walked across the fields and came out near the primary school and walked back along the road," Lydia says, wiping the dog's paws clean from the wet and mud.

"It was lovely, wasn't it Peppi?" Lydia says, making a fuss of her.

"Go on then, go lie down girls, in your bed!" Lydia commands, and the dogs trot off to their baskets in the corner of the kitchen.

Lydia takes her Le Chameau wellies off, and reopening the door, places them on the Farringdon welly rack outside the backdoor. She comes back in and shuts the door behind her. Florence sits, exhausted after last night's arrival of Ava.

"Is Ava up yet?" Lydia asks as she fills the whistle kettle at the sink.

"No darling, she's still sleeping. Clare's popped home to take the girls to school and Katelyn is on her way back from London as we speak."

"Mum, please don't be cross with me anymore," Lydia says sitting down opposite her at the table.

"Oh darling, I'm not cross, it's done and we are all here now. All we can do is be there for her," Florence decides patting Lydia's hand across the table.

"I know you all think it was irresponsible of me to tell her, or *want* to tell her I should say, but she would have never thanked us in the future for knowing and never telling her. She would have wanted to know even if it was a shock," Lydia pauses, "and mum, *he* can't hurt her anymore. This is finally closure for her."

As she finishes her sentence Harry walks in through the back door.

"Good mornin," he says.

"Good morning, Harry. You're here exceptionally early, I'm not sure anyone has any appointments or any outings scheduled for today?" Florence informs him and then sips her coffee.

"I'm aware of that, Mrs Turner, but that in't why I'm here. I need to tell you suffin' that I feel you should know. I weren't able to sleep last night, so I wandered up from mine to the games room and Ava was in there. We played pool and she got upset. Miss Ava told me last night, Richard weren't only just an alcoholic but he was doin' drugs an all!"

He then gestures to the plate he's holding, covered in foil, "And my Mable has made a Victoria sponge, Miss Ava's favourite," he says without taking a breath and places it on the centre of the table.

"Oh Harry. No!" Florence cups her face with her hands and leans her elbows on the table.

"So that's why. That's why she upped and left the way she did, she'd had enough!" Lydia adds.

Katelyn arrives. She has a grey faux fur coat on, leather trousers and a face that is fully made-up.

"Mum!" she heads straight for her mother and hugs her.

"Oh Katelyn, you're here already. How are you sweetheart?" she says patting her arm.

"Don't worry about me. Where's Ava?"

"She is still sleeping. Although Harry here informs me that she was up halfway through the night in your father's games room."

"Hi Harry. Morning Lyds. Is that one of Mable's famous sponges?" Katelyn greets them while eyeing up the cake on the table. Lydia strolls over, hugs her elder sister tightly, who returns the gesture.

"Miss Katelyn. It certainly is." Harry responds.

He leaves the Turners to allow them to talk privately. Lydia continues to make coffees for the three of them, and Clare makes an appearance after her motherly duties are finished with her girls.

Ava enters the kitchen at 10 a.m. She is still wearing her father's gardening jacket. She looks utterly exhausted. Her hair is unwashed, her face pale and there are dark rings around her eyes. Clare is cooking bacon to make sandwiches, and Lydia continues making another round of teas and coffees. Katelyn and Florence are sitting at the dining table.

"Ava, you're up. We left you to sleep for as long as you needed," her mother says.

"Do we know where Richard's body is?" She addresses everyone.

Lydia replies sheepishly to Ava's question. "When he fell ill, Ava, his sister informed me he was at the Jonathan Pryce Hospital." She pauses, "But he discharged himself before any investigations were carried out, so I'm unsure."

"Right... well. I need to phone the Chapel of Rest there first then," Ava says.

Florence glances in Ava's direction. "Is that wise Ava?" She says softly.

"Of course it is. I need to see him, I'm struggling to believe he's dead. Lydia, do you know if his mother has returned?"

"She got back from Ireland when he fell ill, I believe. Why do you ask?"

"Because Lyds... she is quite frankly the last person I want to be confronted with right now. I will make the phone call to the hospital and then I'll get showered."

Ava leaves the kitchen.

Florence rises from the table, and follows Ava to the entrance hall. "Sweetheart, do you want me to come with you? I don't need to come in, just be there for support. What if Janette *is* there?" Ava turns to look at her mother, rubbing her face and then her eyes with both her hands unable to decipher what her mother is saying.

Chapter Seven

Harry drives Ava and Florence to the Jonathan Pryce Hospital. He pulls up to the drop off area. "Are you ready, Ava sweetie?" Florence holds her hand tightly.

"Yes." She sighs.

They slide themselves from the car and make their way to the entrance. Ava's body feels like it is shaking from head to toe. Her mouth is dry. Her stomach is empty. Her body has nothing left to give. She moves her resistant body one step at a time, knowing each step is bringing her closer to seeing the man she deeply loves, who she would always love.

They approach the front desk of the hospital. Ava continues trying to swallow in an attempt to produce moisture in her mouth. Her mother links her arm with great strength, trying to be the crutch, to hold her up. The receptionist calls the Chapel of Rest. A woman approaches them. She is dressed smartly and wearing a lanyard. Her name is Michelle and underneath it says Bereavement Coordinator.

They follow her to the Bereavement Suite.

"Miss Turner I am sorry for your loss. You are going to go through this door. Richard won't be in that room as it is a seating area should your mother prefer to wait there." Michelle looks compassionately at Florence.

"There will be another door in front of you. When you are ready you can enter... Now Richard *is* dressed in a shroud. He looks very much at peace. Please take as long as you need," she explains calmly and sympathetically with a warm face.

Ava and Florence approach the door. Florence turns the handle, wraps her arm around Ava's waist and supports her through. Ava pauses and stares back at Michelle who then shuts the door for them. Ava's head feels light, as if she could pass out. Her heart is beating so hard it feels like it could burst through her rib cage at any moment.

Florence takes her hand.

"Sweetheart, do you want me to come in with you? " Looking at the white door ahead of them.

"No, No…. I need to do this on my own." Ava replies in a whisper then takes in the deepest breath. She approaches with tiny steps feeling as though her ankles could give way from underneath her. She rests her hand on the door handle and her face tingles with fear and anxiety. As she opens it, a soft light glows and there is Richard laying on a pall cloth and dressed in a shroud up to his neck. Ava feels sick, and pauses. She hears her mother close the door quietly behind her.

"No! No! No! Richard. No," she says, broken, in complete despair.

There he lies totally at peace. He looks asleep. Ava slowly walks towards him, taking one slow step at a time. She is physically shaking.

Next to him, there is a chair. The atmosphere is completely still. Sitting isn't a choice. Her body won't let her. She stands silently. She isn't sure whether to touch him. She is in complete shock. Ava tries to speak but no words come out. Tears begin to fall and she breaks down. She whimpers to begin with, which then become gut wrenching screams. She lays her head on his stomach and sobs hysterically.

The tears keep coming and there is nothing she can do to stop them. They come with such ferocity. She wipes her face with her finger tips and removes her head from his body. She looks at his face and moves her hand to touch his hair, doing this incredibly gently. She fears he'll wake. Ava feels incredibly scared and alone.

"Only you aren't going to wake, are you Richard?" She whispers through her tears.

She picks up the chair, moving it closer to him and places it down as quietly as she can. Ava strokes his hair with deep affection and sits quietly for a moment. There is a ghastly silence that surrounds them. The room is still, the candle flickers and she is mesmerized by its movement. There is an aromatic smell in the air.

"It wasn't meant to be like this... It was never meant to be this way," she murmurs to him. The tears begin to flow down her cheeks again..

"I love you Richard, and I will probably never love anyone again, the way I love you. The decisions I made were never easy. I didn't want to leave, I didn't want us to ever come to an end. Leaving you was probably the... hardest... decision... I have ever had to... make," she tries to say through her sobs.

"The day I took those vows I meant them. Every word. But our marriage became harder and I was... sacrificing myself, every inch of my soul watching you slowly lose yourself... and for what?" She begins to laugh with the tears.

"For what, huh? For this? You beautiful man, you beautiful, beautiful man," she begins to cry again. Ava leans forward and strokes his hair again.

"You are the one and will always be the one, Richard. My heart is completely broken. What have you done?" She touches his face and admires it. It seems smoother than usual. His eyes are closed. The tip of his nose is shaped like the end of a love heart. His lips look as they always do, his top lip full shaped like a cupid's bow. She leans towards his face, and places the most gentle heartfelt kiss on his cheek.

She thinks of all their happy times and finally reaches for the phone in her pocket. She swipes to her playlist and clicks on their wedding song. She rests her head on his arm which is covered by the shroud, laying there listening to the song, mouthing the words through her tears. The song comes to an end and she looks up at him. She gives him a final kiss on his cheek and whispers in his ear.

"I love you, and I will... always... love you."

As Ava and Florence are making their way out of the hospital they bump into Janette. Janette is Richard's mother and the shock on Ava's face is evident as she approaches them. "Ava," she says, clutching her arms around her.

"You came. I didn't think you would."

"Janette. How are you? I'm so sorry. I should have called but it came as a complete shock. I flew back as quickly as I could."

"You flew back. What do you mean you flew back?" Janette asks, darting a look in Florence's direction in confusion.

"I've been in America for three months now. I've been working for my uncle." Ava replies reluctantly.

"Oh right, I see," Janette replies, "Well... I must... well you know, I'm now going to see my boy. Will you wait? Or can I get you on your mobile?"

"I'll go. If that's okay? I've just been to see him." Ava's eyes well up. "I've said my goodbyes to him."

"Of course. It must have been extremely upsetting for you, I need to start making the arrangements. Would you like to have any input Ava? After all, you were his wife once upon a time and neither of you had moved on and I also know he still very much loved you, darling." Janette says.

Ava bursts into tears, and walks off towards the exit.

"I....I didn't mean to upset her," Janette says to Florence, growing increasingly upset.

"I know you didn't Jan, it has been an emotional twenty four hours. She is in complete shock and heartbroken. I know they weren't married anymore but the love was very much still there for her too."

"I know Flo."

They hug each other, mother to mother, a mutual understanding and compassion.

Ava has no involvement in the funeral plans. She is barely speaking to any of her family and spends hours alone, sitting quietly in her father's games room or walking the dogs. Her phone has rung several times but she had no interest in answering it or listening to the voicemails. She is skipping all three meals daily and has taken up smoking again with a vengeance. Coffee and cigarettes are getting her through the days and her appetite is diminished.

One evening, Ava climbs out of bed and decides to have a cigarette and a stiff drink. Her father's drinks cabinet is quite astonishing. Every drink imaginable is stored there. She explores through all the drinks, and at the back is the scotch. She slides all the other coloured and differently shaped bottles out of the way and pulls the bottle towards her. The glasses live on the other side of the cabinet. She grabs a Glen Cairn whiskey glass and places it on the top. Ava pours herself a dram, goes to screw the cap on and decides to pour even more into the glass.

She heads to the sideboard where her mother stores the photo albums. She flicks through the numerous albums - Ava's 16th birthday,

Family holiday 2000, Katelyn's 21st birthday, Clare's wedding... And there it is, Ava's wedding. She carefully pulls at the album and removes it from the white birch cabinet. Sitting on the lounge floor with her whiskey bottle, glass and album, she flicks through one photograph at a time, stroking Richard's face and kissing it. This is how she wants to remember him, not how she had seen him a week ago.

After half a bottle of scotch, Ava decides she will play her wedding song on her phone. She dances in the lounge by herself. She is drunk. She sways slowly and does not have full control of her limbs. She sings the words hysterically. When the song finally finishes she grabs a cushion from the couch and lays on the floor next to her wedding album. The room is spinning. She finally drops off into a drunken sleep.

"Ava baby, wake up, Ava!" He says shaking her.

"What Richard? It's in the middle of the night." Ava replies agitated.

"Oh don't be like that, you grumpy cow. I thought I'd wake you to let you know I was home." He slurs.

"Richard right now I couldn't care less if you are home or not. It's five in the morning!" She says moving herself away from him in their bed.

"Oh Ava, just because you don't know how to have a good time! I like to go out and party! You... you bore me!" He retaliates.

"Boring... you call me fucking boring! Your version of partying is going out with guys from work and drinking yourself senseless, and sticking that shit up your nose! It's a waste of money. You repulse me!" She yells, lifting her head off the pillow.

"I fucking repulse you? Why the hell are you married to me! Huh?" Richard becomes extremely agitated with Ava. He throws the duvet off them and jumps out of bed.

"Richard, what on earth are you doing?" Ava says, sitting up. He flicks the ceiling light on, and she sees the state of her husband. He stands there swaying from side to side unable to control his jaw. He glares at her and she begins to cry and then cups her hands over her face.

"What's the problem Ava? Huh? Why are you crying?"

"I can't do this. I'm going to sleep in the spare room." Ava gets up to move into the spare room but Richard tries to stop her.

"Ava, please don't, I'm sorry. If you really don't like it then I won't do it again," he pleads.

"Please Richard, I am absolutely exhausted. I just need to sleep. I have work in the morning." Ava shrugs him off and heads for her new bedroom.

"Oh fine Ava, fine!" He slams the door.

"Ava. Ava, wake up!" A voice says. Ava stirs and tries to shake off the interruption.

"Go away, I'm sleeping."

"Ava, you slept on the floor, and downed over half a bottle of scotch!" Katelyn says.

Ava lifts her heavy body from the floor and rubs her eyes.

"Oh my," she says, yawning, "so I did." She lies back down.

"Ava we're really worried about you. This can't keep going on! Ava May! Do not ignore me!" Katelyn shouts. "You aren't eating, you aren't showering, you aren't talking to anyone! This has *GOT* to stop! Get up *NOW!*" Katelyn demands.

"Okay, okay Katelyn," Ava sits up.

"Get showered and meet me in the kitchen. GO!" Katelyn demands.

Ava lays in the bath, silent, still. Today is the day and it's the final goodbye. She sinks into the water completely immersed, then opens her eyes. The vision is blurry. She lays for as long as she can, and then shoots up out of the water and catches her breath. Ava wipes her face and scrambles out. She decides to wear the traditional black in the form of a smart black suit dress and black heels and no makeup at all.

"What's the point?" She says to herself, staring at herself in the mirror for a long time.

"You can do this!" She sighs to herself, putting on the matching black jacket and making her way to the kitchen to meet the others.

"Are you ready, Ava?" Florence asks.

All the Turner girls are dressed in black. They make their way to the front door.

"Ava sweetheart, we are with you every step of the way," Florence says lovingly and hugs her tightly.

Harry is waiting at the car to open the doors. This is it. They make their way to Richard's funeral, united and to support Ava.

Chapter Eight

TAC resides in its own high rise building, and James has over seven hundred staff. He spends the majority of his time overseeing his empire and attending meetings. On the ground floor there is a large glass sign with Turners' Architectural Corporation (TAC) engraved in silver. It is lit up brightly and very eye-catching to anyone who enters the building. Ava works on the top floor alongside her uncle and the other corporate members, but in the time Ava has been there, she has never come into contact with them. Anyone who visits TAC has to check in at the visitors' ground floor reception before making their way to any other destination within the building which has eighteen floors and there is security throughout.

Michael is standing at the reception desk on the top floor.

"Thank you, if you could bring it to my office, that'd be great," he says to Betty.

Ava emerges from the lift and Michael turns to face her.

"Ava... hi. How are you?" He asks, confused by her appearance.

James interrupts before Ava gets the chance to reply to him.

"Ava, sweetheart, you're back?" He says embracing her for a long moment.

Michael slips away and returns to his office leaving them to talk.

Ava stands there in an oversize jumper, greasy hair and no makeup on her pale face.

"I got back last night, I've barely slept, and have serious jet lag. When do you want me back?" She asks solemnly.

"Darling, I'm *not* entirely sure you are ready to come back. I think you need to take some more time?"

"Uncle James, I need to get back to work, I need a reason to get up, my days are long, draining... and *lonely*."

"I know what you're saying but you need to get stronger. Throwing yourself into work isn't going to make the pain go away."

"Fine! I'll just drink myself senseless instead!" She says turning on the spot and storming towards the lift.

"Ava... Ava, please?" James says striding after her to the lift. The doors open, someone steps out as she steps in, then turns to say "Screw you, Uncle James!"

The doors close before he can reply to her.

Ava feels unwanted and lacking a sense of purpose. Her work has always been the most satisfying thing in her life. When her father passed away, she only took the weekend off and returned to work the following Monday morning. Ava doesn't want to be swallowed up by her emotions. Retracing her steps and returning to the apartment, she knows that with no distractions, her grief will consume her.

Michael knocks on the glass door. "Come in," James says.

"Hi, Mr Turner. I have the draft drawings you asked for?" Handing them over.

"Ah brilliant. They called this morning and want to see them, asap."

"I hope you don't mind me asking... but is Ava okay?"

"Hmm," he says looking up, "Ava... yeah, she had some business to attend to, back in England. She'll be okay," he replies overlooking the technical drawings.

"These are good Michael," James compliments.

"Oh thank you, I mean, they're the first drafts, so there's bound to be changes made by the client, of course."

"I'm impressed, I have to confess. I think you'll do well here Michael."

"Well thank you, Mr Turner," he smiles and heads out of James' office.

Ava sits silently in her apartment. She has opened a bottle of white wine from the fridge, and she flicks on the TV and selects the music channel for background noise. The more she drinks the more the idea grows of going out. Stomping to her bedroom in her baggy jumper, she decides to go through her wardrobe and picks an outfit. Scrapes her hair up with a clip and puts some clear lip gloss on. Slipping on a pair of black denim jeans and a black low-cut top with long sleeves, her breasts are on show more than she would usually allow. Ava digs through her shoe collection and selects a pair of slingback black heels to match her top.

After paying, Ava stumbles out of the cab and heads towards LAVO nightclub. She joins the long queue of clubbers waiting to get in. The doormen greet Ava as she enters through the doors. The music and the dance area is downstairs in the basement. She can hear the music booming so she follows the sound. Already intoxicated she tries to hold herself together. The club is heaving with people dancing and throwing their drunken bodies in time to the music. Making her way through the clubbers past the lounge seating area towards the bar, she stands patiently waiting to get served. The bar is in the corner of the club and lit up by lighting underneath the bar counter. The space looks bigger than it is due to the mosaic mirrors decorating the area where the spirits are located. As she looks around she sees erotic dancers on podiums being oggled at by drunken, sleezy men.

"You want me to head to the bar?" Michael shouts through the music to Mia.

"Yeah sure!" Mia is smiling as she moves her Mexcian body to the rhythm of the music.

"You wanna come with me?" he shouts, trying to be heard.

"Yeah okay!" She grabs Michael's hand tightly so he doesn't lose her as he leads her through the crowd.

As Michael stands at the bar ready to order he scans his surroundings and spots Ava on the other side.

"Mia, come with me!" He grabs her hand again.

"Where are we going?" Mia asks as Michael drags her with him.

They make their way through a sea of people and approach Ava from behind.

"Ava." Michael taps her on the shoulder. She turns to face him. Ava stands there and stares at him, so intoxicated that it takes her a moment to register who he is.

"What do *you* want?" She says annoyed.

"Michael, who's this?" Mia chips in, waiting for an introduction.

"Mia, this is Ava."

"Hi, I'm Mia. Nice to meet you."

Turning back to the bar, Ava says nothing, leaving Michael and Mia just standing there.

Arms wrap around Mia and Michael. It's Joey.

"Joey. No way! How are you?" They both say hugging him. Mia chats away with Joey and Michael slips back to speak to Ava.

"Ava!" Michael says, in her ear standing behind her and clutching her waist.

"What Michael, what do you want?" She turns and yells to be heard through the loud music.

"You looked pretty upset at the office today. I just wanted to make sure you were okay?"

"I'm fine. Just leave me alone, Michael." She spits.

"Who are you out with, Ava?"

"Myself. Shouldn't you get back to your girlfriend? Now go away!" She turns back to the bar, and orders her drink. After paying, the shot is swallowed in one and her mouth is wiped by the back of her hand.

"What? My girlfriend? Mia isn't my girlfriend." He laughs. "Ava, you don't look okay. You shouldn't be out by yourself!" He says, concerned.

She turns back to face Michael.

"What why? Why shouldn't I be out by myself?"

"It's a big club, and there's a load of guys who could take advantage."

"Well, maybe that's why I am here, Michael!" She retaliates as she stumbles.

"Okay I think you've had enough to drink," he says as Ava stares at him blankly.

"Mia, I'm going to take Ava back to her apartment," Michael says as she dances away.

Michael interrupts Joey dancing, "Joey, can you make sure Mia gets in a cab okay?"

"Yeah sure! I'll look after her!", as he grabs and hugs her tightly. He plants a kiss on her cheek and Mia squeezes him back.

"Okay, we'll catch up soon, Joey," he says as he pats him on the back and says goodbye. Michael supports Ava through the club, holding her by her waist. Mia is drunk and too busy enjoying herself to take much notice that Michael is leaving.

Michael has no other choice but to hail down a cab. He helps her in and makes sure her drunken body doesn't fall out as he shuts the door and walks round to his side to get it. Ava's body sits slumped and motionless.

"Where ya headin?" the taxi driver asks.

"Ava, where do you live?" he asks the half asleep woman next to him.

"Pedro.... House," she mumbles.

"Ah, 34th Street, I got it." The cab pulls out onto the road.

They arrive at Ava's apartment building, and Mr Truman is at the Reception. Ava stumbles in through the door.

"Mr Truman," whilst holding her finger to her mouth. "Shhh", she gestures, as Michael and she head towards the lift. Michael feels awkward and stays silent as they are the only ones walking through the echoing lobby.

Ava stumbles into the lift and laughs at herself.

"Are you okay?" Michael asks, supporting her.

"I'm fine! You really didn't need to escort me back, I'm a big girl and could've got myself home, just fine," she slurs.

"Well the state you're in, I very much doubt that!"

Ava fumbles for her keys in her bag as she sways from side to side. Michael takes the bag off her.

"Let me take a look," he says, finding them immediately.

He unlocks the door and opens it for her. Ava falls forward into the apartment floor. Michael scoops her up and helps her to the couch.

"I'm fine!" She pushes him off her.

"Well, you're not, are you? You're in a state!" He admonishes as she slumps down.

Michael slides Ava's shoes off for her one at a time and stares at her. Her eyes are glazed. He heads to the kitchen cupboards and grabs a glass.

He places a glass of water on the table in front of her.

"Will you be okay?" He asks as she sits there motionless.

"Sit down," she says, trying to pat the seat next to her.

He raises his eyebrows in surprise, "Okay..." and he sits on the other side of the couch feeling increasingly awkward.

"Isn't it strange? That you are here, in my apartment." Ava starts.

"Strange. I don't understand what you mean?" Michael replies.

"It's been an awful few weeks," she says, reminiscing.

"Well, you do seem pretty upset. Mr Turner said you had some business to attend to back in England."

"Was that all he said?" Ava prompts.

"Yeah why?"

She begins to cry and Michael is unsure of what to do, so he slides across the sofa and wraps his arm around her and awkwardly hugs her.

Ava pauses, and looks up at Michael with her dampened cheeks. She stares at him for a long moment. He stares back at her and bravely wipes a tear from her face.

"Please don't cry." Michael now feels heady but not from alcohol.

Ava moves in for a kiss but Michael holds back momentarily, before kissing her back. He places his hand on her cheek and kisses her deeply. He wants this, he wants her, he wants this to happen but then he withdraws.

"I'm not sure this is a good idea. You've been drinking, you're clearly upset and I don't wanna take advantage!"

She looks at him in shock.

"You're not. I *do* want this!" She purrs and she goes in for another kiss. Michael fights the urge to take her there and then. He stands up to put space between them both.

"Ava, I'm gonna go!" And he heads for the door.

Throwing her spinning head back against the sofa too drunk to argue, the door closes and she falls asleep.

"Good morning sleepy head. Budge over!" Mia says to Michael as she tries getting on the sofa next to him. He slowly pushes himself to one end to make room for her.

"And where'd you sneak off to last night?" Mia teases.

"I didn't sneak anywhere, I took Ava back to her apartment," he replies.

"Ah... yeah, I remember her now. Who is she?"

"She's the one I told you about. The one from the flight? She works at my office."

"Wait! What! That's her? And she works at your office? So did you...?" Mia giggles.

"What. No, she was really drunk. I just made sure she got home okay!" He replies unconvincingly.

"And that's it, nothing happened?" Mia asks excitedly.

"She kissed me and my *God* I wanted it, like really badly, but she was so drunk. I felt like I was taking advantage, so I left!" He says rubbing his hand through his hair.

"You left. My God, you like her! You really like her!" Mia retorts.

"Shut up you!" Michael playfully shoves her.

Michael and Mia decide to go for breakfast at a nearby cafe in Queens. The cafe is run by a family who live locally and is one of the best in the area. They both order bagels with streaky bacon and a strong coffee, trying to lift their heavy hangover heads. They sit opposite each other as Frank Sinatra is playing in the background. Small groups gathered at other tables talk enthusiastically and loudly. A waitress appears frequently from the kitchen calling out the orders of the hungry customers. The clatter of cutlery on plates and rattling of newspapers surround them.

"So... Mike," Mia says, eyeing him whilst sipping at her coffee, "what are you going to do about this Ava, then?"

"In all honesty I'm not sure I'm going to do anything, right now. She seemed pretty upset when she came to the office yesterday and she is off work too." He takes a bite of his bagel.

"Oh really?" She says covering her mouth, "That sounds pretty deep. Perhaps you're best off out of it then," continuing to eat.

"Yeah and she's been back to England too. Mr Turner said she had some 'business' to attend to," he continues.

"That sounds ominous, don't you think?" Mia implies, reaching for her mug again.

"Exactly. I didn't ask anymore, obviously, as it's not my business. But I think she's going through some stuff right now," he pauses taking a bite of his bacon, "but that's why I wanted to escort back to her apartment last night. She was a drunken mess."

"Yeah right," Mia nods, agreeing as she takes another bite of her bagel.

Meanwhile, there is a pain and throbbing sensation as Ava lifts her head off the couch. She rubs her eyes and closes them again for a second, sighing loudly. She rubs the sleep and hangover away from her eyes, remembering very little of the night before. Glancing at her coffee table, the empty bottle and wine glass stand together. On the edge of the table is a glass of water half drunk. She slowly sits up and decides to try to drag herself to the kitchen to make coffee. Flicking the coffee machine on, she heads slowly for a shower.

Her head is spinning. She gradually undresses and climbs into the shower in the corner of the bathroom. It is a power shower so she turns the heat up and rinses away the hangover and major headache. Feeling worse, Ava decides she needs more rest and goes to her soft sheeted bed where she clambers under the covers on the bed and gently lays her head on the soft feather pillow.

"Richard, can we talk?" Ava sits on his lap while he's working his office desk.

"What's up baby?" He replies lovingly.

Ava gulps knowing that this could develop into a blazing row between them.

"Why have you been shifting money around from your overseas accounts?" She caresses his chest trying to soften the blow of what she has just asked.

He tilts his head in annoyance, pushes her off his lap and stands. Striding away from her, he begins to run his hand through his hair. He turns to face her. Ava can see by his expression he isn't happy.

"You went through my stuff, in order to find this out?"

Ava panics. "No I didn't," she goes to him and tries to show him affection.

"Well you must have done. How else would you know this? My financial affairs have nothing to do with you Ava May."

She sighs and sees she has overstepped the mark.

"I'm sorry, I didn't mean to break your trust, Richard."

He storms out of the office and heads upstairs. She turns back to his office desk and the bottom drawer is open. Something catches her eye. She can see a clear resealable bag and curiosity gets the better of her so she looks in the drawer more closely. Not touching anything else, she removes the bag and in it is white powder. Panic runs through her body and she shakes her head in complete disbelief, and she quickly puts it back.

Ava lifts her head off the pillow and lays there for a while. She is still hungover and rubs her face. The dreams of the past are haunting her frequently these days. On her phone she searches for therapists in Manhattan. She fleetingly looks through various names but clicks off it again. Then she decides it's time to get up and get ready.

Ava has finally managed to get herself together. Locating her keys, she shuts the door and makes her way to the lift. Needing some fresh, air she decides to see some of the sights of Manhattan.

Stepping out of the lift, she sees Mr Truman at reception as usual. Ava thinks to herself *'Does that man ever sleep?'*

"Good Morning, Miss Turner. Alone this morning I see. Your guest left last night?" He asks disapprovingly.

"My guest?" Ava asks, confused.

"Yes Miss Turner. You arrived last night, with a guest!"

The panic rises in her chest and she becomes lightheaded because of a flashback.

"Oh of course, Michael. Yeah, he left last night. He only saw me home," Ava says defensively, and then makes a dash for the door. She can still feel Mr Truman's eyes burning into her.

Ava bursts through the door trying to gasp for air. She is in a blind panic. The memories come flooding back with full force. She remembers trying to kiss him.

"Oh Ava, what were you thinking, what were you doing? He doesn't look at you in that way. He is virtually a stranger!" She questions herself as she paces back and forth at the top of the stairs outside Pedro House. She starts walking with no idea of where her legs are going to take her.

After some time, Ava comes across a swimming pool called the 'Recreation Center' on East 54th. She has been brought up to be a strong swimmer and her father made her attend swimming lessons as a child. She gave them up aged fourteen because she was no longer interested and socialising with friends became a greater priority. The Center is an old building and doesn't look anything like the swimming pools back home in Suffolk. The facade has four pillars with arches in between and a touch of Art Deco. On the roadside there are many black bin liners full of rubbish and a leafless tree standing on its own. Ava walks up the concrete steps and enters.

"Good morning ma'am, how may I help you?" Says a grey haired, middle aged woman.

"Hello there. Yes I was wondering if I could possibly have the pool's opening times and a price list, please."

"Yeah sure," she replies as she reaches for a leaflet and hands it over the desk.

"The pool opening times are there and our membership price is there. It's $150."

Ava takes the leaflet and shoves it in her jacket pocket, "Thank you so much for your time."

⸻◆◆⟨⟩◆◆⸻

Chapter Nine

During her time off work, she makes an effort to rebuild her confidence. Visiting a hair salon, she has it coloured a rich chocolate brown and the shine is intense and glossy. She also attends regular facials and has her nails manicured.

It's Monday morning, and Ava is finally returning to work after having had eight weeks off. She hasn't seen Michael since their encounter three weeks ago. She has made an extra effort today. To hide her embarrassment, she has put on her poker face. She means business when it comes to Michael. She isn't trying to impress him, but to prove she was in a bad place at the time of her coming onto him.

The lift doors ping open and Betty is sitting at the reception. She is now doing some of Hannah's hours, so is a more regular fixture within the office.

"Good Morning Miss Turner, nice to see you back!" Betty welcomes, fumbling around at her desk. "Can I get you a coffee?"

"Good Morning Betty. It's good to be back, I have to say. And yes please, that would be wonderful."

"Have you had your hair coloured? It looks awesome, I love it!" Betty compliments.

"Oh yes I did," she says touching her new hair, "I'm really happy with it," swooshing her long glossy, curly locks.

Michael strolls out of his office and sees Ava standing at the reception. Under his breath he says, "Oh my God," and freezes. His heart is racing as he checks out every inch of her.

Ava is wearing a black double breasted, long sleeved blazer dress, with black patent court heels and bright red lipstick. She turns to head to her office and is greeted with the sight of Michael.

The shock is very present on her face.

"Michael..." she pauses, unable to say anything else.

"Hi..." he replies, smiling broadly.

Ava says nothing else and pulls her shoulders back and strides to her office. Michael glances at her from the corner of his eye, noticing that her dress fits in all the right places and sighs appreciatively.

In her office she whispers under her breath, "*Ava May Turner, you've proven your point,*" pleased with herself. She places her bag down and switches on her computer. Betty saunters in with her coffee. As usual she is as pristine as ever, "There you are... one coffee," placing it down on Ava's desk. Betty then perches on the edge of the desk.

"You wanna know a secret?" She pauses and Ava looks up from her screen.

"Do go on..." Ava coaxes.

"I'm gonna ask Michael out for a drink, he's *sooo* hot! He's been working here for ages now and I've put a lot of effort into flirting with him and... I think he is finally picking up on the vibes!" Betty is pleased with herself as she twirls her hair between her fingers.

"Oh really?" Ava says, sitting back in her chair, "Is there not some rule about people dating within the office?"

"Oh I don't know?" She pauses, "I won't tell if you don't!" She giggles and Ava smiles back at her.

'Of course not!... I'd best be getting on," Ava says, feeling awkward.

"Oh of course," Betty replies as she goes to leave.

Ava's morning is busy. Booking meetings with clients and catching up on draft technical drawings as well as 3D models and countless emails. Putting pen to paper is her favourite part of the job and being in a new city has given her fresh ideas. She has a lunch meeting with a rather important client today. James knocks on her heavy glass door and Ava glances up and signals him in.

"Ava, how are you?" James asks.

She steps from behind her desk and walks round to embrace him tightly.

"I owe you such an apology Uncle James, I was awful to you and you didn't deserve it, especially after everything you have done for me," she says shamefully.

"There is no need to apologise. You were in a bad place and not out the other side completely. You've been through a lot, more than most, but... now look at you!" He fans his hands out and Ava twirls displaying her new look.

"A little more respectful, hmm?" Ava scoffs.

"You look beautiful my darling," he says approvingly at his niece's beauty.

"Thank you. I'd completely let myself go, so I went shopping and had my hair done," she says with a smile.

"The clients will love you, especially today!"

"Ah yes, you said he was a special client?"

"Yes... he is, his name is Donald Clarke, aka Donny," James reveals.

"Oh right, anything I need to know?" She asks, grabbing her bag from under her desk.

"Yes! He's highly obnoxious and loves the ladies. He is from a very wealthy and powerful family. Your job is to win him over so he chooses TAC. He has three other companies doing drafts as we speak. He is a big contract and would be a great asset to this firm," he explains. So Ava agrees and makes her way out to meet him.

As she approaches, Michael is leaning over the desk talking to Betty.

"So... Michael," Betty starts. As Ava hears this, she rolls her eyes, knowing what's coming.

"You wanna go for a drink sometime?" She asks through her lashes flirtatiously. Michael sees Ava from the corner of his eye and stares at her. She looks away and strides meaningfully to the lifts. He feels a pang of disappointment and turns his attention back to Betty.

"Yeah sure... that'd be great!" He says distractedly standing up tall and broad.

"Okay, well I'll give you my cell," and slides her number across the top of the desk.

The lift doors slide shut. Ava feels a swirl of jealousy rise through her, but she shakes the feeling off.

Ava is sitting in the restaurant waiting patiently for Donald Clarke to arrive. She checks her watch, he is late. The restaurant has ambient soft lighting from the ceiling and a glow from the candles at the centre of each table. These are covered in immaculately ironed tablecloths and the look is completed with a freshly cut rose from the restaurant garden. Each table is sectioned off into private wooden booths. The floor is covered with a rich burgundy carpet. The diners are being serenaded with soft classical music playing in the background.

A rather handsome man approaches the waiter who greets each customer as they arrive. Ava sits up straight as the waiter escorts her dining companion for the evening to her table. He reaches out his hand and introduces himself.

"Donny Clarke and you must be Miss Ava Turner?" She returns the handshake.

"Please, take a seat, Donald," she says, gesturing opposite her. Ava can feel Donny eyeing her all over. He is clearly pleased with her appearance. He waits for Ava to be seated and he seats himself.

"It's Donny, please, Miss Turner."

Ava understands she needs to use her femininity to her advantage. She knows he is one of 'those' men. He sits opposite her with a relaxed posture, but arrogantly. He places his hands on the table and links his fingers waiting for Ava's pitch to begin. She takes a breath and goes to her bag to withdraw the technical drawings. Placing them down without saying anything, she waits for him to reach for them.

"So, I'm of the understanding you're one of the best?" He says teasingly, his eyes burning intensively into her.

"I too, have been told that on more than one occasion, Mr Clarke," she replies confidently, leaning forward, letting him feed off of her body language. They sit silently as he goes over her ideas. After placing them down and leaning back in his chair, he places his hands on his lap.

"Let's eat. I can't make any rash decisions on an empty stomach, now can I?" as he reaches for the menu.

"Of course." Ava reaches for her menu too.

The waiter reappears at the table to take their order, and on this occasion, she lets Donny make both their orders.

"We'll have the lobster and a bottle of your finest red, please?" Donny orders and then turns his attention to Ava. "I know we shouldn't drink at a lunchtime meeting, but I won't tell if you don't," he winks playfully.

"Mr Clarke, you are the second person to say that today," leaning her elbow on the table and resting her chin on her knuckles. She has well and truly turned her seductive charm on because she has to win this deal for the company.

'Is that so Miss Turner? Well, that says a lot about you. Clearly good at keeping secrets," he smirks.

Ava's stomach does an unexpected somersault. She is enjoying flirting with this man and she only returns a smile.

"So... you're from England? How are you enjoying it here in New York City?"

"Yes, I am. New York is quite different from where I'm from. I come from a rural county called Suffolk, and I lived in the countryside surrounded by fields and greenery."

The waiter returns with their wine, and he pours a small amount for Donny to approve. He swirls the dark red liquid around, brings the glass to his lips, and takes a sip, not taking his eyes off Ava.

"That's perfect, thanks," he says appreciatively. The waiter then pours Ava a glass too, and places the bottle in the centre of the table.

"Please," Donny gestures to Ava's glass, "try some, it's incredible." Ava picks up her glass and brings it to her mouth, Donny eyes her like an eagle.

"It's smooth and full bodied," she says placing her glass back on the table and he nods to her approval.

Their lobster arrives. It is rich red in colour and the sweet marinade and seasoning wafts aromatically. Ava's mouth salivates at the presentation of her meal. They talk about her ideas over dinner including the structure and the materials they'll use if TAC gets the contract. Donny nods enthusiastically when he agrees and opposes other ideas if he is uncertain. They finish up their succulent meal and their wines.

"Would you like desert Miss Turner?" Donny asks.

"Oh no thank you. I'm completely full. That was mouth wateringly delicious and a great choice I must say," complimenting him.

"You're most welcome. The company has been... exceptional," Donny replies invitingly.

"It's been lovely, thank you," Ava says as the waiter returns.

"Would you like to see the desert menu or may I get you a coffee?" the waiter asks.

"No, we won't be requiring the menu, thank you." Donny turns his attention to Ava, "Unless of course... you have something else in mind Ava?" His eyes burn into her. Ava can feel her cheeks flushing and her stomach roll. She knows exactly what he means and it feels most tempting, but she is aware that this is all a game. This flirting is completely out of character for Ava.

"Not today, thank you," she replies playfully not losing eye contact with him.

"Then I'll have the bill," Donny demands, to the waiter.

"This has been most invigorating, Miss Turner. I have to say, you intrigue me," he says coyly, leaning back in his chair. Ava can see him undressing her with his eyes and she is unnerved by it.

"Then, Mr Clarke, until next time. I shall leave you with the technical drawings, until you have come to a decision." Ava stands and Donny stands with her. He shakes Ava's hand and feels her whole body tingle.

"Until we meet again Miss Turner," he holds her hand for a long moment.

"Mr Clarke, it has been a pleasure," and leaves the restaurant feeling flushed.

Arriving back at the office Ava feels intoxicated after her lunch and she isn't sure whether it is *just* the wine. She is greeted by James as she steps out of the lift.

"Ava, you did it! We have the contract. I've just got off the phone to Donny. He's impressed. However did you do it?" He asks quizzingly.

"Let's just say... I played him at his own game!" She says laughing.

It's late and the office floor is nearly empty. Ava finishes up making amendments to her drawings and decides it's been a long enough day. She rounds up by switching off her computer, then grabs her bag and phone from the desk. As she heads out of her office she bumps into Michael.

"Ava..." he pauses, "are you avoiding me?" Awkwardly running his hands through his hair.

"No, no of course not. What makes you think that?" Replying quickly.

"Well, you know," he pauses, "after...", Michael runs his hand through his hair for the second time, "that night, we haven't seen each other."

"Oh right, yes, that. Um, well. I was drunk and...," Ava says and he interrupts, "Of course... of course, I understand." Michael nods, feeling embarrassed that he'd even mentioned it at all.

"Right... well."

"Well... night, then?" Michael says.

"Night," Ava nods. He slowly makes his way to the lift, while Ava stands still. *What does she do? Does she get in the lift with him? Does she take the stairs?* Feeling silly, she heads for the lift too.

"Hey," she says stupidly, knowing full well she had seen him just moments ago.

"Hey," Michael laughs. They stand silently waiting for the lift to arrive. Ava can feel her heart thumping in her chest and cheeks getting redder by the minute.

"Where's the lift?" She says, tapping the call button repeatedly, chuckling nervously.

"I don't know," Michael replies. The atmosphere is burning between them and Ava's body is growing increasingly hot from the embarrassment.

Arriving at the Recreation Center for her regular swimming session, Ava leaves the changing area and makes her way to the pool side. Today the pool is empty so she can really get some lengths in. Entering the water, she gasps at its coldness. Immersing herself under, she sets off for her first length in front crawl. Coming back in breaststroke, Ava reflects on her encounter with Donald Clarke. Never been one for many boyfriends, she cringes at her behaviour with him. She really does consider him to be an obnoxious sleaze and someone to be avoided at all costs. After an hour and a half, Ava steps out of the pool refreshed and goes to shower, dry and dress.

Michael rushes through the apartment door, in a fluster.

"Hey, how was your day?" Mia asks as he places his case on the African style sideboard.

"Yeah good. Ava's back and... she looked...well - sexy. Really, really sexy!" He recalls appreciatively.

"Ahh, so the mysterious wanderer has returned?" Mia intimates.

"Yeah, she certainly has, and definitely made an impact, that's for sure," shaking his head.

"And turned you into a hot mess too, Mike!" Mia teases.

"I need a stiff drink and a *cold* shower!" He laughs.

"You shower and I'll start dinner. Spicy fajitas okay? Or will that send you to boiling point?" She taunts.

"Ha, ha, very funny, Mia Garcia!" He calls out entering the bathroom and hears her laugh hysterically as the door is shut.

Michael is standing under the lukewarm beads of water. He can't get Ava out of his mind. Rubbing his face under the spraying water, he tries to get the image of kissing this woman out of his head. His body burns for her and his stomach churns. Leaning his forehead and forearms against the tiled wall, he lets the water drench him.

He heads back into the kitchen. Mia is dishing up dinner.

"Mexican, Mia style!" She says, shrugging.

"Great, because I'm starving!" They sit down together and feast.

Ava settles down on her sofa after an eventful day, throws her head back on her grey cushion and flicks the TV on to watch the news. Now she lives in New York, she needs to keep up to date with the latest events. There had been a shooting in Brooklyn. Ava watches it for a while and then switches off. Richard's death is still too raw to watch anything like that.

Ava suddenly realises that she is feeling hungry so she heads to her cupboards and finds some bagels. She checks the large fridge and gets the soft cheese out. As she cuts the bagels she nicks her finger slightly.

"Ouch!" She says, nipping her finger to stem the tiny amount of blood. She goes to the bathroom sink, rinses it and grabs a plaster from the vanity cabinet. Heading back into the kitchen area, she continues preparing the snack.

After eating, Ava places her plate in the kitchen sink and decides to wash up tomorrow. She's tired because the first day back has taken it out of her. She walks to the bathroom and begins running a bath, adding lots of bubbles. As she undoes every button on her dress one at a time, she stands in front of the vanity mirror and is greeted with her reflection, standing there in her plain black matching underwear. She admires herself and notices after the loss of Richard that she is gaining weight again having regained her appetite. Ava flicks her bra hooks and removes her bra. Her breasts are returning too, she thinks to herself. She grabs a clip from the side of the sink to hold her hair up. She slips her panties off and puts one foot in the bath followed by the other. She slowly sits down immersing herself into the hot bubbly water.

Michael lies on the couch, under the blanket. Mia has already gone to bed. The room is dark and quiet and so silent that he can hear his own breath. He begins thinking about Ava again, and the growing feeling swirls in his stomach even stronger. He shuts his eyes and is instantly greeted with Ava. She is strolling past him in her sleek, sexy, black blazer dress. He sees her pert ass and her long bare legs walking away from him. He reaches into his pants and touches himself. Growing in the anticipation of his own touch, he groans, he removes his hand and sighs heavily. He sits up and tries to shake this feeling off.

"Ava, what are you doing to me?" He thinks as he lies back down and gets himself comfortable finally shutting his eyes.

Ava slides into bed, flicks her large side lamp off and gets comfortable. Her phone pings. She sits up and turns to her bedside table, picks up her phone and reads the text.

'Miss Turner, it was a pleasure meeting you today, I would very much love it if you would join me for dinner? But of a personal nature instead. Donny'

Ava blinks, astonished!

"How on earth did you get my number?" She says out loud. She clicks off the message, rolls back over to get some well-deserved sleep, but as she lays there she thinks to herself, 'I know your game Mr Clarke.' Shutting her eyes she drifts off into a deep sleep.

Ava strolls on site and is greeted by the site manager.

"Hello there, I'm Richard Burton," he says putting his hand forward.

"I'm Ava Turner. Pleased to meet you."

"If you'd like to follow me this way, you can come and meet the team and see the plot."

"Brilliant, lead the way," Ava says to Richard, gesturing to him to go ahead.

Ava is wearing steel toe cap boots, a bright yellow high vis jacket, and a white hard hat with jeans and a white t-shirt.

Richard is chatting away with Ava about the plans. It's a hot day and he removes his hard hat to wipe his brow, then he runs his hands through his hair and replaces it back on his sweaty head. Ava admires his stubbled face and piercing blue eyes. She looks him up and down. He has blue denim jeans that are ripped on the thigh area and a white t-shirt on, which is grubby. She continues to listen to the plans for the weeks ahead, intensely staring at him and recognising his organisational skills.

As they head back to Ava's car, Richard stops her.

"Hey Ava, would you like to join me for dinner sometime?" She opens her car door and pauses, "Thank you for your offer, but I don't mix work with pleasure, sorry!" She gets in, shutting the door and starts the engine.

Michael steps out of the lift and James approaches him.

"Michael, could I have a word?"

"Yeah sure thing, how can I help?"

"Michael, I'm going to put you on the same project as Ava, if that's okay?"

"Uh… yeah sure, not a problem," Michael says pleasingly.

"Brilliant, I'll let Ava know the plan and she'll pop in and see you with her first drafts."

"Okay, sure," Michael heads back to his office, shutting the door. He stands there and runs both hands through his hair frantically.

"I cannot be around her, I just can't!" He thinks to himself, shaking his head.

"Betty, when Ava gets in, can you send her to my office?" James requests.

"Yes of course, Mr Turner," watching as James struts towards his office.

Ava arrives at the office at her usual time.

"Good Morning Miss Turner. Mr Turner wants to see you in his office," Betty informs her.

"Oh okay. Did he say what it was referring to?" Ava asks.

"No he didn't, sorry."

Ava knocks on her uncle's door even though it is open. James can feel Ava's presence looming at the door and he looks up from his desk.

'Ahh Ava, come in," he says warmly.

"Uncle James, you wanted to see me?"

"Yes, I've put Michael on your project. He has some fresh ideas and it's always good to work in a small team so you can bounce off each other's creativity just to polish the final drafts for Mr Clarke," he replies.

"Uhh... right, okay. Of course, good idea."

"Don't you want to work with him? He had the same reaction."

"No honestly, it's not a problem."

"Great, I said you'd go and see him with your first drafts. I won't be about this morning. I have a meeting to attend off Manhattan."

"Okay, I'll see you later. I'll check in with Michael now," Ava says as she leaves her uncle. En route to Michael's office she takes in a deep, slow breath.

She knocks on the glass door and he waves her in because he's on the phone.

"Yeah okay, we'll do lunch," he laughs, "Yeah okay Mimi, I'll see you at twelve," and he hangs up.

As Ava enters the office, there is a strong scent of his aftershave and her senses are heightened by it. He is wearing a dark navy blue suit with a matching tie and a crisp white shirt. He runs his hand through his hair. "Ava, morning, come in, take a seat," he says in a fluster, removing the junk from his desk and piles of paper from the guest chair.

Ava awkwardly sits down and remains silent, not knowing what to say.

"So... you have the first draft with you?" he asks, gesturing towards the neatly rolled paper resting on her lap.

"Oh of course." She laughs nervously, unrolling the papers and laying them out for him to analyse.

He spends a minute casting his eyes over them.

"These are brilliant! The cornice has great detail. What material are you going to use on the architrave?" Michael questions whilst studying in great detail.

James bursts into the office, "Sorry to interrupt you. Mr Clarke wants to see you today. It doesn't matter which one of you sees him, but he has some questions about the draft." He explains.

"Okay, did he say where he wants to meet?" Ava asks.

"Yes, Macy's at 1 p.m." Shutting the door after him and leaving Ava and Michael alone.

"Would you like to meet our client?" Ava asks, turning to look at Michael.

"Yeah good idea. It would be good to meet him and get the feel for what he likes." Michael agrees.

They spend the rest of the morning making changes and alterations to the second and final proposed draft.

The clock hits 11.50 a.m. and they decide to take a well-deserved coffee break. As they head out of Michael's office they see Mia standing at the reception. Betty has now left and Hannah has taken over on reception. Hannah is chatting with Mia as they approach.

"Good morning Mike, I know I'm early," Mia says.

"Oh Mia, I completely forgot! Lunch!" As he runs his hands through his hair.

"You forgot? We spoke at nine this morning, how could you forget?" Mia laughs.

"I have to go to a business lunch with a client instead," He says apologetically.

"Ava, you remember Mia, from the club?" He reminds her and re-introduces them.

"Oh... of course, Mia. Nice to see you again," Ava smiles awkwardly.

"Well Mike, as you can't lunch with me I'll take your work colleague instead?" Mia teases. "That's if you don't mind, of course, Ava?" Mia looks at Ava.

"No, of course not. That would be lovely, some female company for a change." They both giggle.

"Okay, Mimi, I'll see you tonight!" He plants a kiss on her cheek, "Ava, I'll let you know how I get on this afternoon."

Mia decides to take Ava to a great Italian restaurant for their lunch.

Michael arrives at Macy's and the waiter takes him to his table. The client is already seated. As he reaches the table Michael is shocked by who he is greeted with.

"Donny?"

"Michael?" queries Donny.

"So you're TAC's client, Mr Clarke?" Michael replies in shock, piecing it together.

"I didn't know you were back in New York? Olivia never said," Donny remarks.

"That's because Olivia doesn't know."

"I was expecting Miss Turner." Donny says, awkwardly.

"Well, I'm working with Ava, Miss Turner, on the project."

"Shall we sit?" Donny says, gesturing to Michael's seat.

Ava and Mia arrive back at the office. They hug and Ava thanks her for a delicious lunch at the Italian restaurant.

"Ava, how do you feel about salsa?" Mia asks, shaking her shoulders in a salsa move.

"Salsa?" Raising her eyebrows in surprise at Mia's question.

"Yeah, salsa. Oh Ava, it's great fun. Mike never wants to go *and* to be honest he doesn't have the moves!" She laughs.

"I don't know!" Ava says anxiously, shaking her head.

"Oh come on, you've moved across the ocean. It's a great way to network. Come on, it'll be fun!" Mia protests.

"Okay... okay. You've twisted my arm." Shrugging her shoulders and realising it could be fun.

"Great. I'll meet at your apartment. It's this Friday. I'll get your address from Mike!"

"Okay great! I'll look forward to it." They go their separate ways.

Michael bursts into Ava's office.

"Donny. Donny Clarke is our client?" He blurts out and Ava lifts her head from a sketch, and turns to look at Michael.

"Yes it's Donny Clarke. I didn't know it was going to be a problem. Is it a problem?" Ava asks calmly.

"Ava, Donny is the brother of my ex-girlfriend of eleven years!" Michael declares.

"Ah...I see why this could be a problem. If you want to remove yourself from the project I completely understand. I had no idea. It must've been really uncomfortable for you this afternoon. I'm so sorry." She says sympathetically.

"No, it's okay, you weren't to know!"

Michael sighs heavily and runs both hands through his hair. Ava turns to face him and rests her bottom against her desk and folds her arms.

"So... eleven years and you didn't put a ring on her finger?" She says sheepishly.

"Oh, I tried, several times, and there was always a reason," he explains, "I wasted eleven years of my life on her and she always moved the goal post." Taking a seat on the couch in Ava's office, she walks over and sits next to him.

"I wasted nine years on my ex-husband too!"

"You were married for nine years?" Michael asks, staring at her.

"No, not married for that long but together." She sighs, staring ahead of her, aware of him gazing at her.

"What happened?" He says, quietly.

"An ongoing sequence of events... that consequently led to the breakdown of our marriage."

"Is that what you were upset about that day?" Michael asks.

Ava stands and walks to the window and takes in the view, watching the clouds moving across the sky.

"Would you mind if we change the subject?" Continuing to look at her view, she feels a pang of sadness building in her chest. They are both silent for a moment.

"Have you seen Manhattan?" Michael asks.

"Hmm, sorry?" Ava says, turning to look at him.

"Well, you've moved here, but have you been to see any of the sights, yet?"

"No, I haven't. I haven't gotten around to it."

"Tour guide?" Michael says, standing and gesturing to himself.

"That would be lovely."

"Okay. Well, we could go tomorrow night? You wanna eat before we head out?"

"Yes, I'd really like that." She replies.

Later that day, Ava leaves work to attend her usual swimming session. She is really enjoying them, as if she was thirteen again. As she swims her lengths faster and stronger, she is aware that her health is returning. After a shower and dressing she is walking towards the exit. A man walks past her and gives her the biggest smile. Feeling awkward she says, "Hello, lovely day out, isn't it?" As Ava walks to the door she is greeted with a downpour of rain. *"Typical Ava. Think before you speak."* She laughs to herself as she sprints down the wet streets of Manhattan.

Chapter Ten

"Y ou look nice. Where're you off to?" Mia asks Michael.

"I have a date. How do I look?" Michael says, doing up the top button of his navy blue long sleeved shirt.

"A date... Ooo! Who with, Ava?" She taunts.

"No... Betty, from work, actually."

"Wait... what? Who's Betty? What about Ava?" Mia asks, shocked.

"Mia! We talked about this. Ava is a no go zone. Remember?"

"Yeah! And then I had lunch with her and she's great!" Mia says biasly.

"Mia, I don't date people just because you've approved them," Michael laughs.

"Yeah I know, but you like her and seeing you around her today just proves that."

"Mia... drop it!" He says putting his black Derby shoes on and lacing them up. Mia stands watching him attentively for a moment.

"Okay well, I'll drop it when you admit that you still have feelings for her."

"How can I have feelings for someone I barely know?" Michael retaliates.

"You said she made you feel alive, Mike? Those feelings don't just go away!"

"Right, well, whilst I leave you to ponder this whole situation, I have a date."

Michael grabs his black bomber jacket, slips his wallet in his back pocket and heads for the exit. Mia follows behind him to the door and kisses him on the cheek.

"Have a great time."

"Don't wait up... Mom," Michael laughs.

Mia shoves him jokingly and shuts the door after him.

As Michael stands outside the 'Top of the Strand' with his hands tucked in his trouser pockets, Betty appears. She looks more beautiful than ever. Long blonde hair is curled and resting on one shoulder. Her complexion looks flawless and she is wearing tight black fitted trousers on with a baby blue breast revealing top. Michael is drawn to staring across her breasts immediately.

"Hey Betty." He says, removing his hands from his pockets. Hugging her briefly, and kissing her cheek briskly, she returns the gesture.

"Hey Michael, you look smart. I'm impressed!"

They take an elevator to the 21st floor.

"Shall we go in?" Michael says confidently and opens the door to her and they head for the bar. Michael orders a Budweiser beer and orders a pina colada cocktail for Betty.

"If you would like to find a table and we'll bring your drinks to you." The bartender informs them after Michael swipes his American Express.

Michael and Betty choose a table on the rooftop terrace. It is overlooking the city under a black sky. The buildings have warm window lights that twinkle like stars.

"This is nice. What a view, huh?" Betty says staring across the Manhattan skyline.

"I know, right? It is something I missed when I lived in England." Michael replies, following her eye.

"So you lived in England?" Betty prompts.

"Yeah, I did, I haven't been home long. I lived there with my recent ex, Olivia. She's still over there."

"Did you find it hard, coming home?" Betty asks as the bartender arrives with their drinks and places them one at a time on the table. They pause their conversation.

"You could say that. It was a massive decision to leave in the first place, but I don't regret it."

"It's a very brave thing to do, Mike. I could never leave New York. It's my home and all of my family is here," Betty adds.

Mike and Betty have an enjoyable evening. After consuming several drinks, both are now tipsy and as the evening draws to an end, they are standing back on the sidewalk. Betty becomes increasingly flirtatious and steps closer to Michael.

"So," she pauses, "do you wanna come back to mine for a drink?" She says stroking his chest and staring at him invitingly. He stands still, feeling that he is a lot more tipsy than he realised. He sighs deeply, knowing that he has reservations on this whole situation when his mind is elsewhere.

"I'd love to, but I better not. We have work tomorrow, and we need a clear head." Michael says, holding onto her elbows, smiling but the guilt is building in his stomach.

"And?" Betty looks at him longingly. Without any hesitation she edges towards his lips and kisses him. He returns the kiss and it becomes intense. Their tongues entwine together and their arousal grows, the kiss becomes more intense by the second. Michael withdraws and Betty smiles at him bashfully.

"Uhhh," he sighs, "we'd better go. I'll grab you a cab." With that, he hails a yellow cab. It draws up next to them, and Michael opens the door for her. She plants another kiss on his lips before climbing in.

"Thank you for a lovely evening. It's been great. We should do this again sometime." She says, and slides into the cab.

"Yeah it's been fun, I'll see you tomorrow?" He says leaning in. Michael shuts the door and taps the top of the cab to signal it's okay to leave. He stands there alone running both hands through his hair and sighs heavily.

Ava is in her office with Michael. They are discussing further plans and materials they'll be using on the Donny Clarke project. Betty knocks on the door and enters, holding an enormous bouquet of flowers. The roses are blood red and the lilies are pure white with the green foliage defining the two colours. It is stunning and quite breath-taking.

Ava's cheeks burn red hot. "Who are they for?" She asks, completely embarrassed.

"For you Miss Turner. They just arrived," Betty smiles sweetly.

"No they are not!" Ava says in disbelief.

"They are... there is a card addressed to you. Look."

Betty carefully passes the flowers over with both hands to Ava who places them on her desk. The flowers are in a water-based bottom to keep them fresh. Reaching for the card and opening the envelope, she shakes her head in total shock that she has received flowers. Michael watches horrified but says nothing.

"Who're they from, Miss Turner?" Betty asks excitedly.

'Ava,

Please do me the pleasure of joining me for dinner tonight?

Donny'

Ava reads aloud and looks up at Betty in astonishment.

"What! As in Mr Clarke? It looks like you have an admirer." Betty teases.

"It would appear so." Ava places the card back in the envelope and puts it back on the card clip within the flowers.

Michael can feel his insides burning, and a fury building. "Would you excuse me? I need to check something?" He leaves Ava's office abruptly as they stare.

"How sweet! Are you going to go?" Betty inquires.

"I highly doubt it. He is a ladies man and I have no interest in playing his games, but the flowers really are beautiful." Ava says, staring at them.

"Okay. Well, I best get back to work. They really are quite something, though!"

Michael sits in a leather chair at his desk trying to concentrate on his computer screen, but slips into a daydream. He is thinking about his meeting with Donny yesterday. He thinks about the letter Olivia left for him on the coffee table in their house. She made herself scarce when she decided to end their eleven year long relationship. Michael had lost his job the day before. He had been to his office to clear his belongings and came home to *that* letter. With no hesitation, he booked the next available flight and was out of there. He didn't contact her, he didn't reply with a letter, just left without a word. He hasn't heard from her since.

He is unaware of how long he has been in a trance until Ava knocks at his door.

"Hi, um... are we still on for tonight?" Ava asks awkwardly.

"Uhh yeah sure!" Michael says, running his hands through his hair nervously. "Make sure you wrap up for tonight."

"Oh... okay," she replies, surprised.

"Oh, and comfy shoes too. We'll be doing a lot of walking."

Ava nods and smiles. "Okay, where would you like to meet?"

"I'll come to your apartment at 6.30 p.m. and we'll head out from there?" Ava smiles shyly and leaves his office. Michael's heart races. He can't believe they are going to spend time together outside of the office. Alone, just the two of them.

Ava returns to her apartment, frantically unlocks the door and opens it. She is greeted with a pigsty. She hasn't washed up for a few days and there are shoes and clothes sprawled all over the furniture and floor. Now she knows that Michael is coming, she needs to tidy it and quickly! In the kitchen she runs the taps, grabbing all the dirty dishes and glasses from her bedroom, dining and coffee tables. She chucks them in the sink and begins washing up as fast as her hands will allow her. She dries everything and puts them where they belong. Straightening the cushions on the couch, the realisation hits that he may need to use the bathroom. She grabs cleaning products and a sponge from under the kitchen sink and begins to frantically clean the bath, basin, shower and toilet. She heads to her bedroom and makes the king size bed, and dresses it with cushions and a throw. Running a hoover around to pick the debris up from the grey carpets, the apartment is straight again. Finally, she gets herself ready after the frenzied rush in sheer panic.

She is spraying air freshener around the open plan living area when there is a knock at the door. Without thinking, she chucks the air freshener under the couch. Casually walking to the door Ava takes a deep breath.

"Hey, are you ready?" Michael says, having no idea of how stressed Ava truly is.

"Hi, yeah come in, I just need to get my coat." Opening the door wider, he strolls in after her as Ava heads to her bedroom.

"Wow! What a view of the city!" Michael calls out.

"Oh yes! ...It's stunning, isn't it?" She says whilst dragging her coat off a hanger in the wardrobe. Ava makes her way back out and sees Michael taking in the view through the window.

"It's a great perspective of the different styles of architecture wouldn't you say? Where are we going?" Ava says, putting on her duffle coat.

"So, we have a table booked for 7 p.m. at The Liberty for a bite and then we'll head to the Empire State Building."

Ava beams from ear to ear, "Sounds perfect!"

They arrive at Michael's chosen restaurant and it's heaving with people drinking and enjoying their meals. It's warm and cosy. There are leather chairs to one side and wooden bar tables and stools to the other. Fairy lights set a romantic ambience.

As they amble through the restaurant they see that the top half of the walls are covered in photographs and the bottom in wooden cladding. The bar staff are buzzing around the crowded bar trying to serve all the customers. It's the type of place where you feel at ease immediately.

"Hi. We have a reservation for 7 p.m. under the name of Johnson," Michael says.

"Sure! If y'all wanna follow me?" Says the waitress. Ava follows Michael and the waitress, thinking to herself *'This is exactly my kind of place. How did he know?'*

They remove their coats, sit down and make themselves comfortable feeling quite at home.

"What can I get y'all to drink?" Says the waitress ready with her notepad in hand.

"Uhhh can I have a... oh what to have?" He says stroking his chin, "Budweiser?"

"Can you make that two please?" Ava adds.

"Yeah sure! I'll be back shortly. Can I get y'all anything else?" the waitress asks.

"Yeah, actually we wanna get a bite to eat, so a menu would be great?" Michael says.

The waitress hands him a menu and leaves to deal with the drinks order.

"You drink beer? Now that surprises me, I have to say, Ava," Michael smirks.

"You make that assumption like everyone else. I'll have you know, I drink beer and I'm partial to a game of rugby from time to time," Ava giggles.

"Ahh yeah, the Brits love rugby. Can't beat a good game of American football, though. That was definitely something I missed back in England, but I gave rugby a look. But soccer, what is that game?" He laughs.

"Ah yes, I totally agree. A bunch of overpaid pansies faking injuries to get a free kick."

"Pansies, huh? What's that?" He laughs.

"A flower, Michael, a flower," she mocks.

"Oh a keen gardener too, then, huh?"

The waitress returns with their drinks and places them down on the table.

"Y'all decided what you'd like to order?" She asks.

"We haven't looked over the menu but I know what I'd like. Can I order a twelve inch pepperoni pizza, extra cheese, Ava?" Michael says staring across the table.

"Can you make that two again please?" Ava says with a grin.

"You got it. I'll get that ordered for you now."

There is laughter surrounding them. People are enjoying themselves, couples sitting intimately, or large crowds of friends or families. There is no particular age group and all kinds of characters have gathered here. The atmosphere is like a drug and Ava laps up the enthusiasm that is cast over the restaurant. She can feel her insides glowing with happiness, a feeling Ava had forgotten.

Their food arrives and Michael immediately cuts his pizza with a knife, picks a slice up and tucks in. Ava follows suit and does the same. The slices create a cheesy mess but neither of them care. They laugh as the melted cheese stretches and falls down their faces and devour their food and chug at their beers.

Light conversation is made about Ava's upbringing and her sisters. Michael tells his story too, how his parents split, as did Mia's, and that was the common ground of their long and lasting friendship. He goes on to say that his father was very demanding whilst he was growing up, and that the expectation to succeed is still there. The conversation flows and they never run out of things to say. Michael pays the bill after they jokingly argue over who is going to pay, and in the end settle it with the toss of a dime. Of course, when Ava's side lands, Michael suggests best out of three. He is adamant that he is going to pay and luckily for him, it ends in his favour.

They leave 'The Liberty' and take a leisurely stroll to the Empire State Building, and Ava takes in, with excitement, the activity on the streets. They continue to make small talk, remarking on the architecture of buildings and Michael points out other great places to eat. He explains that The Chrysler Building is great to see at some point too. Ava finally feels free. She is really enjoying the company of Michael and realising that he is completely different away from work.

"So, here we are. We're gonna head up to the 86th floor to the Indoor Observatory. The views are great from up there." Michael explains.

"I love the Art Deco architecture, I have to say. That's what makes it really unique," Ava says.

"You know that it was built in the 1930's by Shereve, Lamb and Harmon? It derived its name from the nickname for the State of New York which was 'Empire State', and the owners didn't profit from it until the early 1950s because of the depression and the war," Michael says informatively.

"I knew that Shereve, Lamb and Harmon were the architects. It really is elegantly designed." Ava agrees.

"Pretty incredible, huh?"

As they enter the lobby of the Empire State Building, Ava is blown away by the beauty of it. The ceiling is endless and the lighting is incredible. The lines on the interior walls are clean cut and totally in keeping with the Art Deco theme throughout. The floor is highly polished and there is a mural on the back wall. Ava analyses every square inch with appreciation. They get in the elevator and it ascends to the 86th floor. Both remain silent as it travels upwards, enjoying a moment's peace.

Michael and Ava step out of the lift and there it is. An astonishing view for miles. Landmarks in every direction. Ava is stunned by it. The sky is dark but the city is lit up by millions of lights, and in the distance you can see the Brooklyn Bridge and the Statue of Liberty. Michael points out where Central Park is. They have a 360 degree view of Manhattan.

"You know you can see up to 80 miles on a clear day?" Michael tells her with pride.

"It really is incredible. Thank you for bringing me to see this, Michael," Ava sighs in astonishment and stares at the incredible vista for what seems like hours.

"You wanna go see the exhibits?" Michael asks.

"Can we just stay here, and enjoy the view?" Ava asks. They stand intimately and silently, watching.

"Richard... my ex-husband always promised to bring me... but it never happened." Ava says.

"Why, are you okay to talk about him? You shut me off the other day when I tried to talk about it. " Michael observes.

"It is incredibly complex." Not looking at him but staring out of the window.

"You don't need to explain complicated things to me Ava. My whole eleven year relationship was complicated!" He admits.

"When I left him, Richard was a different man to the one I first met. He had... issues." Ava mutters, picking at her fingers.

"Right. What can I say? I would never judge anyone's circumstances. Jeez, the mess I left behind in England was far from normal."

"He had troubles... he was a drinker... and then the dilemma became even bigger and he started taking drugs. It started off recreationally but then it became a problem, a really big problem. I had no choice in the end but to leave him. I didn't want to... I had to. He and the addiction left me with no other choice."

"Holy shit, Ava. I... I don't know what to say."

"The business I had to attend to, back in England, was his funeral. He passed away..." She pauses, her eyes filling with tears.

"What happened to him, if you don't mind my asking?" Michael murmurs edging closer to her.

"A pulmonary embolism. A blood vessel in his lung was blocked by a blood clot and it killed him." Tears fall from her eyes and she wipes them quickly. Michael is aware that Ava is upset, so he moves even closer and embraces her tightly but says nothing.

Chapter Eleven

Mia is occupying herself making coffee and reading the news updates on her laptop. Michael comes out of the bathroom after a shower and she asks.

"You were home late last night. Where'd you get to?" As he heads to the kitchen.

"I was out with Ava."

"What on a date you mean? What about Betty?" She mocks.

"No! ...Not a date. I was showing her the Empire State Building, and we got a bite to eat. As for Betty, nothing else has been arranged." He says tucking his shirt into his trousers.

"It so was a date and you know it Michael!"

"Michael, now is it? Now I know I'm in trouble!" He teases.

Michael makes himself some lunch for his day ahead. Deciding on a turkey salad, he grabs an empty lunchbox. In the refrigerator he finds everything he needs. Taking out a chopping board and a sharp knife, he begins cutting up the turkey followed by some tomato and pepper.

"You're quiet this morning, Mike," Mia notices.

"Am I? I'm just making a turkey salad, Mimi. I'm tired and work is incredibly busy, and to top things off... Donny is our client!"

"Donny! Donny, is your client? Are you freaking kidding me?"

"That was my reaction, and no I'm not. He is who I had *that* lunch meeting with," Michael tells her, cutting up a cucumber and waving his knife around as Mia rolls her eyes.

"I take it Ava has met him, too?" She asks curiously.

"You know it, and he sent her like a massive bouquet of flowers to her office. The sleaze!"

The conversation falls silent. Mia continues staring at her screen and Michael finishes up making his lunch by drizzling ranch sauce over it.

"I'm sure he enjoyed that!" Mia spits, "He is the biggest jerk imaginable!"

"He did ask after you though, Mia," Michael says.

"Yeah, but I haven't heard from him in months. Mike, he used me!" She withdraws from the breakfast table while Michael pauses to press the lid on his container. "I hate him with an absolute passion, 'gilipollas'! I don't wanna hear another word on the subject, do you hear me?" She is clearly agitated.

"Mia... I didn't realise he had hurt you so much!"

"Well he did, I'm now going to shower myself. I have some serious studying to do because we have our mid-term exam soon!" She stomps to the bathroom.

When Mia was seeing Donny, Michael always hated it. Yet at the time, Mia played down the relationship. Michael warned his best friend several times of Donny's intentions when it came to women, but Mia had always said she knew this and was in control. Michael now knows by her reaction, that this wasn't at all under control and she had strong feelings for the sleeze bag.

At TAC, there is something different about the atmosphere between Michael and Ava. They are both working on the 3D model of the Donny project, whilst devouring their lunch from 'At the Deli' that Michael had grabbed for them. Gluing all the intricate details to the miniature version takes patience and skill.

"So Ava... are you free tonight?" He says with a mouthful of food.

Ava continues gluing and ponders his question.

"I don't have any plans for tonight." She says looking in his direction.

"Well... do you fancy doing something?"

She smiles sweetly and nods.

"Okay... well do you wanna go straight from work tonight?"

"Sounds great!"

The work day ends. They have finished the first stage of the model. It is a painstaking task leaving materials everywhere. Donny the client is paying so he gets what he wants. Ava quickly tidies her office knowing that if she finds it in the current unorganised mess when she walks in tomorrow, she will be in a foul mood for hours. Standing at the door, Michael waits patiently for her to finish.

"You ready?"

"Yes of course… there isn't much more I can do."

"So I was thinking we could go and watch the sun set, sound okay?"

Ava says nothing but smiles at him.

As they exit TAC tower, there is a man waiting for them with two bags of food. Michael had already suggested that they take something with them for their sunset stroll and had ordered two salads dishes. Michael then flags a cab, asking the driver to take them as close as he can to Brooklyn Bridge. After a short journey, the cab pulls up at the intersection of Tillary Street and Boerum Place. Both climb out and the cab pulls back into the busy traffic. Ava looks at the view of the bridge, she has a warm feeling inside, '*or is it just more romantic than our last encounter?*' She wonders.

They begin strolling along the Brooklyn Bridge Pedestrian Walkway that allows people to walk across the bridge into Brooklyn. The water glistens on either side of them. Ava is struggling with what to say and how to begin a conversation. Half way across, Michael hands over her salad in the brown paper bag, suggesting they eat and stroll. '*Ah this is why he ordered the food!*' She thinks. Walking, talking and eating is tonight's plan.

The crossing takes just over forty minutes and they finally reach the other side. Michael looks back at Manhattan skyline and Ava follows his eyes.

"Oh… my… that really is incredible, Michael. Now that is a view!"

"It's something huh?"

Looking in his direction for a long moment she catches his eye.

"Very romantic, Michael. I'm impressed!" She says basking in the beautiful view.

They adjourn to the River Cafe where there are more stunning views of Manhattan, especially as the sun sets and the lights come on in the buildings. The majority of the evening's conversations are about their personal lives. Michael gives Ava a detailed account of his relationship with Olivia and feels that for some reason he can really open up to Ava about everything. He talks of his fears when he left the U.S. and started his new life in Cambridge, England. Ava can relate to this because she is doing the same thing in reverse.

The night finally comes to an end. Michael puts Ava in a cab and pays for her journey back to Manhattan while he gets one to Queens. Entering her building, Ava skips to the elevators feeling butterflies in her stomach. *'Was that a date?'* She thinks to herself.

Michael enters Mia's apartment. Mia is already in bed. It is late, really late. Michael feels exhausted but settling down on his sofa bed, he can feel a happy glow bursting from inside him. *"Another successful night with Ava Turner!"* he mutters to himself.

Ava is sitting at her desk and Betty brings in her coffee as usual. Betty leans over the desk itching to say something, and Ava can feel her presence towering over her as she is typing an email.

"So, I had a date with Michael the other night." Betty reveals excitedly.

Ava freezes and her heart sinks, but she remains poker faced and composes herself to ask more.

"Oh, lovely and how did it go Betty?" She tries to ask as cheerily as possible, continuing to stare at the screen pretending to not be overly bothered.

"Well... you can't say anything, but... we kissed, and when I say kissed, I mean we... *really kissed.*" Betty boasts.

Ava's eyebrows raise and she can feel the fury building inside her and a sickness swirling in her stomach. She says nothing but wonders to herself why he went to such efforts last night, if he was kissing another woman.

"Well that clearly sounds promising." Ava replies curtly.

"Well I think so too. *Aahhh,*" Betty says, clapping her hands, "can I get you anything else?"

"No that will be all. Thank you Betty," as Betty leaves the office.

Ava grabs her phone from her bag under the desk and clicks on her text messages. She scrolls through and selects Katelyn. She types:

Hey Katelyn!! How's things back home? I'm in a much better place.

Finally saw the Empire State Building!! Wahoo. It was amazing, just as you said it would be.

I miss you all soooo much. X x x

She clicks 'Send'. Due to the time difference, Ava doesn't expect an immediate reply. She has missed her family a lot since returning to the US. Katelyn was always her agony aunt when it came to matters of the heart or dating, but of course when it came to Richard she went to her eldest sister Clare, as she has always been far less judgemental.

Katelyn was the highflyer of the four girls. She went to London to start her career as a novelist. It was a slow process but she is finally getting somewhere with it and one of her novels has finally been published. She loves the life that London has given her and she has so many friends there that she rarely returns to Suffolk. Having two daughters at home was very time consuming for her mother, Florence, and it wasn't always easy for her to get away to London to see Katelyn. Ava tried her best to see her sister as much as she could. When they were growing up the two were very close but as time passed, they grew apart especially after all her problems with Richard. Lydia only saw Katelyn on her own terms. If she wanted to go to a concert at the O2 arena or a West End show, she would use her sister merely as a base.

James enters her office, he is smartly dressed as usual. Reminding her very much of her father, he has the same posture and eye colour, and his button nose is exactly the same as Ava's. He has a cropped haircut and is clean shaven. Ava always wondered why he never married or had children. It wasn't something that had ever been discussed within the Turner family and they just accepted it for what it was.

"Good morning, darling," he says.

"Hello uncle James. What can I do for you?" she says sweetly.

"Well you've been back here in New York for a while and now you've settled back in, I realised that we've only eaten together once. I haven't wanted to encroach on your personal space, but I'd like to see you more than just in the office?" he explains.

Ava smiles back, completely understanding that he wants to get to know her on a more personal level, as a member of his family rather than of a boss and employee.

"That would be lovely. When and where?" she replies.

"Would you like to come to mine for dinner?"

"Oh that would be lovely. Which day?"

"Can you make it tomorrow night?" he enquires.

"Uhh, what day is it tomorrow?" Ava says aloud scanning her brain.

"Friday, Ava," he answers, laughing.

"Oh I can't. I'm meant to be going to a salsa night with Mia," Ava remembers.

"Not to worry my darling. We'll do a night next week?" He suggests.

"Perfect, sounds wonderful. I look forward to it," and James lets Ava get back to work. He awkwardly leaves her office knowing he has put himself out there to which is very out of character for him. Ava sits and smiles to herself thinking how sweet her uncle had just been. Yet, she could sense that this conversation was incredibly awkward for him.

The morning passes and Ava has nipped out to 'At the Deli' to grab her lunch. Heading back to her office, she can feel the fury growing in her stomach again. The snack bar brings back memories of Michael and his latest antics with Betty. She is furious with him and she can't shake these feelings off.

She is finishing her last mouthful of food and screws the sandwich bag up and chucks it in the bin next to her desk. Michael knocks on her glass door. She chews quickly and reaches for her bottle of water to take a sip and waves him in.

"What is it Michael?" she says shortly.

Michael stands stunned at her tone and runs his hands through his hair.

"Uhh... well I had... an.." Michael tries to say, sensing her hostile tone that's disarming him. Ava intercepts.

"Oh come on. Out with it!" she says exasperated.

"Have I upset you or something? Because I'm so confused with your tone right now." he says shaking his head in disbelief.

Ava stands and heads to close the door. Turning to face him, the distaste of what she is about to say is apparent on her face.

"What?" he says, fanning his hands questionably.

"I opened up to you last night Michael. *You* created what I'd describe as a perfect evening, a date in fact... and... well, you've been for a drink with Betty... and *kissed her*, and didn't think to tell me?"

"Wait?! What?" he pauses, "Just hold up a second! You thought last night was a date?" Completely confused with the conversation he is having with a woman he finds completely insatiable.

"Well... I... I don't know... was it?" Ava tries to reply confidently but fails.

"Hang up a sec!" Anger is building within Michael. "I tried to talk to you about that night and you... you Ava... specifically told me, you were drunk and..." he shakes his head in disbelief.

Ava stands voiceless and feels her cheeks redden with embarrassment.

"You're a hypocrite, Miss Turner. You're the one receiving flowers off that *son of a bitch,* who is a sleaze, may I add!" he pauses again. Ava struts to the other side of the office to create some distance as the fury builds between them. "And you're gonna lecture *me* about a *kiss* that happened between me and Betty. Are you for real?!" he says running a hand through his hair again.

Ava unfolds her arms and has nothing to say in return as she is gobsmacked by his response. Silence falls between them and they stand staring at each other, both wearing furious expressions on their faces.

Ava breaks the silence. "How dare you speak to me in this way? Who do you honestly think you are?" Unfolding her arms she points a finger in his direction.

The staff are beginning to notice the raised voices coming from Ava's office. They stare through the glass and Ava can sense they are attracting some spectators.

"Can you get out of my office now, please?" she says slightly calmer as to try and deter more attention.

"With pleasure!" he says and turns to leave. "You wanna know something," he turns back to face her again. "You are a complete hypocrite Ava Turner!" He goes to the glass door and storms out, completely furious with her.

Ava is completely taken back with what has just happened. *How did this manifest into such a hideous argument like that?* The realisation hits her that she is jealous of Betty. *But why?* She has never looked at Michael in this way. *Yes he has nice eyes, that you could certainly get lost in. Yes he has a handsome face and yes of course she has kissed him.* Ava knows, however, that she is still mourning her dead ex-husband. Walking to the office door to see where he is heading, she is fully aware that the spectators are still watching this scene unravel.

Betty sees Michael heading in her direction, but does not notice that he has a furious expression on his face. "Hey Michael!" she asks, "You wanna hook up again, tonight?" flirtatiously. He storms past her and turns to face her.

"You wanna know something Betty... I'm busy tonight!" He turns back to the direction of the stairs.

"Huh?" Betty says, confused, staring after him. She is feeling extremely silly, so she sits herself back down in hope that no one else saw that.

Ava stands at her open office door, and watches Michael disappear from view.

"Is everything okay?" her uncle has appeared next to her.

"Uh yeah, it wasn't anything really... we just had a disagreement, work related."

"Are you sure that's all it was?" he questions. Everyone nearby is staring and whispering to each other.

"Yes honestly. It wasn't important. It's fine... I promise."

"Where's he gone?" James asks.

"To cool off I imagine," Ava says smoothly, knowing full well she had created his fury.

"Okay, everyone! There is nothing to see here. Back to work!" James says authoritatively and the spectators return to their desks.

Michael heads home to Queens via the subway. As he stands amongst the commuters squashed like sardines he can feel his anger subsiding. He stares at different people. Old, young and a couple kissing. Ava has made him furious and he needs to unwind. As he enters Mia's apartment it is silent. She's obviously at the office. He finds his running gear of black shorts, fluorescent yellow lycra top, socks and running shoes. He also straps on an MP3 player and headphones. Michael hasn't been for a run since returning to New York. It was always his escape from Olivia in England and when he was having problems at work he would run twice a day. Turning the music up loud he begins jogging the blocks of Queens. The streets are busy as he passes local stores and restaurants. Michael needs to run his temper off. *How has a woman that he barely knows, annoyed him so much?* Reflecting, he's not sure if it was Betty, Donny or Ava that set him off.

Mia enters the front door of Pedro House at 8 p.m., and she notices Mr Truman at the reception desk. As she walks through the lobby, she notices how beautiful it is. Mr Truman addresses her sternly, "Can I help you?" making Mia's visit to Pedro House *his* business.

"Hi, I'm going to see Miss Turner, on the eleventh floor. Is that okay?" she replies sarcastically. He gestures for her to continue about her business. Mia cheekily winks back at him and goes to the elevators.

Mia is fully aware of her looks and tonight is no exception, especially as she is wearing a short black slinky silk dress with matching shoes. She also chose a blood red lipstick to compliment her Mexican dark features. Her hair is down which Mia only allows on nights out or when she needs to look sophisticated. Mia has naturally curly hair and she has emphasised them this evening.

She knocks loudly on the apartment door and waits. Ava eventually opens it in her dressing gown.

"Mia! Bugger!... I completely forgot about tonight! Come in," Ava gestures to her to enter and Mia makes her way in. Ava has the TV on Netflix and a pizza half eaten with a glass of wine sitting on the coffee table.

"Sorry to disturb your date night for one!" Mia laughs.

Ava shuts the door and pulls her dressing gown up tighter.

"Sorry, it's been a few stressful days at the office and you, tonight, completely slipped my mind." Ava explains.

"Well, you look in exactly the same state as Michael does! Your boss sure works you hard," Mia laughs and Ava copies her, knowing that there is a lot more to this story. It is obvious that Mia is not aware of this.

"Come on! We have an hour to get you ready." Mia says clapping her hands.

Ava perches on the back of the couch facing the door.

"I'm just not sure I'm up for tonight Mia."

"Are you crazy? Don't say that. You are going to love it! Now go get ready!" Mia protests.

"Okay!" Ava slips off the sofa and slowly dawdles to her bedroom.

Mia sits down on the couch and takes a slice of the pizza.

"You got any more wine?" she shouts to Ava in her room, changing.

"Yes!" Ava yells, "Have a look in the fridge. Help yourself to some pizza, won't you?"

"Don't worry I am!" Mia says with a mouthful.

Mia strolls to the kitchen area and looks through the cupboards for a glass. She pours herself a large glass of wine and Ava strolls through. She is wearing black jeans and a smart casual top, but appears bland and lacking any enthusiasm.

"Are you gonna be wearing that?" Mia asks, with a displeased expression on her face.

"Yes, why?" Ava replies confused.

"No! No! No! It's all wrong. Show me to your wardrobe!"

After a painstaking hour and half of organising Ava's outfit, hair, makeup and lots of wine consumption, they arrive outside the club in their cab. Ava pays, and they step out and shut the door. There is a line of people waiting to get in. Mia and Ava join the back of the queue. Ava continuously tries to tug her dress down lower.

"Chicka! Quit tugging it down. You look hot. Trust me," Mia says confidently.

"I feel like it's a little short!" she says, feeling conscious.

"Are you kidding me? Stop it! Look, if I was a man I'd be eyeing you *all* over right now!" Mia laughs.

Ava has a red ruched bust silk milkmaid mini dress on. Her shoulders are on display and the dress hugs her figure tightly. The dress is Lydia's and she lent it to Ava a long time ago but she has never worn it. It isn't her style, but she packed it anyway. Ava's hair is tied up smoothly in a high ponytail with the ends straight. Like Mia, she too, has a blood red lipstick on. Ava's shoes and bag are matching. The bag is a Ted Baker clutch bag and has a gold-tone chain that rests on her shoulder. Her shoes are ankle tie stilettos. Deep down, Ava knows she's an attractive woman but this is not her style and she doesn't dress up very often. When she packed for America she packed with haste. Half the things she brought with her haven't been worn or have been replaced.

After a long wait they finally enter the Salsa club. The lighting is dark but there is an orange glow. It is very lively. People are erotically dancing everywhere and Ava doesn't know where to look. Mia guides them to get a drink and at the extremely busy bar, they order four shots straight off.

Ava bursts into laughter seeing that Mia has no hesitation in ordering on her behalf.

"What are these for? Are you trying to get me drunk?" Ava takes two from the tray.

"Oh trust me Ava. You're gonna need them!" Mia says confidently.

Ava doesn't argue with Mia's advice and knocks them back without hesitation.

Led to the dance floor, Ava can instantly see that Mia is completely in her element. Ava stands awkwardly, not knowing what to do and watches Mia do her stuff. She moves her body to the music and it is in complete tune with the beat. Ava realises that Mia really can dance and is incredibly sexy when she does it. Taking Ava's hands, Mia pulls her in close.

Ava has never really been a clubber. She has always been a pubber and a get out and do-er. Ava did gymnastics as a child, while Katelyn was the dancer, and Clare had ballet. Ava gave up her beloved gymnastics when she suffered an injury aged eleven and instead, put all her energy into swimming. Much to Florence's complete disbelief, Ava went on to join the Army Cadets but it was really just to see the handsome boys who attended. She was a bit of a tomboy growing up, so this for her was completely out of her comfort zone.

"Relax Ava... let it go. With hips like that, I know you got the moves!" Mia says through the loud music. Ava starts off tense but slowly loosens her body and they dance in time with each other. After lots of dancing and laughing, they head back to the bar and order two more shots. Ava realises the more they drink the more she loosens up. They continue this pattern all night.

Mia attracts lots of attention throughout the night from rather attractive men of all ages. She replies to them in Spanish. Sometimes Ava isn't sure whether it is aggressive or just the tone of the language. Mia continues to dance with Ava, as she has no interest in the male attention and Ava wonders if there is a man on the scene. After all, she doesn't know her all *that* well, yet. The music is loud and Ava is completely intoxicated by the atmosphere and the alcohol, but in a good way. Her feet are killing her from the dancing in high heels and her forehead is perspiring from the constant dancing. Her body is now dancing freely and she feels much more confident. She has no idea she could dance like this and realises that

Mia is right. By releasing the tenseness, your body will inevitably move freely.

The night is drawing to an end. One more song is played for all the dancers to a last dance. Ava is now completely intoxicated and just lets her body go to sway with Mia in time to the music. *'To think that it just took alcohol to do this?'* she thinks to herself. The music comes to a halt and the lights brighten up, but not completely. It's time to go home.

As they drunkenly walk out of the club, there is a sea of people on the street. A row of yellow cabs are waiting for customers. Mia suggests that Ava go back to hers and Ava is far too drunk to remember that Michael lives there. The taxi ride is just over half an hour to Queens and all the way back they talk and laugh, acting drunk and silly.

Mia opens the apartment door and she falls on the floor. Ava bursts out laughing and falls on top of her. They are both rolling around giggling.

"Mia? What time is it?" says a groggy voice. Ava stops laughing and Mia puts a finger to her own mouth trying to stop herself from laughing.

"So sorry Mike. I don't know, but it is way past my bedtime." And the girls begin to laugh again. Michael drags his sleepy body off the couch and flicks on the lamp beside the sofa. As the light fills the room, the girls are greeted with him just in his boxer shorts. He can finally see who has accompanied Mia home.

"Ava?" he says shocked.

Ava stops giggling and stares seriously in Michael's direction.

"Michael!" Dragging her drunken body off the floor, she rapidly sobers up.

"Michael, we have a guest. Go put some pants on, Ava doesn't need to see you half naked!"

Michael can see Ava admiring his body. "Uh, of course," he says confidently, staring down at his practically naked body and strides to the bathroom in his boxers.

"Let's drink!" Mia proclaims, rifling through her cupboards.

"Would you mind if I sit on the worktop?" Ava asks.

"Be my guest," Mia says, as Michael comes back wearing his sweatpants but leaving his top half naked.

After several drinks contribute to the continuous chatting and laughter between the three of them, Mia breaks the tension between Ava and Michael. She checks her phone for the time.

"Maldita sea! Is that the time? ...It's 3 a.m. I have got to get some sleep. I have my midterm exam on Monday, and I have *got* to study. Ava I'll leave you to finish up your drink and you can jump in with me." And stumbles to Mike and plants a kiss on his cheek and attempts to hug him.

"Night." Ava musters through her drunkenness and Mia drags herself off to bed.

Michael and Ava sit in silence for a moment. Ava is still sitting on the kitchen worktop. Michael stands up from his seat and slowly edges towards her from the breakfast table.

"So... you seem to have enjoyed salsa tonight?" he asks running his hand through his hair. Ava stares at him through her lashes.

"Oh I did, very much so. Mia can really dance!"

Michael edges even close to her. He stands a metre directly in front of her, staring at her. His pupils are dilated with appreciation of what they see.

"Sorry that we woke you." She says shyly looking away.

"It's okay. Mia has a tendency to wake me when she goes to the club. I want to apologize for the way I spoke to you."

"That's alright. It wasn't my place to cast any judgement on you and Betty." The atmosphere is growing increasingly intense between them.

Michael can't take his eyes off of Ava and she can sense it.

"You look incredibly sexy in red." he says seductively, stepping even closer. Ava freezes and can feel his gaze burning into her skin, making her cheeks feel flushed.

She is drunk and confident. "You approve of red do you?"

Neither take their eyes off of each other.

"I do, but especially on you!"

"Well... I'll have to remember that," returning his intense gaze.

He moves even closer, inches away from her. She can feel the heat radiating off his naked muscular body with the light framing every inch of his contoured frame. His skin is smooth and ripped in all the right places. Her eyes draw heavy and she becomes breathless. Michael places his hands either side of her hips on the worktop. Anticipation grows in her stomach at the closeness and he looks directly into her eyes.

"Is this too close?" he asks.

"No, not too close," Ava pants breathlessly.

"Then I gotta do this." He places his mouth on her soft lips, holding her head in the grasp of both his giant hands and begins to kiss her deeply, passionately. She returns the kiss and enters her tongue into his mouth and he sighs with gratitude.

They both grow intensely breathless, panting at their eager bodies pining for each other. He runs his hands up her thighs. She watches as they glide towards her sweet place, but then he moves his hands to grasp her hips under her dress pulling her closer to him and she rolls her eyes at the sensation. She coils her arms around his neck and ruffles her hands through his hair, kissing him. He gropes her hips roughly thrusting himself against her, eager for more, insinuating what he wants. He knows what he wants.

He stops and looks at her, completely aroused.

"You sure you want this?" he suggests breathlessly; he waits for her to agree to what he started. She leans in, placing her hand at the nape of his neck, drawing his lips to hers and kisses him again.

He moves his kisses away from her mouth and moves his way down her neck with his lips.

Ava's arousal is ignited inside her, "Oh my God... yes!" she moans as her body is burning for him.

Michael slides her dress down to reveal her breasts.

"No bra?" he teases and takes her nipple into his mouth. Ava throws her head back in appreciation and Michael groans agreeably at her pleasure.

With the intensity that grows, Michael reveals his manhood and shows how his body agrees with the presence of hers. Ava pupils enlarge and her body yearns for him. Ava pulls her knickers to one side and takes him in her hand, and enters him inside her, slowly. He stares into her eyes as he glides in. She groans with intense pleasure as he withdraws again.

He places his hand over her mouth to silence her, "Shhh," he murmurs and removes his hand again. Michael breathlessly moans in her ear at his own growing pleasure. They kiss erotically, ferociously as their bodies become one, as Michael thrashes himself inside her again and again. He takes her there and then.

Ava and Michael are asleep on the sofa. She suddenly stirs with a startle, still tipsy and with panic growing inside her, thinking *"where am I? What is the time?"* She then slowly and quietly removes herself from Michael's grasp. Luckily, she is on the outside edge of the sofa, so she can do this easily. Noticing she is dressless, revealing bare breasts and only a pair of knickers, Ava, quietly hunts the apartment in the dark for her red dress and heels. Having found them, she slips the dress on as quickly as she can. Finding her bag and heels together, she grabs them and makes her way silently tiptoeing to the door. She opens and closes the door quietly making sure not to wake Michael. Outside, she eagerly checks her bag for her phone and checks the time. It's 6 a.m. She rushes down the flight of stairs, shoes in hand and makes her way home.

Chapter Twelve

M ichael stirs and goes to wrap his arms around Ava, but pats her empty space instead. He sits up and rubs his eyes and then heads to Mia's room and slowly opens her door. She lays silently alone in her bed and he closes the door again, quietly. As he re-enters the open plan living area he notices Ava's belongings have gone. He stands and rubs his face, then goes to the sofa and sits down again. Resting his elbows on his knees and his fingers on his lips, he sighs deeply. He is confused. *Why did she leave without saying anything?*

Ava sits on the base of the shower, cupping her legs with her arms with tears streaming down her face. The hot water runs over her body as she sobs. Ava feels like she has been disloyal to Richard and the guilt is foremost in her mind. Michael is the first person she has been with since the split three years ago. She begins to scrub herself, over and over again, removing all remnants of Michael and what they had done. Ava feels dirty. She gives up and sits there silently as the water rinses over her and drains away down the plug.

It's past midday. "You're alive then?" Michael says as Mia makes an appearance.

"Oh don't even go there. I feel terrible, but what a night! What time did Ava leave?" Mia asks slowly, delicately seating herself on the couch.

"Uhh, I'm not sure. She was gone when I woke up." Michael says solemnly.

"She looked really hot last night, don't you think?"

Michael is seated behind Mia at the breakfast table.

He sighs silently remembering last night, "My God she did," he replies.

"So... did you make a move?" Mia asks and turns to gauge his reaction.

Michael doesn't see Mia staring in his direction as he sits quietly staring at nothing in front of him.

"Michael!" Mia says to get his attention.

"Hmm, sorry... I wasn't listening. What'd you say?" he asks turning his attention to her.

"Okay! I've been your friend for too long... What's up?"

"Nothing, I'm okay."

"No you're not. What's happened?" Mia asks, growing increasingly worried.

As much as Michael hates to admit it, Mia does know him well and he finds it incredibly hard for him to hide anything from her.

"I have well and truly screwed up!"

"Why? What happened?" she prompts.

"Something happened last night," he frantically runs his hands through his hair.

"Okay, well I could see that coming!" Mia jokes.

"We fell asleep together last night and when I woke up she was gone."

"Okay... well... don't panic! She's probably freaking out a little!" Mia reassures him.

Michael takes a walk to clear his head and before he knows it, he is heading to Ava's apartment in a cab. Paying the driver, he clambers out the back and shuts the door. Michael stares up at her windows. As he enters the building, there is a different man standing behind the reception desk. His head is down, working, so Michael strides quickly past to get to the elevators.

Knocking on Ava's door loudly, there is no answer, so Michael knocks again.

"Ava! I know you're in there!" he calls through the door impatiently.

Ava is in there wearing pyjamas and hears him but refuses to answer the door. She sits silently, listening. Not sure why but she feels sick with guilt at hearing his voice. She can't face him and she doesn't want to. Not right now.

"Ava... please... just answer." Michael is leaning his forehead against the door. Ava gets up from the couch and sits closer to the door. She has a solid barrier to protect her but she still wants to hear what he has to say.

"Ava... if you're in there, then please listen." He sighs and takes a nearby seat to her door and leans his back against it, pulling his knees up to his chest.

"If you have any regrets about last night then I understand. I'm not a complete jerk. I..." he pauses. Ava slides closer to the barrier and strokes the door quietly. Tears are rolling down her face and she closes her eyes.

"I... know you are going through some stuff right now... and I don't wanna put any pressure on you. But I also want you to know..." he sighs again, "I don't regret a single second of it!" Rubbing his stubble on his chin. Ava sits and listens, still refusing to open the door.

"Well, if you're in there, I hope you heard that, because if not, I look like a complete idiot talking to a door."

Ava giggles silently but begins to cry through her laughter.

"Well... that's it! That's all I came to say!" Michael rises from the door, replaces the chair and slowly walks away. Pausing, and he turns back, hoping she'll open the door to him, but she doesn't.

Ava sits there alone and sobs. She lies at the door and eventually falls asleep,

"Happy one year anniversary, Ava baby." Richard says pulling Ava onto his lap. They are at Richard's apartment. She straddles him.

"Can you believe it's been a year?" Richard remarks.

"I've never stayed in a relationship this long... but you... Miss Turner, you do something to me!" He says, picking her up and slamming her on the bed so he is on top of her.

"Well, what can I say Mr Burton. The feeling is somewhat mutual," Ava says seductively.

Richard leans in for a kiss and Ava wraps her legs around his waist. Their kiss grows more meaningful. Ava pulls Richard's grubby white work T-shirt over his head and strokes the hairs on his chest, appreciating his body that she has come to love.

He pins her arms above her head and begins kissing her slowly. He withdraws and whilst kneeling, he undoes her jeans slowly watching her and she grows excited of what is to come next. In one foul swoop he rips her jeans from her legs. Her sweet spot eagerly waiting for his touch.

"Ahaa, my favourite panties," he pauses, "How did you know?"

He lifts her top and plants kisses on her stomach, slowly making his way to her panty line, Ava squirms at every kiss.

"You want it do you? You want me inside you, Ava?" He licks her sweet spot through her lace underwear. He lifts his head. Her excitement grows more by the minute.

But something is wrong, she tries to decipher the face. It isn't Richard.

"You sure you want this?" It's Michael!

Ava starts to feel the panic again.

Ava wakes with a complete shock, she can feel her mind racing and her heart is thumping.

"No! No! No!" she exclaims with tears building in her eyes. Scraping herself off the floor, she walks around the apartment, back and forth, retracing her steps again and again. Shaking her head, pausing to rub her face and running her hands over her tied hair, the turmoil and disbelief is engulfing her. She frantically hunts for her phone and finally finds it under the couch. She scrolls and scrolls until she finds the name. It rings and is then answered.

"Hey mum. How are you? I miss you!"

"Ava sweetheart. I'm so glad you called. How's things?" says Florence soothingly and Ava then bursts into tears.

"Where have you been? I was going to send out a search party. You've been gone for hours!" Mia says.

"Yeah, I... uhh... I went to Ava's."

"And? Was she there?"

Michael shakes his head and sighs heavily, "No, so I sat at her door, talking to it for a while."

"You did what?" Mia asks, trying not to laugh at Michael's desperate actions.

"Well I had it all planned what I was going to say, so I just said it. Her neighbours across the hall are gonna think I'm crazy!"

"I'm surprised you got past Mr Nosey at reception!" Mia remarks.

"I know who you mean.... Uhh, what's his name... Mr Truman. He wasn't there!"

"Oh Ava darling, you sound tired and overworked. What you need is a hot chocolate, a bubbly bath and an early night. Everything will seem brighter in the morning." Florence suggests. Ava hasn't explained everything going on in New York. She completely left out Michael and that whole scenario which had been the whole reason for her call in the first place.

"You know mum, you're right. Thank you. I feel a whole lot better. I love you!"

"I love you too, sweetheart. Now go and get some rest."

Mia pampers Michael for the rest of the evening. She cooks for him and they snuggle on the couch under a blanket and watch an action-packed film. Michael is in no state to talk so Mia doesn't force him.

It's been a few days since Ava and Michael slept together. Ava arrives at the office exceptionally early and leaves early as well to ensure that they don't cross paths. She has passed the whole Donny Clarke project on to Michael and asked her uncle to break the news. With the project coming to a start on site, Michael will be out of the office a lot more.

Ava completes an email and clicks the 'Send' button. She feels famished. Pushing herself back from her desk, she fumbles for her bag and heads to the door to check if the coast is clear. She quickly heads through the door and darts down the corridor at high speed. She decides to take the stairs to avoid bumping into Michael.

Entering 'At the Deli,' Ava selects something different. There is a special 'root vegetable soup'. Approaching the counter she hears a familiar voice. Turning, she sees Mia, and someone else with their back to her. It's Michael! Ava steps out of the line and goes to leave.

"Hey!" Mia calls.

Ava pauses, sheepishly says, "Hi." and leaves in a fluster.

Making her way back to the office at lightning speed through the busy street and trying to weave past pedestrians, she rushes up the stairs as fast as her legs will carry her. Then runs back through the corridor and into her office. She is breathless. Her head is spinning and her chest feels tight. Her breath becomes shorter and she tries to gasp for air. She even sits on a couch to try and calm her breathing, Ava's panic grows stronger.

Michael appears at her office door and walks straight in.

"Ava! Are you avoiding me? You passing the Donny project onto me seemed a coincidence, but after that, back there, it's clear you don't want anything to do with me. You can't even look at me."

Ava is paying no attention to anything Michael is saying. She is having a panic attack.

"Are you okay?" He rushes over to her and kneels in front of her. In broken breaths she tells him she can't breathe.

He sprints to the ladies toilet and rips a paper bag from a dispenser as fast as he can. Running back into her office he gives it to her, telling her to breathe into it. It will slow the breathing. She eventually calms down and begins to feel incredibly foolish.

"How are you doing?" he asks, sitting next to her, concerned.

Ava nods, continuing to breathe in the paper bag.

Once she has calmed completely, she removes the bag away and holds in her lap, looking down shyly.

"How did you know what to do?" asking quietly.

"My sister Chloe suffered from panic attacks as a kid. I used to see my mom do it all the time." He shrugs, knowing he had always been understanding and supportive of his younger sister's illness.

"I've never had one before," she pauses, "it frightened me!" Ava confesses softly.

"Yeah, they're pretty scary and you feel like you're gonna die... or so my sister used to tell me."

"Yes, that's exactly how it felt!"

The conversation falls silent. Ava stares at her fingers not knowing what to say and Michael begins to pace back and forth in front of her running his hands through his hair.

"Did you feel like that after seeing me, in 'At the Deli'?" he finally asks, but Ava sits silently, not daring to look in his direction.

"Well as long as you're okay?" he pauses, Ava still says nothing.

"Okay... well...are you gonna be okay? I'll leave you in peace, then!" And awkwardly leaves her office.

Michael heads to the elevators and presses the 'call' button. He waits impatiently, but it is taking too long so he heads for the stairs instead, descending them with speed until he reaches the ground floor lobby. He strides towards the exit, but accidently barges past a woman.

"Pardon me, ma'am, I'm sorry," he says apologising as the lady raises her hand to say 'it's okay'.

Outside the towering building, the Manhattan streets are swarming with people. He runs his hands through his hair, sighs, and decides he needs a drink. Joining the moving crowds, he weaves through them at high speed, trying not to bump into anyone, eventually stopping outside the first bar he comes to.

He slumps himself on the bar stool and realises that the bar is virtually empty. The decor is gloomy and dark. There is a juke box directly behind him and nearby are two men that look as if they could be regulars, both middle aged and sitting alone.

"I'll have vodka," Michael orders.

"Coming right up," the bartender says.

He turns and grabs the bottle of house vodka off the shelf, pours a short and plants it in front of Michael, who picks it up and gulps it in one.

"I'll have another."

"Okay," so the bartender refills the glass again. Michael requests a refill several times and what seems like hours pass by.

"Well, you won't find your answers at the bottom of that glass, you know?"

Michael turns to see who is addressing him.

"I can't believe it takes a drunken call to find out my son is back in New York. Why haven't you returned any of my calls or texts, Michael?"

"You came then?" Michael slurs.

"So... what's going on? It's five in the afternoon and you're up at a bar, drowning your sorrows," George asks.

"This is my life, dad, I'm sleeping on Mia's couch." Michael sighs heavily.

George orders himself a drink, takes the stool next to Michael and sits himself down.

"So, you back, for good?" George asks.

"Yeah, I lost my job back in England, Olivia called things off... I had nothing, so I just left."

"Why didn't you call me, Michael?"

"Because, dad... I'm embarrassed, I'm never gonna be like you!"

"Michael, you have this idea in your head, that I want you to be this high flying businessman with a flash car, when actually, all I have ever wanted... all your mother and I have ever wanted is for you to be happy."

Michael sits gormlessly staring at his empty glass.

"You know" George continues, "When you were a kid, you were always the sensitive one. When the twins grazed their knees, you were always there, making them feel better... and when Chloe had her panic attacks, you were always there with your mom, making sure she was okay."

Michael sits and listens, gliding his finger around the rim of his glass tumbler.

"Your mother and I always worried about you. Christ, when you moved to Massachusetts your mother was worried sick!"

"And, you?" Michael asks.

"I have never been more worried than I was.... when you made the leap to England, with Olivia," George says.

"You never liked her!" Michael retaliates.

"No it was never the case of your mother and I, not liking her. We just knew that Olivia wasn't right for you, son. She was far too selfish!" Michael nods to his father, still staring at his glass.

"So, you want me to take you back to Mia's?" George asks.

Michael turns and looks at his father, "I wanna go home dad." Michael replies.

"Okay son, I'll drive you back,"

Michael's mother comes to the door, and he walks past her and heads straight up the stairs.

George follows him in.

"How is he?" Cora asks her ex-husband.

"I picked him up on 34th...and he was at a bar, so I swung by Mia's and grabbed some of his stuff, I don't know if he's just staying the night, or maybe a few days."

"So Michael called you?" she says.

"Yeah! He's had quite a bit to drink," George admits.

"Has he eaten?"

"I dunno. He hasn't, with me." George shrugs.

"You wanna a coffee before you head back?" she asks.

"I better not, Vanessa will be wondering where I am. Thanks anyway."

George walks back to his black mini van, turns and waves Cora. She returns the wave and heads back into the house and shuts the door.

She gets her phone out and sends a text to Chloe, Asha and Andy.

Hey guys, I wanna let you all know. Michael is home with me. He isn't in a good way. Perhaps we could all have dinner? Your big brother needs you right now. Love mom x x

She clicks 'Send'.

Chapter Thirteen

Ava knocks on the door and waits for an answer. The solid wood door is black and very grand with it's brass knocker. The large house is detached and covered with wall climbing ivy. The front garden, full of flower beds and shrubs, has a quaintness. To the left of the house are her uncle's double garages where the chauffeured cars live. Ava realises that she doesn't know if the chauffeur lives on site like Harry does back home.

James answers the door and greets Ava with a kiss and a warm hug.

"Ava, darling, come in, come in,"

She hugs her uncle and plants a kiss on his cheek as she enters. Immediately Ava is mesmerized by the decor in the hall.

"Wow! Your home is stunning. It's spectacular!" As she takes in her surroundings.

The hallway has a grand spiral staircase framed by an iron decorative railing that is painted an aged white. The metal is bent in an elegant design and the steps on the stairs are a pearl colour marble, glistening with a high gloss shine. There is a round pillar that is obviously in place for structural support, but it really goes with the theme of the grand traditional design. In the centre of the extremely large entrance hallway is a beautiful wooden cream table with a glass top surface to finish, displaying the most beautiful bouquet of lilies in a crystal vase. The ceiling is double height and hanging from its centre is an enormous twinkling chandelier.

"Thank you. We have used good interior designers from England, actually, but the architecture was obviously designed by me." he boasts.

Ava thinks in her head *'we?'* as she removes her shoes.

A gentleman then walks through. He is around the same age and build as her uncle, and has a smooth head with a salt and pepper beard. His belly is slightly rounder as well. The man is wearing an overpowering aftershave and dressed incredibly smart. He has a newly pressed dusky pink shirt, crisp black jeans and an unlikely matched floral waistcoat, that has an air of a modern fashionista twist.

"Ava, this is Daniel, my partner." James introduces him, and Daniel leans forward and gestures his hand. Ava beams at him and instead of giving her hand she leans in for a full blown hug.

"Well Daniel. It's an absolute pleasure to meet you." she says as she releases from his embrace.

"You too Ava, I've heard so much about you. What's it like working for your uncle? I bet he cracks the whip." he laughs, then looks in James' direction and winks at him. He then leads her through to the lounge and James follows them behind.

"Ava darling, can I get you a drink?" James asks, rubbing his hands together.

"Oh gosh," she says, "what's everyone else having?"

"Well, I'm drinking a fine Sauvignon blanc," Daniel says, gesturing to his glass.

Her uncle describes the contents in his drinks cabinet and Ava settles for the Sauvignon blanc too. She sips it while James gives her a tour of his homes and Daniel busies himself in the kitchen preparing their meal.

The house is tastefully decorated. There are lots of different textures and warm tones, but it is also airy and bright throughout. Every room is based on different shades of creams and beiges. Ava is taken aback by his colour choice because the office is white and clean cut, and her apartment building is based on various shades of grey and modern. The interior of his house is very traditional and grand which is completely different to what she expected.

Heading upstairs, James leads her to the bedroom which is absolutely stunning and it takes Ava's breath away. The walls are lined in gold baroque bead pearl wallpaper, and the bed has a traditional Victorian button tufted upholstered headboard set with a pearl white jacquard fabric. It has been carved from solid wood in an intricate design and the bedside cabinets and dressing table are made from the same wood. The drapes hanging from the windows are cream with a golden embroidery pattern sewn into it. The darkness of the oak parquet flooring complements the furniture harmoniously.

The guest room has a golden wainscoting decorating the walls and painted in antique cream. The bed has an upholstered button tufted leatherette headboard, and all the furniture is solid birch wood coloured pearl white. The bed linen has a golden accent to it throughout the embroidery and in this room there are antique cream voiles hanging from the windows. The parquet flooring is a light oak.

"You're welcome to stay any time you like, Ava."

"It's so beautiful," she says as she strolls around the room, sliding her fingers across the end of the bed.

"Uncle James could I use your bathroom, please?"

"Yes of course. It's down the hall, the end door to the right. I'll show you."

The bathroom is as spectacular again, but with a slightly different twist to it. The style is modern and very luxurious and imported from Dubai. The tiles are made from Italian granite, and the double vanity sinks are set in a high gloss antique cream unit with an enormous mirror sitting in the centre, and subtle lighting finishing its elegance. Brilliant white towels are neatly rolled and neatly placed within the unit too. The flooring too is made of the Italian granite with two steps leading up to a very large bathtub. The ceiling is decorated with inset mood spotlights. Such small detail has gone into every inch of the house and Ava can sense the pride they both take in their home.

"Wow! Uncle James, your home is truly magnificent!" Ava acknowledges.

"Ava, thank you sweetheart." He leaves to go back to the lounge.

In the bathroom, her phone pings in her pocket and she goes to reach it. Donny's name lights up the screen,

'Ava, I will continue to contact you until you at least reply! I'm a patient man,

Donny x'

Ava rolls her eyes, ignores the message, places her phone back in her pocket and goes back to join her uncle.

Daniel comes through to the lounge area and says that lunch is ready. Ava doesn't have far to go, as there is only an archway separating the lounge to the dining area. The kitchen can be accessed from either the main entrance hall or from the dining room via another arch. There is a spectacular pool outside the double bi-folding doors.

As Daniel and James begin to bring in the food, Ava takes more of the decor. There is a cove fireplace with a tray design complimented with moulded twisted spindles and a warm light glowing from a concealed place. The ceiling also has a tray design made from a decorative mould, which merges it and the fireplace together. In the centre of the ceiling is another crystal chandelier, that hangs elegantly over the centre of the dining room table which seats ten people. There is also a Litchfield traditional two drawer server and a traditional glass door china cabinet both coloured in an antique taupe tan.

They sit at the dining table to enjoy a Texas style brisket which, juicy and succulent, lies on a wooden serving board. Roasted potatoes with a golden crispy coat, sit in a dish with the aroma of rosemary. There are vegetables of all kinds, in individual serving dishes covered in knobs of rich butter and Ava's mouth salivates at the thought of eating.

"This looks incredible," Ava says, appreciatively as she looks at the effort that Daniel has made. "Daniel is an amazing cook," James replies, dishing potatoes onto his plate.

"It's nothing. It took no time," he says modestly.

Ava serves herself a little bit of everything and takes her first mouthful of the brisket.

"Wow... this tastes amazing!" Ava tries to say with a mouthful of food and nods agreeably with the flavours.

As they all enjoy the food together, the conversations begin to flow.

"So Ava. Your uncle tells me that you've had a pretty rotten time back in the UK. I was in a relationship with a real ass before I met James. I decided to go down the therapy route, and got myself a shrink," Daniel chuckles, as he takes a sip of his wine.

"Funny, you should mention that. I looked into therapists here in New York a while back, but never saw it through," Ava declares.

"Oh really?" James chips in, "You never said?" looking in her direction.

"Well, it's a bit embarrassing really, but my past has been haunting me in my dreams," she admits.

"Well… Ava, my therapist is called Annette and she is really good at what she does. So if you ever want me to put you in touch with her, just ask. Okay?" Daniel confides.

After dinner, they all retire to the lounge which is cream with a Georgian bath limestone fireplace. There are textured drapes woven through with subtle silver embroidery that match the Litchfield beige button-tufted couches and loveseats in antique taupe. Sofa cushions help to coordinate the colour theme. There is a dark espresso wooden flooring with a large traditional antique cream rug in the centre of the room, and a Lichfield coffee table sitting in the middle.

Ava and her uncle reminisce over the past when James lived in England. They both make Daniel laugh with the tales being told.

"Do you remember the time you fell in the hedge drunk? Dad had to rescue you!" Ava laughs.

"Oh yes I do. He never let me live that down!"

"Why does that not surprise me in the slightest?" Daniel laughs, and affectionately squeezes James' shoulder who perches by his feet.

After the evening draws to an end and Ava stands at the door, they say their goodbyes to each other, and James and Daniel see her out.

"I really want to thank you for a lovely afternoon and evening, it *really* was lovely," Ava says. She makes her way down the steps and James waves her off, as she enters the chauffeur's car.

It's midday on Saturday in Albany, and there is a knock at the door. Michael calls to his mother,

"It's okay, I got it." And he opens the door.

"Oh my God, Asha, Andy. What are you guys doing here?"

"Are you gonna let us in?" Asha asks.

"Or are we gonna have to stay out here?" laughs Andy.

"Uh, my bad, guys. Come in, come in." He steps aside and as he lets them through the door, another car pulls up. It's Chloe.

Michael walks down the steps and stands with his hands on his hips as he watches her get out of the car.

"Let me guess. Mom beckoned you all here because I need you?"

"Mike, you know what mom is like. What are you doing back? Not that I'm not pleased to see you, and all that. It just came as a surprise."

Chloe is a very pretty woman. She has her mother's eyes and her father's lips, which are full. Her long straight, sleek hair has subtle blonde highlights in it. She is tall but petite. Chloe is slightly hippy and loves nature, practicing yoga daily and trying to feel spiritual. She trained as a veterinary nurse and she drives around Brooklyn saving animals that are sick or at risk.

"Hey mom, I'm home!" she calls up the stairs.

"Okay! Be right down!" Cora calls.

In the kitchen, Chloe finds her twin brothers.

"Asha, Andy. How are you guys?" she says hugging them both.

"Hey Chloe. All good here. Where's Mike?" Asha asks.

Andy is raiding his mother's fridge for snacks and finds some seasoned chicken legs in a container.

"Is he in the lounge?" he ponders with a mouthful.

Chloe finds Michael there sitting on the couch watching ice hockey. She leans against the door frame.

"How you doing? Why are you hiding in here?"

"Chloe, I'm not hiding... I'm watching the game!" he says distractedly.

Asha and Andy burst through the door nudging Chloe to join Michael on the large cream couch to watch the rest of the game.

Cora comes down the stairs and embraces Chloe with a motherly hug, she calls to the boys who are all engrossed in the game.

"You wanna help your momma make a start on dinner?"

"Yeah, sure thing mom. Ice hockey is so boring." Chloe taunts.

"Hey!!" They all shout at her. Michael throws a cushion at his sister and misses her.

In the kitchen Cora gets out the peanut butter and pop tarts for starters, then starts to heat a pile of waffles. Chloe finds the maple syrup in a cupboard.

"You wanna get the Mountain Dew for the boys, Chloe?"

She grabs three cans of soda and takes them through to the lads who are shouting at the TV screen.

"Hey! You losers want something to drink?"

They all turn to her, and Michael holds out his hands for the cans.

"Oh jeez. Have I missed this stuff!" He receives them with a cheeky grin.

"Mom has gone all out on the kiddie snacks." She laughs.

Cora loads up the serving platters with bacon, scrambled eggs, waffles and fruit..

"Take that through for me, honey. I've got your peanut butter and pop tarts here unless of course you're not a veggie anymore?"

"Thanks mom. You know I'll always be a veg!"

They all sit around the table eating and chatting. Afterwards, Michael suggests going into the yard to throw a baseball and goes to get his leather glove from a bedroom.

"Michael!" Cora calls, "Your glove is in the garage!"

He comes back down the stairs. His brothers scurry after him. Asha and Andy are twenty-six and are identical twins. The only difference is their hair colour which has changed with age. The twins look more like George than Cora because they have his green eyes, lips and chiseled jawline. As teenagers, they were very mischievous, but never objected to Michael correcting their bad behaviour. They have always looked up to their older brother. They still do everything together, renting an apartment on the edge of Queens near Manhattan Island and also working for their father George.

Cora and Chloe are sitting on the decking watching the boys playing around with the baseball.

"You wanna play Chlo?" Michael calls.

"Absolutely not! What are we, ten again?" everyone laughs.

"We have meatloaf for dinner. That okay with everyone?" Cora adds, "Chloe you have a veggie loaf."

"Sure!" The men reply breathlessly as they run to catch the ball.

Later, Cora is in the kitchen preparing the meatloaf. For the first time in years she feels whole. All of her children are back at the nest, where she feels, they belong. Michael comes through the door and plants a kiss on his mother's cheek.

"Thanks mom. Just what I needed!"

Cora smiles to herself and continues the preparation. She begins to think of the past and her marriage breakdown. The twins were very young when it happened, and this is all they have ever really known. After the separation, Michael withdrew from both his mother and father. He had always hidden his emotions as a child and this carried on into adulthood. Cora feels that people confuse his sweet nature as a weakness.

"Dinner!!" Cora calls.

All of her children appear like toddlers, dishing up their own meals with hands flying everywhere. The aroma from the meatloaf fills the air. They all feast together. Cora watches Michael silently as he chats with his siblings. She wonders to herself *'What really happened to get him to come back to his home?'*

It's Monday morning and Ava arrives at the office early after a relaxing weekend and she sets straight to work. It isn't long before she's interrupted.

"Good Morning Ava," James says, entering.

Ava is completely engrossed on her screen.

"Morning," she replies as her fingers tap away on her keyboard.

"I have some news. You'll need to take over the Donny project again,"

Ava doesn't take her eyes away from the screen.

"How come? I thought Michael had it taken over."

"Well he had, only... I had his letter of resignation sitting on my desk this morning," James explains.

Ava pauses and swallows hard. "He's... resigned?" she says, in complete shock.

James perches on the corner of her desk. "It would appear so."

"Did he give a reason?"

"No he didn't, but..." he says as he shakes his head, "the letter was very thankful for his opportunity here at TAC."

"Oh... oh right."

"You wouldn't happen to know why he resigned do you?" James asks curiously.

Ava's heart skips a beat, but she says nothing and shakes her head in response.

"Anyway, I'll need you to head out on site and oversee things," he says as he stands and knocks her desk with his knuckles, "I'll leave you to crack on as you seem to have things under control." With that he sees himself out.

The hectic day whizzes by in a flash. She skips lunch because she can't shift the uneasy feeling in the pit of her stomach. Ava feels that Michael's departure is down to her. The guilt of her recent attitude towards him is eating her up. She says her goodbyes to the reception staff with the intention of making her way to the Recreation Centre with her swimming bag.

By the time she exits the office building, Ava has changed her mind. She flags a cab down instead. "Main Street, Queens please," she says as she climbs in, shutting the door. Ava sits in the back watching the driver weaving through the busy rush hour traffic of Manhattan. Her stomach whirls with anticipation, as she heads to Mia's apartment instead of her swimming session.

The taxi draws up outside Mia's building. Ava pays the cab driver, then lets herself out. Surprising herself that she has remembered where Mia lives, she hurries through the doors into the small lobby and makes her way to the stairs. The building is far less attractive than Ava's but it has a homely feel to it. The dark stairwells have a scent that is welcoming with aromatic cooking smells coming from different apartments. She continues to climb the stairs, one at a time, as fast as her legs allow her.

Arriving at Mia's door, she knocks louder than she means to, but there is no answer. She knocks again. Mia finally opens it and she is wrapped in a towel and beads of water are still sitting on her golden skin.

"Ava," she pauses, in surprise, "What are you doing here?" she asks looking puzzled.

"Is he here?" Ava asks, trying to look through the door past Mia.

"No... Ava he isn't. He's gone!" Mia sees the upset appear on Ava's face.

"What do you mean, he is gone?" she whispers.

"He's gone back to Albany. He's moved back to his mom's. I'm sorry, but he's gone. He made the decision yesterday."

Ava's panic grows. She places her hand on her brow and strokes her forehead, while pacing.

"You want my advice, Ava," Mia says and Ava pauses staring at her, waiting for what she is about to say.

"He isn't the monster you think he is. I don't know what is going on between you two but, what I do know is he is a good guy. He's kind," Mia pauses "and sweet hearted. I don't know if he is coming back and I'm not one to judge any situation. But... but you are really suited to each other. Whatever has happened to you in the past Ava, is stopping you and getting in the way of your feelings!" Mia finishes.

Tears roll down Ava's face and she turns to leave the apartment. She doesn't hear the door close behind her but knows that Mia is watching her. Ava doesn't know what to say. She has let him go and forced him away by her actions. One thing Ava does know is she will never chase after him. It is over.

As Ava exits the building she sends a text,

'Uncle James can you please get Daniel to send me his therapist's number, please? Love Ava x x'

She clicks 'Send'.

The next day Ava has her steel toe cap boots and hard hat on. Donny is on site, waiting for her arrival.

"Miss Turner," he says as she approaches him.

"Donny, good morning."

"I'm shocked to see you here. Where's Michael? I thought he was taking over."

"He was meant to be, but there has been a turn of events and he has handed in his resignation." Ava says bluntly.

"Well... I won't pretend I'm not pleased," he grins.

"Right, well, shall we get to work?" she says changing the subject.

Both Ava and Donny stroll around the site deciding the layout and referring to the drawings that Michael had finalised. Ava can feel Donny's eyes burning into her as she discusses the plans with him. She chooses to ignore his sleazy behaviour but it reminds her that Michael was completely right about him.

"Ava." Donny calls after her, as she goes to leave the site.

She rolls her eyes and turns to face him, "Everything okay?"

"I was wondering if you were free for dinner tonight."

"I'm really sorry but I'm not. I have plans this evening."

"Okay, well maybe some other time then?" he replies smiling.

"Yeah, perhaps." Not really sure what else to say.

The gunmetal Dodge truck is a business vehicle owned by TAC. Ava climbs in and sits there with her hands on the steering wheel. A tear falls from her eye. She isn't sure why she's emotional but she doesn't feel herself right now. *Is she crying because of Richard? Is she crying over Michael? Are the dreams dragging her down? Or is she just home sick.*

She turns the key to start the engine and roars off with the car wheels spinning off the rubble car park. The tears are now flowing from her eyes. Something she does know is she is really struggling with everything that is being thrown at her recently and does not feel like swimming today.

Michael is standing in his mother's kitchen making a hot drink when she walks through.

"Coffee?" he asks.

"Are you going to tell me why you're really home, Michael?" Cora pauses. "What or who are you running from?" She asks her son, folding her arms waiting for a response.

"I'm not running from *anyone* or *anything* mom... it was time to come home."

Ava stands at a door. The rain is falling relentlessly from the darkened sky. She is knocking frantically and a light flicks on through the window pane of the door. It finally opens.

"Ava, what the bloody hell are you doing here?" Harry asks, shocked to see her.

Ava is drenched and her eyes are black from the mascara smudged around them.

Mabel appears at the door. "Who is it at this unearthly hour?"

Taking one look at Ava, she says, "Harry, you head along to the house and get to work... Ava my darlin, I think we better have a little ole chat," and she gestures to come inside.

"Does your mother know you're here?" Harry asks, on his way out.

Ava shakes her head.

"Then... your secret is safe, I best be off," and he makes his way to the Turner's house.

The relief hits Ava as she enters into her safe zone where the familiar smells instantly calm her inner chaos.

Ava and Mabel are in the kitchen and it's very late. Mabel is around the same age as Harry. She is a plump homely woman, with a short grey wiry bob who dresses herself older than her age. Mabel's regular attire is of blouses of every colour and pleated skirts which are grey or black. In the summer the skirts change to cream. She always wears an apron.

"Where's Harry going?" Ava asks.

"Your mother is out for dinner, my darlin. He's got to go along and pick her up!" Mabel says, pouring hot tea from her antique china teapot into a cup.

"I take it you'd like some of my famous sponge?" Mabel asks, placing the teapot on the table.

"Please."

"You're lucky. I made a fresh cake just this afternoon," Bringing it through in a cake tin from the pantry. She places it on the table and takes two china plates out of a cupboard. Mabel lays them on the table and cuts two generous slices of Victoria sponge. Placing them on the two plates and passing one to Ava, she places the cake knife in the sink and re-covers the cake with the lid.

Mabel sits silently but comfortably opposite Ava. "So are you gonna to tell your Aunt Mabel why you're here? Or am I gonna to have to guess?" Ava sits twiddling her fingers ignoring the cake sitting in front of her. She attempts to speak several times, but nothing comes out.

She stares intently at Ava, watching and waiting. Mabel has watched all the sisters grow up from babies, but she was always closest to Ava as a child who would always pop in for tea and cake once a week after school. This continued until she married Richard. Then the ritual changed to occasionally. Mabel and Harry never had children of their own so Mabel took a great interest in the girls.

"I....I," Ava bursts into tears.

"You what Ava May? What you tryin' to get away from? To come knocking on my door late at night, when you're meant to be in America," she reaches over to stroke Ava's hand.

Ava sniffles and Mabel stands up and walks around to her side of the table to take a seat next to her, wrapping her arm around Ava and hushes her tears.

"Start from the beginning my woman. You know you can tell me anything," she coaxes.

Ava tells Mabel all that has happened in New York including Michael and the flashback dreams regarding Richard. Mabel says nothing and just sits and listens without interrupting, letting Ava get it all off her chest through the tears.

Mabel makes more tea and cuts more cake.

"You must be starvin', travelling all that way in a hurry?" she says placing the second round of cake on the plates.

Ava picks up the cake and devours it without thinking, while Mabel nods agreeably.

"Now, let's start with them dreams." Mabel says.

Ava stares at her, as she chews a mouthful of cake, pleased to have finally told someone of her predicaments.

"Ava... my darlin'," Mabel pauses, "The dreams are your brain trying to process what it's been through. You're tryin' to make heads from tails of it all."

"Your marriage fails through no fault of your own... you're left with no choice but to leave..... and then he goes and dies suddenly. You never had 'the chat' so to speak." Mabel continues, "When a marriage ends, a lot of ex-couples talk about it. I guess they do this to close the door on what is broken and unfixable. You never had that chance, my woman. It was taken from you. The truth is, my darlin, he had already left you when he chose drugs and alcohol."

Ava sits and listens to her closest ally talk. Ava always went to Mable about her troubles if Katelyn wasn't around because she always had words of wisdom.

"So, you dream instead," Mabel explains.

"But..." she pauses, "but... how is that helping me?" Ava asks.

"Well... my darlin. Only you can answer that. You left Richard suddenly. You upped and left. Perhaps your brain's trying to decipher the exact moment you left him?"

"Well I know when I left. Why would I need dreams to tell me that?" Ava asks, confused.

"My woman, that's when you left him physically. I'm talking about, emotionally," Mabel says and Ava sits completely stumped, analysing Mabel's suggestion.

Mabel leaves Ava with that thought and clears away the plates and washes up.

She turns back to Ava, as she wipes her hands on her apron and sits back down.

"And.... as for this Michael chap... well, from what you've said, he's nice enough. But you're having a battle going on inside you right now." Mabel pauses and Ava sits childlike hanging on every word.

"So you and him canoodled. These things happen. He *has* moved away now and there *int* much you can do about that. But you can't run away from your problems Ava May!"

Ava nods like a small child being told off.

"But from what you've told me... you need to deal with your issues regarding Richard, first and foremost," she speaks as Harry walks back through the door.

"You're still up? Heck it's late!" Harry remarks, yawning.

"Right you are Harry. We're gonna head to bed ourselves, aren't we, Ava?" Mabel suggests.

Ava nods and Mabel makes up a bed for her on the couch and they all settle down for the night.

"How could you!" Ava says through her hysterical tears.

Richard paces the kitchen, back and forth. He has nothing to say to justify what he has done.

"You! Richard" She pauses, "You stole my bank card, disappear for the weekend, with no word as to where you are? Or even if you are coming back." Ava continues to cry. Richard tries to comfort her and she pushes him away violently.

"You used my money to take another woman to a hotel, to have a dirty weekend away together and you didn't think I was going to catch on? Do you honestly think I'm that fucking stupid?" she screams.

Richard stands there blankly, "Just let me explain."

"Explain!" she says incredulously. "Explain why you're having an affair with another woman and I'm paying for it? You really are the most unbelievable bastard I have ever known."

Richard falls to his knees in front of Ava and pleads "Ava baby, I love you. I'm sorry, I have only ever loved you. I will only ever love you. You have to forgive me, I'll change, I'll do whatever it takes. Just please forgive me."

The next morning Ava is woken by the sweet smell of bacon being fried. She stretches her limbs and sits up, fully aware that the dreams are still haunting her, this one was the most painful by far. The day she found out about Lily. They had met at a party. It started with a few messages from what Ava could gather. Then every time Ava and Richard fought he went out of his way to seek her and the affair went from there.

Ava rises from the sofa, and heads to the kitchen. Mabel is cooking the bacon at the stove and Harry is at the kitchen table reading a newspaper.

Ava pauses at the doorway.

"Morning," she says, rubbing her eyes.

"Well good mornin' sleepy 'ead," Mable remarks turning back to the sizzling bacon.

"Mornin', Miss Ava. Take a seat," Harry offers over the top of his paper.

"It's Ava, remember Harry." she says as she sits down.

Harry says nothing and continues reading.

Mabel places a bacon and tomato sauce sandwich along with a cup of tea down in front of Ava. "After you've demolished that Ava, you'll be booking yourself a flight back across the pond'" Harry watches Ava's reaction, as he folds his paper and places it down next to him on the table.

Mabel puts his bacon sandwich down in front of him and sits down herself.

"My Harry will sneak you back to the airport and no one need know you were ever here."

Ava later checks her phone. She clicks on Donny's name and sends a text:

'Donny, I'm sorry that I have ignored all your messages but at the moment I have no interest in seeing anyone and I certainly don't mix business with pleasure. I am your architect and that is all it will ever be. Ava'

This has been something that she has been ignoring for some time and it needs to be nipped in the bud, once and for all.

To her surprise her phone pings.

'Ava Turner, I appreciate your complete honesty and if anything, I respect you even more for it. There isn't much more I can say to your response, other than take care. Donny x'

The relief rinses over her. This isn't going to be the only thing that she addresses from here. One thing she does know is Mabel is right. She can't run anymore.

Chapter Fourteen

Thanksgiving one year later

It's Thanksgiving and Ava is standing with James and Daniel near Macy's, patiently waiting for the parade to start. The sun is shining but there is a chilly wind. There are heavy crowds and a sea of people gathering to watch New York's famous Thanksgiving parade. It is Ava's first Thanksgiving in America and she can feel the excitement of the people in the city waiting for the event to commence. There are all ages gathering to watch and she really appreciates that this day is incredibly important to the Americans.

"Are you excited to be a witness to our crazy holiday celebrations?" Daniel asks Ava enthusiastically.

"I am actually. This is quite something!" she says eyeing the scenes around her.

"I felt exactly the same way, the first time I watched it." James admits.

"How is it going with Annette?" he continues.

"It's going well I have to say. I really like her and she really is helping," Ava replies.

"Well I'm so happy to hear that." With that Daniel wraps his arm around her.

The parade is broadcast live across the whole country and is a *big* event. The parade begins and the gigantic helium cartoon balloons move down the streets of Manhattan, above the heads of the crowd. Kids scream with excitement as they glide by. The parade lasts a long three hours and Ava enjoys every second of it. There are Broadway shows and featured dancers too. High school bands perform in the parade too. The crowds cheer as each different performance passes by. More novelty balloons float through the air, held down by individual people. Nursery themed helium balloons pass by and Ava points these out to her uncle, feeling like a child again and excited by everything she sees. As the parade draws to an end, the streets begin to disburse people heading home, but they are still exceptionally busy.

"Don't forget we have our table booked." Daniel reminds Ava and James loudly as they make their way through the crowds.

They leave the restaurant completely satisfied by their turkey Thanksgiving dinner. The streets are still packed. Ava is dodging and weaving through crowds of people and chatting away with Daniel when she walks straight into a man.

"Michael!" She yells, shocked by their encounter.

"Ava... hey," he pauses, in shock too. "How are you?" he asks running his hand through his hair.

They stand awkwardly in the presence of each for a moment, as if no one else is there with them and the streets are empty.

"You're back in Manhattan?" Ava asks, finally.

"Uhh, yeah," he pauses again, "I moved back about a month ago now."

A dark haired woman interrupts him, wrapping her arm around his waist affectionately. She has pale flawless skin, light hazel eyes and long mousse brown hair tied up away from her pretty face. She's wearing a very stylish red jacket with oversized hoop earrings. The woman places her hand on Michael's chest. "Mike, we need to get back."

The air falls silently around them, an atmosphere that could shatter at any moment.

"Ahh, Ava this is Olivia. Olivia, my..."

Ava cuts in, "Fiancée, what a beautiful ring." She gestures to the glistening ring sitting perfectly on Olivia's ring finger. Michael stares at Ava for a long moment, realising that there is a pain slipping into her eyes.

"This is Ava. I worked with her at TAC about a year ago," he says, uneasily.

"I heard a lot about you. It's good to put a name to a face," Ava replies.

"It's great to meet you. Michael we really must be going," and Olivia slips away from him to join the rest of their party.

"I, uhh... Perhaps we could go for a coffee sometime?" Michael suggests, nervously.

"That would be lovely."

"Okay, well... I..." Michael says, using his arms to indicate in the direction he needs to leave in.

"Yes of course."

Michaels stands for a long moment.

"It's really good to see you Ava," he finally says.

"You too, Michael, you too," she says with a growing lump in her throat.

Michael turns and heads towards Olivia and their friends. Ava watches him disappear into the crowd with her.

"Who was that?" Daniel asks, intrigued.

"Oh that was Michael. He used to work at, TAC."

"He is *hot,*" Daniel replies and Ava shoves him playfully with her shoulder.

"You wanna come back to ours, Ava?" Daniel asks.

James is talking to a couple he knows, so he is completely distracted.

"No, it's okay. I think I'll head back. It's been a really long day."

Daniel plants a kiss on her cheek and wraps his arm around her, saying goodbye. Ava interrupts her uncle's conversation with the couple to say her goodbyes to him.

Back at her apartment, Ava reclines on the sofa and lets out a massive sigh. Her phone starts vibrating in her bag which is still hooked on her arm next to her. She dives into it trying to locate the vibration, finds it and pulls it out.

It's a video call from Katelyn, so she slides the green telephone symbol up to answer it.

"HAPPY THANKSGIVING!" all the voices shout at her.

It's Ava's mother, Clare, Katelyn and Lydia.

Ava beams at them all and shouts back, "HAPPY THANKSGIVING, I can't believe you've all called!"

"Did you go to the parade?" Katelyn asks.

"Yes I did. It was so much fun, I felt like a child again. I've never seen anything like it!"

"It's great fun, isn't it?" Katelyn adds.

"How are you? How have you been?" Clare asks.

"Yeah, really good. I went with uncle James, and we went for food too." Ava pauses, "I miss you all so much. I wish you were all here to see it!"

They all catch up over a lengthy conversation. A pang of heartache forms in Ava's chest, and she wishes she was at home with her sisters and her mum.

"So now that I have all you girls together, there is something I need to discuss with you." Florence announces.

Ava sits patiently waiting. Florence's face is now on the screen alone.

Ava's sisters quieten down and Florence begins, "So I have to say that the partner of your fathers company is being a pain in the arse. He has been hounding me for some time regarding my share. How would you all feel if I was to sell up? Especially now that you, Ava darling, are in New York." Anger fills Ava and without any hesitation she scorches, "Don't even think about it!"

Florence's face is shocked by Ava's response and her sisters stay quiet.

"Ava May! You cannot speak to me in this way. This was your father's and your passion. Not mine. Don't forget that. You aren't here and I back your decision 100%. Yes, we earn a decent income from it but, -"

Ava interrupts her again. "I said no. It isn't up for discussion mum. I'll come back if I have to. Or I'll speak to uncle James but what I can tell you is it isn't for sale!"

Clare's face appears on the screen and she tries to defuse the situation. Given that none of the other girls have any idea of what being an architect really entails they feel they can't comment.

Ava continues, "Look. Dad invested everything he had to build this business and if the partner doesn't like it because he is an arrogant prick, then he can sell his half back to us. We'll find the money from somewhere. But we are not selling!"

"Okay. Look, come on you guys. It's Ava's first Thanksgiving."

"Clare, you're right. Ava sweetheart, we best leave you to enjoy the rest of Thanksgiving," Florence declares. They all say their goodbyes and end the call.

Ava decides that she needs to talk about this with her uncle. After all, he too was a founder once upon a time. His older brother, her father, had encouraged James into this field in the first place. He'd know what to do.

Ava sits in her quiet, empty apartment. For the first time in a while she feels lonely. She walks over to the large, glass sliding doors, grasps the metal handle and slides the door back with force. Stepping outside and she leans her forearms on the black metal railings linking her fingers and sighs. She wishes her father was here so she could ask him what he would do. She doesn't want to see the family business being sold off to an irritating stranger.

A million thoughts run through Ava's mind. She has been in New York for over a year now and realises she hasn't made many friends. Feeling that she needs someone to vent to, she wonders who to call. She lost touch with Mia after Michael moved back to Albany and she now spends a lot of time with her uncle and Daniel and their social circle. However they're a lot older than her and she sometimes feels a burden.

An idea enters her head. She has never been to the Rooftop Terrace or stepped foot in the 'Oasis' gym. Both are on the top floor further above her. Ava walks back into the apartment, slides the heavy door shut again, grabs her bag and leaves.

On the Rooftop Terrace, Ava is greeted by a black sky with the stars glistening back at her. There are several seating areas spaced out on the terrace. The grey rattan sets have light grey cushions and there are potted olive trees scattered. Ava finds a seat and slowly sits herself down. Nobody else is there and it's completely silent. Beneath her, she can hear the distant sound of traffic on the streets of Manhattan and the occasional horn. She sits just enjoying the silence.

"You alright?" There is a man, fairly tall and he is dressed in all black gym wear.

"Oh, hello." Ava replies.

"I've never seen you up here before?" The man smiles.

"In all honesty, I've lived here a year and this is my first time coming here.

"I was gonna say, I come up here most nights and I've never seen you, I'm Jacob, by the way." In a friendly voice.

"I'm Ava, nice to meet you."

He is tall and slender, tanned and his facial hair matches his very dark brown hair. Jacob sits down uninvited.

"So, you're not American?" Jacob concludes.

"And neither are you," she giggles.

"No!" he laughs, "I'm not and I'm pretty sure you can work out from my accent that I'm from Australia. Well, Brisbane actually. And you?"

"England," Ava replies smiling.

"Well, Ava from England. It's nice to meet you."

"So, how long have you lived here, Jacob from Australia?"

"Well," he pauses, and chuckles at her witty response, "I travelled around South America. Then, I explored a few states up here and ended up in New York about three months ago. I landed a job and got myself an apartment down below and haven't yet left."

"So, you plan to move on, eventually?" Ava asks.

"I haven't decided, if I'm honest. I like New York and the people are friendly. What about you? How did you end up here?"

"Well... my uncle owns this apartment block and he runs a large corporate Architectural company and I work for him."

"No way! Crazy! So you're an architect then?"

"I am indeed," she says nodding and smiling.

"Well Ava the Architect. It's been nice chatting with you. I'll leave you with your own thoughts, and perhaps I'll see you around?" He smiles and rises from their rattan sofa.

"Nice to meet you too, Jacob."

After Jacob has headed downstairs, Ava sits for a while, enjoying her thoughts and realising that she isn't alone. Millions of people move around this world, for work or for pleasure. The world is everybody's oyster.

Chapter Fifteen

Michael and Olivia sit at breakfast. Christmas is only a week away and Olivia is discussing the gifts she has already purchased for their relatives.

"Michael. Are you listening to me?" She asks tilting her head and gazing at him intently.

"Hmm sorry," he says coming round from his daydream.

He was miles away, "Uhh, what did you say? Sorry."

"Shall we get your mom anything else? Or will the perfume and Macy's voucher be enough?" she repeats.

"You know my mom. She's always grateful. That should be more than enough."

Olivia stands from her chair opposite Michael and walks to him around the breakfast bar.

She leans herself on his back, wraps her arm around his shoulders and strokes his suited chest. Michael touches her hand while continuing to hold a bagel in the other. She ruffles her hand through his hair, then leans forward and kisses his cheek with affection.

"Right, Michael. I had better get myself to work. Don't forget we are meeting my parents at The Plaza at 7 p.m. and please don't be late." She reminds him.

"The Plaza at seven. Got it." He takes another bite of his bagel.

"Are you okay, Michael? You seem distracted. Is your father working you too hard? Don't forget you're a partner now and you can take control a bit more."

"Sorry Liv. It's been quite full on at the office lately. I'm okay," he says taking a sip of his coffee.

"Okay, well, I'll see you at seven, then," she says kissing him briskly on the lips. "Love you."

"You too," Michael replies, distracted as Olivia grabs her keys from the counter and leaves.

Olivia turned up at Michael's mother's door six months ago, tail between her legs, declaring she had made a mistake. Michael moved back to his mother's and stayed. His dad offered him a partnership at his company. It isn't the size of TAC but the money is good and it was more than his father had ever offered previously. His mother isn't happy about Olivia but says she will support her son in whatever decision he decides to make.

Olivia had left England apparently because Franko had put her on the 'back-burner' when a younger woman became his 'PA'. Michael believes there is more to it but Olivia was here, and she returned to the United States for him, to save *their* relationship. This time Michael wears the trousers and controls everything. This time, Olivia hankers after him and he likes the power that he had never had before. Michael asked her to marry him because it was the right thing to do and after eleven years it was time to take the relationship to the next level. There would be no more waiting around. He was edging towards forty now and he wanted to settle down and start a family.

Michael's phone pings in front of him and he picks it up,

'*Good morning Mike! LUNCH DATE? Love you x x x*'

He smiles and replies.

'*Mimi! Is that you asking or demanding that we meet? X x x*'

His phone pings again.

'Michael you should know by now it's me demanding! Haha. x x x'

He laughs and replies again.

'*Got it! I'll meet you outside 'At the Deli' at 1 p.m. X x x*'

Another ping.

'*Okay, but you know that we're not eating there, right? You're treating me! See you then! Have a good morning. Love you x x* '

Michael arrives at his office on 39th West Street. His father, also an architect, is already at the office. George set up the business when Michael was born. Bankruptcy threatened several times but scraping by, the business was saved mainly due to his father's determination. Michael's younger twin brothers, Asha and Andy both have been working for their dad since leaving College having followed their older sibling in the family footsteps of architecture. On most days, Michael deals with the clients and their requests making phone calls, writing emails and delegating work to the staff. He misses doing the design work but this is what his father needs to be done.

Michael arrives outside 'At the Deli'. Mia is already there waiting.

"Hola!" She kisses him on his cheek and hugs him.

"Hey, Mimi! How are you? So where does senorita wanna eat?"

"Mike! You know you sound odd when you try to speak Spanish. Why bother?" she laughs.

"What! I sound Spanish?" he laughs back.

"Okay, well, now you're a partner, I want somewhere fancy."

"Mia, you have graduated. You're on some pretty decent money at the District Attorney's Office as well, you know." he smiles.

"Ahh, yeah, but I'm not a partner," she pauses, "and you, Michael Johnson, upped and left me for a whole year! You *owe* me!"

He wraps his arm around her neck and kisses her head.

"Okay, you got it. We'll head to Carmines at Times Square."

Carmines has a real family restaurant feel to it. It is filled with dark wood tables and matching chairs. Crisp white tablecloths have menus sitting in the centre. There are mirrored pillars making the interior appear more spacious. Photos are displayed on the yellow walls. The restaurant is always busy but Michael and Mia are given a table in a snug corner. They view the menu, and both order their meals. Mia chooses the meatballs and Michael opts for the lasagne. They both have to return to work so order soft drinks. Colas all round.

"So, how's the wedding plans going?" Mia asks, genuinely interested.

"Yeah good! We've got a meeting at seven, at the Plaza." he says sipping the cola that the waiter has just placed on the pristine table.

"Oh wow! Things are really moving forward then."

"Yeah... I guess they are."

Mia stares at him, and raises her eyebrows.

"What? What?" He looks uncomfortable.

"You wanna tell your face to look a little more excited then, Mike."

"What's that supposed to mean?"

"Well," she pauses, "You don't look very happy about it. I mean, this is what you wanted, Mike, right?"

"Yeah, it is, only..." he pauses.

"Only what?" she fires back.

"I saw Ava. At the Thanksgiving parade."

"What? No way. She's still here then? I thought she'd head back to England, by now." Mia stammers.

"I know, but she hasn't and...," he pauses again.

"You can't still have feelings for her Mike. Not after all this time. Surely?"

"No. No I don't." he says unconvincingly.

"Then what?" Mia replies as their food arrives.

"Saved by the bell, as they say." Michael laughs as his food is laid in front of him.

"Michael Johnson you won't get out of it that easy." she laughs.

The meatballs are sitting on a bed of spaghetti soaking in a rich red tomato sauce with basil that fills the air. Michael's lasagne is neatly stacked layers of pasta sheets and mince topped with a crispy grilled golden cheese topping. A colourful side salad accompanies. The smells make their mouths water. Michael leaning in to take a mouthful of salad leaves, continues the topic.

"It's making me question myself Mia. Am I doing the right thing marrying Liv?" he says as he begins to chew.

Mia pauses, completely dumbfounded at his last sentence.

"You're probably just getting cold feet. You're about to look at wedding venues. You're making that jump, Mike. It's scary!"

Michael changes the subject and begins to talk about work.

After paying and leaving a handsome tip, they are standing outside the front door sheltered by a canopy.

"Oh, Michael. I forgot to say. I told Joey that you were back in Manhattan and he wants to hook up on Friday night, for some well-deserved drinks."

"Sounds great. I'll be up for that."

"Awesome. I'll let him know, and Mike... don't stress about the wedding planning. It's exciting!"

"I know, I know, you're right, I'm just panicking, I guess." he accepts.

"Exactly! Right so, I'll text the plans for Friday?" Mia says.

"Friday?" he repeats absentmindedly.

"Yeah. Joey? Drinks?" shaking her head.

"Oh, of course! Friday. Joey. Got it," he confirms and wraps his arms around his best friend. They return to their offices in different directions.

Chapter Sixteen

Ava is sitting on the rooftop terrace. It's her new favourite spot. She is wrapped up warm because New York is freezing around Christmas time. The thick black duffle coat is helped by a grey fleece blanket wrapped around her legs to keep the warmth insulated. A cup of hot cocoa steaming in front of her on the table. She sits silently with her notepad instead! Ava has been working on a letter to Richard. Even though he is no longer alive he has been haunting her dreams and this is her way of addressing some of those demons. It is personal and this is something she will never share with anyone.

'*Richard,*

This feels so strange doing this. Where do I even start? There is so much I want to say.

The first few years of our relationship and our marriage were just perfect. . . You really did make me so happy! I'm not entirely sure where it went wrong, I feel I should have said these things when I left! Only... I couldn't! You cheated on me you bastard! You disappeared for days at a time so you could go on drug and drink benders! How could you put me through that? Why did you put me through that?

I gave you so many chances and every time I did, you... well... you screwed up in another way.

You stole from me. More than once. You used my money to rent hotel rooms! You got yourself in debt because of your habit! I wasn't there for you! I gave up too easily... I can't change that now! I forgave you too easily!

I'm not entirely sure why I am writing all this... but I guess this is the final goodbye?

No one will ever know of this! I love you, but you can't hurt me anymore.

I forgive you, for everything. I can only hope that you are now at peace?

I know how mad you were when I adopted my maiden name after the divorce. But that is who I am.

Ava May Turner.

Ava sits reading over her draft letter when she is interrupted.

"Alright, Ava from England?" Jacob says approaching her.

She glances over her shoulder and sees him out of the corner of her eye.

"Oh hello. Jacob from Brisbane, wasn't it?"

"Well done for remembering. Up here again I see?"

"Yes. I come up here all the time and in all weathers. As you can see." Laughing, she raises her hands to reveal her blanket. Jacob sits down opposite her.

"I can see that." he gestures to her thick protection.

"So," he pauses, "Do you like to party?" he links his fingers together in front of him.

"Party? What do you mean?" she says placing her phone down on her lap.

"Yeah, exactly that. There's a club. LAVO. You want to come with me? I don't mean like a date." he laughs, "Just as mates? It'll be a laugh."

"Oh my Gosh. I'd love to!" Ava beams. "I spend a lot of time with my uncle and his partner Daniel. Clubs aren't really their thing. They like to dine and go to Broadway shows, I've only ever been to a salsa club since I've been here." she reminisces.

Jacob stands.

"Well, it's a mate date, then." he smiles. "We'll go Friday? Sound good? What apartment are you? I'll meet you at yours?"

"Sounds great! 1107."

"Great, well, if I don't see you before, I'll see you Friday. Shall we say 9 pm? Clubs in New York don't really kick off till late."

"Perfect. I *actually* can't wait!" Ava says excitedly, clapping her hands with enthusiasm.

"Awesome.., Well, I'll catch up with you later and let you get back to your hot cocoa." He waves a hand above his head as walks to the double doors.

Ava stares back and yells, "Bye, Jacob from Brisbane," and hears him laugh as he disappears.

Looking through her draws, Ava finds a lighter. Tearing off the letter she has written to her dead ex-husband from the notepad, she opens the balcony door and sets the letter alight until she can no longer hold it. Once it is consumed by fire, she smiles to herself, knowing she is finally making a positive step.

Michael runs up to the tall white brick building embedded with rectangular windows. The front of The Plaza, on 5th Avenue, has flags hanging boldly at the front of it. He catches his breath and strides up the elegant red carpeted stairs, through a revolving door into the entrance lobby. There is an arched ceiling that towers above his head with detailed coving of gold leaf features framing a grand archway that draws his eyes above. In front of him lays a grand antique regal red Axminster carpet. Standing at the centre of it is a bespoke Victorian dark inlaid mahogany table, with six conjoined intricately carved legs and an ornate flower display in the centre. Above it is a grand crystal chandelier with a soft but powerful lighting. The whole lobby is spectacular.

Olivia struts up to Michael agitated. "Where have you been? You're late, Mike."

"Sorry! I got held up," he sighs equally annoyed by her tone.

Olivia's parents approach them both.

"Michael, Olivia, shall we not keep them waiting any longer?" Olivia's father firmly interrupts.

The concierge is waiting at a glass arched doorway for the party to follow him into the Grand Ballroom where the wedding could be held. Michael still feels angry but sighs and nods to his future father-in-law.

As they stroll through the grand interior of The Plaza, Michael breathtakingly notes the architecture of the stonework with its neoclassical style and white and breccia marble and appreciates the work and effort to achieve the effect.

Olivia nudges Michael as they approach the gigantic ballroom.

"What do you think Michael?" she asks beaming at him.

"Yeah, I like it, Liv." he replies, paying more attention to the building than her.

"Our event specialists' can help you take your wedding to extraordinary heights," the concierge says giving them the tour. "You can have the choice of the Grand Ballroom or the Terrace Room."

At one end of the Grand Ballroom is a stage, and the room is designed symmetrically. There are carved pillars evenly spaced with arched windows between them dressed with rich fabric drapes. The ceiling has gorgeously carved patterns painted in gold leaf to emphasise them.

"The ballroom can seat up to 500 guests." The concierge explains.

Michael stares up at the chandelier and the enormous ceiling. It isn't as grand as the crystal chandelier in the entrance lobby, but is still a focal point in the Grand Ballroom.

"So, now we shall take a look at the Terrace Room." he says informatively.

As they enter, Michael is dazzled by what he sees.

"Holy crap, look at this place!" he says aloud and Olivia darts him a look of disgust.

"What?" he says, shrugging, "What? This is incredible. The history this room holds is indescribable, Liv. This is the original architecture."

"I agree. The crystal chandelier by Charles Winston, is an original piece and it really is quite exquisite, don't you think?" the concierge concurs.

"I've never seen *anything* like it!" Michael takes in the true beauty.

The Terrace is broken down into sections, with horizontal barriers. One side of the room is largely mirrored and the other has golden railings broken apart by pillars. At the far wall is an ornate statue that is the main focal point. On either side of it are two enormous curved top mirrors. The ceiling is covered in designs of hand painted art. The lights in the ceiling alcoves give a soft lighting and feel very romantic standing amongst the ambience of the architecture.

It, again, is spectacular but in a completely different way to the Grand Ballroom.

"Now, you can hire this too. You can use it for the ceremony and the Ballroom for the wedding breakfast, but either way the choice is yours?" the concierge says.

Olivia's father interrupts, "Money is no object here, sir."

"Of course, of course. Well, we can give you a brochure which you can take with you and discuss your ideas amongst yourselves."

Olivia and Michael arrive back at their apartment. She slings her coat on their cream couch.

"I can't believe you were late Michael! You *knew* we were viewing the venue tonight. Do you have any idea how embarrassed I was?"

"Oh Olivia, so I was late! At least I turned up!" he says shutting the front door behind him.

"What's that supposed to mean?" she asks quietly.

Michael freezes and runs his hands through his hair.

"I mean, so I was late. My meeting could have run even later and that would have meant I couldn't have come at all." he says trying to convince himself.

Olivia strolls over to him and wraps her arms around his neck linking her fingers at the nape of his neck and begins to kiss him tentatively.

He pulls away, "I need to shower. I feel dirty."

Olivia pulls away, putting her hands on his chest.

"Of course. You shower and I'll order in. Pizza okay?"

"Yeah sure." he strolls up the stairs.

Michael is at his office and his phone pings next to his computer. He continues tapping away on his keyboard, pausing to check his phone. It's Mia.

'I hope you're still on for tonight? We're meeting at the cocktail bar near LAVO. You know the one, at 10 p.m. DON'T BE LATE! See you later, can't wait!! LET'S PARTYY. Love you x x x'

Michael smiles and turns the screen off. It's been ages since he and Joey had caught up properly. It is even longer since the three of them have been united all together as a trio.

Back at his apartment, Olivia is waiting for him on the couch. She is dressed in sexy red lacy underwear.

"Hey, how was your day?" she seductively asks him.

He shuts the door.

"Oh, what's this?" and strolls towards her, dropping his case on the floor. He slips his black leather Derby shoes off one at a time. Then lays on top of her body, her legs either side of him.

"Well, as you've been working hard, I thought you'd like a little reward."

He looks into her eyes, her pupils enlarged with arousal. He kisses her, wrapping a hand under the nape of her neck then grabs her hair and tugs it. He kisses her again. Deeply, passionately.

"I want it," she murmurs through their kisses.

"Oh do you now?" he teases.

He lifts himself on to his knee, over her body. She gropes her breasts through her single layered bra. Taking the hem of her knickers, he slides them down her legs, slowly watching her. Olivia watches intently. Michael reveals her sweet spot, eagerly waiting for him. She looks at his approving eyes and undoes his black leather belt, button and flies. Sliding her hand into his pants she feels his hard manhood and reveals it. He groans as she does this while she guides him to her entrance. He forces himself into her pool of moisture. Both are groaning loudly at the pleasure. He withdraws and slams himself into her again with pleasurable force.

"Again," she tells him. He groans and waits.

"Again." He does it again, picking up his pace.

"I'm coming for you."

He continues to pound her sweet spot until his own satisfaction pours into her.

Ava is ready standing in front of the mirror, to check her reflection. Tonight, she has a full face of makeup, making the extra effort. Her hair is curled and sits over one shoulder. She purchased a dress online for tonight. Not just to impress Jacob but to the whole of LAVO nightclub. She hasn't been out in over a year and wants to feel feminine. The short black silk spaghetti strap backless dress makes her feel sexy. She slips on a pair of black pump heeled shoes with pretty velvet bows at the back. She eyes them in the mirror.

"*Great choice, Ava,*" she tells herself and there's a knock at the door. Placing her deep red lipstick in her black bag, she heads to the door.

Ava opens to Jacob.

"Holy shit, Ava the architect, you scrub up well mate."

She laughs loudly, "Thank you, Brisbane."

Before leaving, she sprays her Gucci perfume over herself.

"Alright mate, not too much, you tart," he laughs hysterically.

Ava nudges him playfully and they make their way to LAVO.

"Honestly Mike, your time keeping." laughs Mia as he approaches the table with Joey and her table. Joey stands and embraces Michael with genuine affection.

"Mikeyboy. How the hell are you?" he says letting go of their embrace.

Joey is a descendant of Italians that migrated to the United States. He is shorter than Michael, but very muscular with dark brown eyes and black hair. He has a clean shaven face and is dressed in a black shirt with black tight jeans.

Mia is dressed in a red dress that rests off her shoulders and is tightly fitted. Her hair is tied in a ponytail and she is wearing open toe heels. Michael turns his attention to her as she stands to hug him and she kisses him on the cheek.

"Looking as good as ever Mia." he says.

"Actually Michael, you're looking extra hot tonight." she admires. "Shame you're soon to be a married man, huh?" And she seats herself again.

Michael is wearing a cream blazer with a white shirt, with the top button undone. He has black tight jeans on and his shirt is tucked in. He sits at their table and they order cocktails on Mia's recommendation. Chatting about their daily lives, Michael explains the architecture of The Plaza and Joey talks about his wife and children. Mia talks of work at the District Attorney's Office.

Ava and Jacob are waiting at the crowded bar to be served. Jacob fills her in on his travels around the U.S and which were favourite places and others he didn't like. Ava tells him of her family back home and what England is like. They both neck back Sambuca shots two at a time. Ava needs to let her hair down and Jacob is great company. She isn't attracted to Jacob and can really see a really good friendship forming between them. She finds him funny and he makes her feel at ease.

Pushing their way through the merry moving bodies, they make their way to the middle of the extremely busy dance floor. All types of musical genres are played at LAVO and Ava lets her body dance to the rhythm of the music. They dance together and he wraps his arm around her shoulder and they bounce up and down to the R&B that is playing at an ear-bursting loudness. Ava is feeling the drunkenness rise through her body and she is loving the atmosphere of the night club.

"I need the restroom." she shouts in Jacob's ear.

"Okay. You want me to come with you?" he yells back.

She shakes her head, "Wait here, I'll find you."

"Okay."

She heads for the restrooms.

Mia, Michael and Joey are waiting at the front of the queue. The doorman nods them in. Mia pays for her coat to be held in the cloakroom. They go straight to the bar and Mia is buzzing to be with her two best friends, Joey is as tipsy as Mia, and Michael is slowly catching up. Mia and Joey got to the cocktail bar on time but Michael turned up an hour late. He had been tied up with his fiancée.

"Let's go straight to the dance floor?" Mia pleads.

"Mia. You and Joey go to the centre of the dance floor. I'll wait here at the bar and get a drink." Michael suggests.

Mia and Joey agree and strut their way to the dance floor while Michael laughs at them as they make their way through the hoards of people. He stands at the crowded bar and patiently waits to be served.

He receives a text:

'I love you Mr Johnson. Have a good night. Now going to bed. Don't wake me, when you come in. O x x x'

It's Olivia. He turns the phone off and places it back in his jeans pocket.

When Ava returns, Jacob is dancing rather closely to a woman. He is grinding his crotch against her backside. Ava is incredibly tipsy and can't see the woman's face because she is facing the other way. She taps Jacob on the shoulder to let him know she has returned. Jacob glances at her, winks and steps away from the woman. He then grasps Ava and picks her up by her waist and spins her around drunkenly. As they come to a stop, she can see who the woman is. It's Mia.

"Mia!" Ava shouts.

Mia takes a moment to register the face and then flings her arms around Ava and hugs her, swaying her side to side.

"Ava!" she exclaims, "How are you? This is Joey," she gestures to Joey. He waves drunkenly and carries on dancing in his own world. Ava begins to dance and a recent hit plays. The crowd roars with excitement. Mia starts dancing with Joey again and Ava joins in.

Michael is making his way through the crowd, and finally sees Mia and Joey. Mia is doing her usual, drunken dancing with men. It never leads to anything but she loves the attention. Next to her, is a woman, a woman he knows. A woman he knows every square inch of. A woman he once loved. He finds himself drawn to her and lets his legs take him. Slowly stepping towards her as if the dance floor was empty, his eyes watch her as she swings her hips erotically to the song. She lifts her hands above her head and flings back her long dark hair back. Approaching her from behind, he strokes her naked back, and dances behind her at very close proximity holds her hips through her silk dress. Ava recognises the touch, she knows the grasp. As she turns she knows who she will find.

They stand staring at each other.

"Michael!" she says, breathlessly.

Chapter Seventeen

va opens her eyes. She doesn't recognise the sheets or the bed. It isn't hers. *Whose is it?* Ava sits up to find the other side of the double bed empty. She is confused. Raising her body up and out of the bed, she grabs a shirt from a chair in the bedroom. The shirt belongs to a man.

Ava can hear the shower running in the en-suite. She follows the sound and the steam floating from the open door. Pushing the door open, there is a naked man in the shower. Ava tip-toes closer, trying to make out who it is. It can't be Richard as she knows he has gone, gone for good. He turns around, "Ava. Good morning." He smiles. It's Michael.

Ava awakes and her eyes flick open. Panic rises in her chest. She isn't in her apartment. Lifting her head off the pillow, it spins from all of the alcohol she consumed the night before.

"Alright mate?" A voice says from behind her. It's Jacob. A wave of relief washes over her when she realises that they are both fully dressed.

"Thank goodness! I worried where I was then." Ava replies.

"You were pretty smashed Ava the Architect," he laughs.

"I know. I can't remember leaving." she is embarrassed.

"You were mumbling some sort of crap in the night, mate. You kept waking me up!" he is laughing again.

Ava's cheek flush as she replies.

"Oh gosh. Was I really? What did I say?" knowing full well what she was dreaming.

"Crikey, I didn't catch that mate! I dunno?" he shrugs innocently.

Ava is laughing. She was so intoxicated that Jacob had to support and escort her back. They stay in his apartment all day. He slings her a sweatshirt and jogging bottoms so she doesn't have to go back to hers to get changed. He makes bacon sandwiches and they watch Disney films.. Ava has started to really enjoy Jacob's friendship and feels really at ease in his company. His apartment is like Ava's, but grubbier. It smells more masculine, is filled with trinkets from his travels and not as tidy, but she feels at home all the same.

It's Monday morning, and Ava is in her office. She's still feeling the effects of the hangover from Friday night antics. It takes a lot longer to recover now, she is past thirty. Ava is standing at her desk looking over a drawing. Daniel knocks at her door and lets himself in.

"What are you doing here, Daniel? You never make an appearance at the office. What a lovely surprise!" As he approaches her.

"Ava, baby girl. Good morning" he says staring at his watch, "As we didn't see you over the weekend, you wanna go to lunch?"

"I know I was out with Jacob! So Daniel. I need you to speak to Uncle James about the family business back in the UK. The partner is trying to buy mum's half. He will get it over my dead body. Can you see if he'll invest back into his old business, please?"

"Oh Ava I'm not sure I can get involved with the business side of things!"

"I... I... just can't see my father's hard work and James's for that matter, be run into the ground."

"Okay... Ava! Leave it with me baby. I'll see what I can do! Say no more about it."

"Thank you Daniel!" she throws her arms around his neck and shrieks with happiness.

Ava and Daniel are discussing where to go for lunch when Michael bursts in unannounced. "Hey!" he says, running both his hands through his hair, nervously.

"Michael?" Ava pauses.

"So... I was passing by and thought I'd come in and say hi."

Ava and Daniel stand there watching.

"So now I've said hi, I see you're busy, so I'm gonna go." Michael leaves her office as fast he did entering it and heads for the stairwell.

"What the hell was that?" Daniel asks.

"I have... no idea." Ava is completely flabbergasted by Michael's appearance.

"When did you two have sex?" Daniel questions, staring in Ava's direction,

"How on earth did you come to that conclusion?"

"Are you kidding me? The sexual tension between you two is on fire. I noticed it when we saw him at Thanksgiving!" Grinning.

Michael arrives back at his apartment. No one is home. Taking his coat off, and hanging it on a dining room chair, he places his briefcase on the table. He pulls a seat out and sits at his laptop, flipping open the screen and turning it on. He searches for florists in Manhattan and selects a website. Scrolling through the different types of bouquets, he likes one of white roses and lilies mixed with green foliage and chooses the 'Deluxe' option. It is possible to send a message as well. He types:

Ava,

"I miss you",

He deletes it.

'Ava, I want to see you.'

He deletes it again.

Ava

Merry Christmas,

Best Wishes

Michael

X X X X

He uses his work credit card to pay and completes the order. After deleting the search history, he flips down the laptop and takes the deepest breath. Michael gets up from the table and goes to the kitchen to make himself coffee.

Olivia and Michael's apartment is spread across two floors and has been recently decorated in cream. The first floor is an open plan living and dining area with a large cream corner couch next to the door. The television which is mounted on the wall. The kitchen is large with high gloss white units, a black quartz worktop and spotlights. The stairs lead to the bedroom and en-suite.

As Michael switches off the coffee machine he hears the front door slam. It's Olivia.

"Anyone home?" She walks into the kitchen where Michael is pouring himself a coffee.

"You beat me home." she says.

"Ahh yeah. I finished work early because Christmas is in a couple of days." Michael grabs another mug from the cupboard for Olivia.

"Coffee?" he asks as she hangs up her jacket.

"Yeah please. Did you pick up the turkey?"

"Yeah I sure did." he says handing Olivia her coffee.

"So have you decided on The Plaza yet?" Olivia asks with enthusiasm.

"Yeah, I did. Whatever you want," he says.

Olivia rests the palms of her hands on the worktop and studies him.

"Michael. Why aren't you paying much interest in the wedding plans?" she asks, bluntly.

"What? I am!" He gets agitated.

"Well, you wanna start showing it."

"You asked me if I wanted The Plaza and I said whatever you want. What else do you want me to say?" he replies abruptly.

"Well, it doesn't seem like you are. Do you want The Plaza or not?"

"Liv, if you want the freaking Plaza, then we'll have the freaking Plaza!" he spits.

Olivia stands shocked at his reaction and glares at him.

"You know what Olivia. I don't work my ass off to come home to you creating arguments about stupid stuff like wedding venues." he yells.

"Stupid stuff? Are you kidding me?" she yells back.

Michael storms past her and grabs his coat from the dining table chair.

Olivia follows him as he speeds towards the door.

"Where are you going?"

"OUT!"

He slams the door behind him.

Michael arrives at a bar a few blocks from his apartment. Swinging the door open, he lands himself heavily on a bar stool. He runs his hands through his hair and sighs heavily.

"You had one of those days huh? What can I get you?" says the bartender.

"A brandy and make it a double!" Michael demands.

"Yeah sure. Coming right up!" The bartender places the drink in front of him. Michael swallows it in one and slams the glass down.

"Make it another!" he spits, throwing $50 on the bar.

"That bad?" The bartender chuckles.

"Yeah! Now how about you stop being nosey and get me a drink!"

"Okay! I think you've had enough!"

"You what!? I said get me a drink!

Two men from another table come over and ask him to leave. They both take an arm and escort him to the door.

Michael is fuming and just wants to let off steam. He wriggles free of an arm, turns and takes a swing at one of the men. Ducking the punch, the man plants his fist hard on Michael's face and they secure his arms again. Outside, feeling dazed, he is thrown to the ground and kicked in the ribs.

"Don't come back, jackass!"

He finds another bar, orders a drink and eventually realises *'My secret temper is back!'* He only ever learnt of this aggressive characteristic because of Olivia. It isn't the first time he has lost it with someone in a bar but it only happened previously because he felt he had lost control of a situation and his emotions were out of sync. *'I've never been good at confrontation. If there was an argument with my brothers I would run and hide instead. I've always tried to be a people pleaser. Maybe this is why the aggressive side comes out when I am drunk. It must be the built up frustration.'*

After a few more drinks and more self-reflection, he eventually gets himself together and flags down a cab.

"Pedro House on 34th," he says stumbling into the car.

After a ten minute journey, the cab draws up outside Ava's apartment building. He pays the driver and drags himself out.

He heads into the lobby. Mr Truman is behind the reception desk.

"Can I help you?"

165

Michael stops short. "I'm going up to see Ava Turner. Now d'you mind."

Mr Truman rolls his eyes and recognises Michael from Ava's drunken return over a year ago.

Michael stands at Ava's door, holding his bruised ribs, and knocks. It's late so she calls at the door before opening it.

"Who is it?"

"It's Michael. You've gotta let me in." Slurring and leaning his drunken head against her door. As she opens it, he falls forward, forcing her to stumble backwards.

"What on earth are you doing here?" Ava is genuinely shocked. "You had better come in." The door is shut.

"You've gotta hear what... I've... me... has to say." he says tapping his chest.

Ava stands in her pyjamas, with no makeup on and her hair tied on the top of head in a scruff. She crosses her arms, agitated by the state of Michael and the time of night.

"Go on!" She says in annoyance.

"We went to see a wedding venue the other night." he mumbles.

"And?..."

"Ava I can't marry her."

Ava stands speechless.

"Have you got any more booze?" he says stumbling to the couch where he takes a seat. His eyes are glazed and he is clearly very drunk.

"I think you've had more than enough." She says firmly and he nods silently.

Ava sits next to him on her couch and turns off the TV.

"I don't understand why you're here Michael."

"I can't marry her!"

"Right, well. *Clearly* you can and it's *quite* clear you love her!"

"Ava! Are you listening to me, I can't do it!" he slurs.

"Why can't you?"

"Because... I am infatuated with you, Ava!"

Ava jumps up from the couch and begins to pace around the room while Michael stares.

166

"What do you want me to say Michael?" Throwing her arms out. "You have come here as another woman's man!"

"I wanna hear you say you feel the same." he probes.

Ava can feel her fury building.

"How dare you! How dare you come here? What? You thought I'd play a part in all of this. You don't want to marry her? Then don't. But you dare make me your reason for not wanting to!" she says outraged.

"Say it, Ava! Say it!" he begs, trying to stand.

"*I will not!*" she hisses. "I have been in the same position where the person you love is hankering after another woman, and I *will not* play *any* part in this charade and I *will not* be culpable for any of *your* decision making!"

He strolls towards her slowly, trying to mask his pain.

"Ava," he whispers.

"No!" She starts again. "Did you *honestly* think I would allow you to come here and for *me* to be the other woman in a seedy affair?" she pauses.

"I want you to leave." She walks to the door and opens it to indicate that it's time for him to leave.

Michael stumbles towards the door, and pauses next to her.

"I'm sorry, I shouldn't have come."

"No you shouldn't have. Now leave!"

She slams the door after him.

Chapter Eighteen

Michael has taken the day off to nurse his hangover and his bruised ribs. His face has also puffed up from the punch. He slept on the couch last night but didn't see Olivia this morning as she slipped off to work without a word. Michael sits slumped on the corner couch in jogging bottoms and no top. He spends much of the day going over the conversations with Ava from the night before.

He receives a message from Mia:

'Hey Mike, I'm now leaving to go to Albany for the holidays. We'll catch up when I get back. What's your plan for the New Year? Love you x x x'

It's the day before Christmas Eve and Michael has previously invited both Olivia's and his parents for Christmas dinner. He needs to patch things up with Olivia to avoid making the meal incredibly awkward. He runs his hands through his hair and sighs.

On his phone, he selects 'Liv'.

'Hey, I didn't hear you leave this morning, I'm off work today. Is there any way you can finish early? I think we need to talk. M x x x x'

He clicks 'Send'.

Patiently waiting over half an hour for a reply, he doesn't get one. *A shower will freshen me up.*

The master bedroom upstairs, has freshly painted all white walls and white curtains in a double lined taffeta material. The wardrobes are fully mirrored units. The bed is dressed in crisp white cotton linen sheets and several immaculate white cushions including velvet, Carissa round ones and Maximo. Finishing the look are two sheepskin fur rugs either side of the beautifully displayed bed and a faux fur blanket laid at the foot of it.

The en-suite bathroom's walls and floor are covered in Calacatta white marble. The freestanding tub with ornate silver taps is to the right and the shower at the far end of the room with an all-encompassing glass door to separate it. There are twin wash basins set in the marble countertop with more highly polished silver taps. Michael stands in front of the mirror and stares long and hard at his reflection and checks the bruises left on his skin.

He sighs to himself *"Oh Michael Johnson. What are you going to do with your life, huh?"* Finally, he can no longer stand his reflection. He whips off his jogging bottoms and underpants leaving them in a heap on the floor and slides the shower door open.

Olivia returns. Michael is in the kitchen preparing a shrimp salad for them. She just stands there, silently.

"Hey," he says, sheepishly. "You got my message then? Look... I owe you a massive apology, I was a complete jerk yesterday, and I don't really have an excuse for how I acted. Only that work is really stressful right now." Running his hands through his hair. "I also got into a fight in a bar and got whacked. My body aches. I am so sorry.'"

Olivia says nothing and walks towards him. Wrapping her hands around him, she hugs him passionately for a long moment.

"I hate when we fight Michael." She whispers.

"Look. It's Christmas Eve tomorrow. Let's talk about the wedding in the New Year. We don't need to rush and book anything. Let's just enjoy the holidays first." Hoping to placate her as he lets go of Olivia and grasps her hands.

After her swimming session, Ava is greeted by the usual man who is walking towards her. They happen to come across each other on the regular basis now. He looks in Ava's direction.

"Hey. We have a habit of bumping into each other, don't we?"

"We certainly do." She giggles.

"I'm Mark, by the way."

"Nice to finally have an introduction, Mark. I'm Ava."

"Well Ava, perhaps we could go for a coffee after a swim sometime?"

"That sounds great. I'd really like that."

"Okay well perhaps the next time we bump into each other we'll make it happen?"

Ava leaves the pool and heads to her appointment.

"So... Ava, how have you been? Tell me about last week?"

The small therapy room has two windows that look out onto a courtyard. There is a bookcase, filled with all kinds of therapy books and a desk with a laptop. There is very little in the room to distract Ava throughout her therapy sessions.

"Well, it's been a funny week, really." Ava is lying on a black leather reclining chair.

Annette, her therapist, is sitting opposite. She is a very attractive but eccentric woman in her fifties. She is wearing a khaki green bloomer suit and never wears shoes.

"I had a night out with Jacob."

"Jacob is from your apartment building?" her therapist confirms.

"Yes, that's right, and we saw Michael out with Mia and it's made me feel, well, confused."

"In what way?" She starts to take notes.

"Well I'm not sure. Anyway, he turned up at my apartment a couple of days ago."

"What did he want to talk to you about?" Annette coaxes, resting her arms on her lap with her legs crossed.

"Well... he is meant to be marrying his long term girlfriend Olivia and has declared that he can't ....because of me."

"And, how did you react to that Ava?"

"Well... I was furious. How *dare* he turn up and just expect me to accept his declaration like that!"

"Right... so at that moment you felt anger... how do you feel about it now?"

"Confused. It brings back so many memories of Richard."

"Okay... so do you think there could be a link there? Has it triggered memories of your late ex-husband?"

"I guess so. I hadn't thought of it like that."

"Have you had more dreams lately?"

"Yes, I had one on Friday night after drinking and another on Saturday night, when I was hungover." Annette sits silently listening.

"In the first dream, I was in a bed I didn't know and a room that wasn't mine. I went to the bathroom and there was a man in the shower and I didn't know who it was. But then I remembered that Richard was gone and when he turned around, it was Michael."

"Okay. So you're dreaming of Michael, but at first you thought that it was really Richard."

"Yes! And it really threw me. I felt confused. Why was I there, with him and why did I automatically think it was Richard?" Annette nods.

"My second dream was of the day I left him. I came home from work, and he was drunk, again, I just flipped and told him I couldn't do this anymore, and was hysterically crying. I told him I couldn't live like this."

"And how did he react to your declaration? Was he... angry or was he... upset?" Annette says, interrupting Ava's flashback.

"Well, he was angry, really angry. He asked why? I explained the trust had gone, that I couldn't handle his lifestyle anymore." Ava begins to laugh at herself stupidly. "I told him that our vase isn't just cracked. It is smashed to pieces and no amount of glue was going to fix our vase."

Aromatherapy scents fill the air. Annette pours Ava a glass of water, sits back down and continues to listen. Taking a sip.

"He just flipped, not being able to see it from my point of view. He had been on a night out in another town, back in England and got himself in a spot of bother with some random local drug dealer. Do you know what he did? He laughed. He thought it was funny that he put himself in danger like that."

"How does this memory feel to you now, Ava?"

"Like a lifetime ago. Like it was a different life."

"So you have distanced yourself from that memory? When you woke from the dream how did it leave you feeling?"

"What do you mean?" Ava questions.

"Okay... well did you feel angry, upset, confused?"

"Ermm, I suppose I didn't feel anything. It was just a dream, I guess.

"Are you still swimming?"

"I am and it is really helping me. It really relieves my stress."

"Good. You must continue finding ways to help you unwind. Okay, so Ava, I'm going to set you some homework. Now that your dreams are far and few between, I want you to write down when you have them. I want you to write how it made you feel, and the next time I see you, we'll go over it. So apart from Michael coming to your apartment, you have had a good week?"

"Yes I have, although I am feeling a little uneasy being away from home for Christmas."

Annette nods continuing to listen.

"I'm going to my uncle's for Christmas so I'll be with some family on Christmas day." Ava continues.

"Okay... so, perhaps you could put some time aside on Christmas day to call home and speak to your family back in the UK?" Annette suggests.

"Of course, I didn't think of that."

"Just because you are away from home doesn't mean you can't make time for them. Christmas is the most obvious time to spend time with our families and loved ones."

"Absolutely. That is very true."

"Okay. Well that's our session over for today. We'll arrange for an appointment after the festive period. I've set you some homework, so we will leave it there for today."

Ava thanks the therapist for her time, leaves Annette's office, and makes her way home.

Ava knocks on Jacob's door and waits. He answers with an apron on and a wooden spoon in his hand,

"Alright? How did your session go?" he asks.

"Yeah good, it seemed to go so quickly today." Ava places her tan handbag and black duffle coat on his couch.

"What are you cooking for me today?" she asks following him to the kitchen area. The air is filled with the sweet smell of chicken frying.

"Ahhh well, Ava the Architect. I am cooking you a chicken and cashew stir fry with Thai rice. It is one of my favourites." Jacob swishes the chicken around the pan.

"It smells incredible. I can't wait to try it, Jacob."

"Would you mind straining the rice, Ava?" As he adds the sauce to the chicken and colourful vegetables.

"Oh course, where is the colander?" She asks looking around his kitchen as if it was her own. She finally finds it and lays the Thai rice on the plates. Jacob dishes out the chicken, cashew and vegetables on top with his wooden spoon. He grabs two forks from a drawer.

"And just like that, dinner is served." He winks.

"So, my uncle has asked if you'd like to join us for Christmas dinner." Ava says with her mouth full.

"No way. That would be awesome, Ava, I'd love to."

Chapter Nineteen

Jacob knocks on the door and Ava rushes towards it with Christmas morning excitement. He starts to sing 'We wish you Merry Christmas', as Ava opens it. Jacob thrusts a massive bouquet of flowers in her face.

It's 10.30 a.m. and they have to be at her uncle's in half an hour.

"Merry Christmas, Ava!"

"Aww, you're so sweet. You didn't have to get me flowers!" She says shocked by the surprise.

"Ava! How many times mate? I don't regard you like that," he laughs "They're not from me. I found them sitting outside your door," he says as he passes them over to her.

"What do you mean they're not from you? So who are they from?" Confused, she tries to shut the door with her handful of flowers.

"I dunno. Why don't you read the card?" Jacob shrugs.

"Aww, I'm guessing they're from mum and family back in England," she smiles, placing the flowers down so she can read the card. She breaks the seal on the envelope and takes it out.

Ava,

Merry Christmas

Best Wishes

Michael

X X X X

She cups her mouth with her hand, shocked,

"What? Are you alright, mate?" Jacob asks, taking the card from her.

"Michael?" He gives Ava a look.

"Who is buddies with the hot Mexican? Why would *he* be sending you flowers?"

Ava shakes her head and leaves them on the coffee table. "I have no idea. Anyway, shall we make tracks?"

They head out of the door and make their way to Christmas day at James and Daniels.

"Merry Christmas... Merry Christmas, you guys." Daniel bellows as Ava and Jacob approach the door. He embraces Ava heartfeltly and shakes Jacob's hand.

"Nice to finally meet you Jacob. Ava has told us so much about you. Come on in. James is pouring champagne, the show off." Stepping aside to let them past.

Ava and Jacob slide their shoes off. They stroll in and hear Christmas songs blaring from the sound system. James is doing exactly what Daniel said he was doing, only there are three extra glasses,

"Who else is coming, uncle James?" Ava calls through the loud music.

The dress code is to wear a Christmas jumper. James has The Grinch on his. Daniel has Kevin McCallister from 'Home Alone'. Ava's has a reindeer while Jacob is wearing the only thing he could find at late notice, a dull Christmas tree.

"SURPRISE!" several voices squeal from the lounge area. Ava goes to investigate and bursts into tears.

"Mum, Lyd, Kate. What are you all doing here? I can't believe it. Is Clare here?" she says through her ecstatic tears.

"Oh sweetheart!" Florence starts, "She really really wanted to be here, but with the girls and work commitments, she couldn't. I said we'd call her later."

Ava wraps her arms around her mother and sobs, and in turn Katelyn and Lydia too. They are all very emotional and so happy to see each other. James then joins in on the group cuddles with his sister-in-law and nieces.

Ava turns her attention to James.

"You're sneaky!" she grins through her tears, "How did you ever manage to keep this quiet?"

"With great difficulty." Daniel interrupts.

"I'd like to introduce you to my dear friend Jacob. He lives in my apartment building," she says, touching his arm.

"Good day. Nice to meet you," he nods confidently.

"Ah, we have an Australian in the house," Lydia points out.

"We do indeed. I'm from Brisbane, so not quite the outback."

James tings his champagne glass to get everyone's attention.

"Florence has already made Clare aware of what I am about to say. So I will just come out with it. I have some news. Well some major news actually. Your mother and I have been in cahoots and she has made me aware of the dilemma with the current partner of Turner Brothers Ltd. After having checked over my finances, I'm going to reinvest in the family business. There is no way I am going to let some jackass buy the business that my brother and I founded and let him change everything your father worked for."

Ava is stunned. Everyone in the room has all their eyes on her, knowing how passionate she felt about the company. How furious she was over it. The emotion in wanting to keep the business within the family. She bursts into tears again. Completely overwhelmed by her uncle's speech she embraces him with affection. Her fear and worry is over.

Daniel and James take turns keeping an eye on the Christmas dinner. Everyone stands chatting and sipping champagne. The atmosphere is buzzing and everyone is laughing and catching up or getting to know each other. Even Florence, Lydia and Katelyn got the memo on the dress code. They are all wearing matching red Mickey Mouse Christmas jumpers.

"Michael, can you get the door!" Olivia calls out, checking the turkey cooking in the oven. He hurries to the door from upstairs, where he is hiding from cooking duties, and greets his mother Cora.

"Mom, Merry Christmas." he says and cuddles her.

She is smartly dressed, wearing a navy blue dress with long sleeves, and tidy hair as always.

"Merry Christmas, Michael. How are you?"

The door goes again. Olivia's parents have arrived. Greeting her mother, Jennifer, he gives her a swift kiss on the cheek before she heads straight to Cora. Michael shakes Olivia's father's hand.

"Merry Christmas, Michael." he says coldly as he enters.

Michael and Olivia's father have had a strained relationship from the beginning. It was bad enough trying to meet the high expectations of his own father, let alone a future father-in-law. Their dislike of each other has been hard to disguise and anyone else in their company can sense the animosity between the two men.

"Cora, how are you?" Jennifer says tenderly, embracing her. Jennifer is nothing like her husband. She is far more loving and caring and is the only one who can soften her husband. Olivia gets her looks from her mother and they have the same hair colour and eyes. Today, Jennifer is wearing a bright pink lipstick to brighten her face.

Michael offers drinks to everyone as there is another knock at the door.

"I'll get it for you Michael." Cora says.

Michael's father George and his wife Vanessa walk in. They all exchange pleasantries. The atmosphere is awkward and intense because Michael and George can't stand Olivia's father but are always polite.

"Okay, are you ready? The girls have been working on this for a few days now." The voice says behind a laptop.

"READY!"

Clare's girls appear on the screen, get in position and perform a little dance for all the Turners in America, as well as Daniel and Jacob. When the two girls finish, everyone screams and shouts "YAY!! WELL DONE!" and clap.

The girls bow and run off to play with their new toys left by Father Christmas. Clare and Ava catch up over the video call and raise a glass to one another. Clare's husband appears on screen every now and then chipping into the conversation. Clare is the eldest of the four sisters and settled down at a young age. She is incredibly happy with her high school boyfriend, now husband. He has his own business as a chartered accountant. Clare is also an accountant but has put her career on hold to be a stay-at-home mother. Out of the sisters, Clare is the most motherly and the least judgemental. Clare has two girls. Victoria, aged eight, and Elizabeth, six. Clare named the girls after English Royalty.

Hours later and everyone has far too much to eat. They play games and Clare does a little quiz for everyone. The team members all become rather silly towards the end as they have far too much to drink. Florence isn't much of a drinker and even she is merry. Finally, the conversation must come to an end as Clare's girls need to bathe and go to bed after a long day. England is five hours ahead of the United States.

"Bye!" The group in the U.S. frantically waves at the screen.

"Bye!" The call disconnects.

The party continues.

"Right well, it's late," Ava says. "Perhaps we should think about getting back, Jacob?"

"Yeah, I'm easy, Ava Architect."

"Where is everybody staying? You don't have that many spare beds here uncle James?" Ava points out.

"Well I can always come back to yours Ava May." Florence slurs.

"Yeah of course you can, mum. Grab your overnight bag. You can sleep in with me and then Katelyn and Lydia can share a bed in uncle James' guest bedroom."

They all say their goodbyes at the door, Florence and James have a quiet word together and hug tightly. Ava notices this and will ask about it in the morning. Daniel embraces Jacob and pats his back, telling him how amazing he is. Daniel and James both hug Ava with affection and tell her they love her. It isn't too far to Ava and Jacob's apartment building so they decide to walk. It will only take them fifteen minutes if they walk fast. Ava can show Florence the streets of New York when they are slightly quieter.

Arriving at Ava's apartment, they leave Jacob in the elevator because he lives on a higher floor.

"Oh Ava, I've missed you." Florence says lovingly, hanging off her daughter's arm as Ava tries to unlock the door. Inside, her mother is drawn to the twinkling city view.

"I'll just flick the lights on." Ava declares.

"No don't. You can see the city better when they're off."

Ava walks towards her mother and embraces her tightly and they stare at the city.

The following morning, Ava appears from her bedroom, wrapped in a white dressing gown and her hair in a towel. The hot shower an attempt to rinse away her heavy head. Florence, in her pyjamas, is in the kitchen making bacon with scrambled eggs and coffee. The aroma of the food floats in the air.

"So Ava May. Who is Michael?"

Ava pauses and winces without her mother seeing her face.

"*The flowers.*" She thinks to herself staring at them on display in the centre of the dining table.

While Ava was in the shower, Florence had arranged the bouquet in a vase.

"Michael," she pauses "is nobody. Well, not of any importance, anyway."

"Well, young lady. You are clearly something of some importance to get a bouquet of that magnitude, wouldn't you agree?"

Ava chooses to ignore her mother's remark and helps to make the coffee. Breakfast is finally ready. They sit and eat while staring at the beautiful bouquet.

Jacob bursts through the door, bright and happy, "Good morning Turner ladies."

"Good morning," Florence replies.

"Everything okay?" Ava adds. "You're here early."

"10 a.m. is not early. Get dressed. Let's go for a walk in Central Park and walk off the hangover?"

"Oh, I'm feeling a little delicate this morning." Florence admits, "I'll give it a miss, I'll do the washing up and make the beds."

"Of course. No worries. Ava?" Jacob says, turning his attention.

She flicks her head back and sighs. "Okay, okay, I'll go and get dressed." she says rising from the table.

Once Ava disappears, Florence checks the coast is clear.

"Jacob, darling, do you know who this Michael is?" she whispers, so not to be heard.

"Um, yeah, I do. But if you are referring to the flowers then, I can't answer why he sent them. She got them yesterday morning. They were left outside her door. When I asked her about it, she shut me down."

Florence nods. "Yes, she did exactly the same to me this morning, when I asked."

Ava comes back through and is wearing a pair of running trousers and trainers. She has a baggy hoodie on and her hair is tied messily on the top of her head.

"Ready," Ava mutters.

She kisses her mother on the cheek and they open the door.

Ava and Jacob stroll around the busy park which is a meeting point for the city's residents. There are families walking, dog walkers and others exercising. Jacob gets into an in depth conversation about Christmas Day and how much he enjoyed it. They are messing around, laughing and joking. Jacob notices a runner heading towards them, "Hang about. Isn't that your mate, Michael?" Ava follows Jacobs eyes to the man wearing black running shorts and a sports jacket that is zipped up to his chin.

"Oh for goodness sake. Yes." she says awkwardly.

Michael, sweating profusely, slows down in front of them, removing an earpiece from his ear. He leans over to catch his breath.

"I'm gonna leave you two to chat." Jacob slowly walks off.

Ava stands there looking unimpressed.

"Ava, I," he runs a hand through his dark blonde sweat sodden hair. He is still trying to catch his breath. He tries again. "I owe you such an apology. I actually don't know where to start."

Michael struggles to find the words. When he is around her everything makes sense, but he can't articulate it. Ava is enjoying watching him squirm. She stands patiently waiting for the explanation of the flowers she received yesterday.

"I should have never turned up at your apartment and in that state. I'm embarrassed... and -" he pauses.

Ava interrupts him, "So why did you send me flowers yesterday, Michael?"

He runs his hand through his wet hair again.

"I can explain."

"Can you really? After I told you to leave? You then send me flowers on Christmas day? Why?"

He shuts his eyes a second, and prepares himself, holding his hands in front of him.

"I actually ordered them before I turned up at your apartment."

Ava crosses her arms and retorts. "I have completely respected your decision to send me away, and I chose to ignore the flowers. I promise you won't hear from me again."

Jacob returns and Ava decides to end the conversation there. They walk away leaving Michael standing alone wondering if they are a thing after all.

The door bursts open and Ava strides in. "Oh gosh I'm desperate," and runs through to the bathroom.

Jacob stands at the open door. "Psst!"

Florence gets up from the couch and walks over to him. "Yes Jacob?" she asks curiously.

"You'll never guess who we just ran into at the park?"

Florence stares eagerly waiting.

"Michael!" he says raising his eyebrows and smiling.

"And?" she asks with growing impatience.

"Well I don't know what was said because I left them to talk. But put it this way. I was standing way back and even I could see the chemistry between them."

Florence nods. "Okay, I think Ava and I need a little chat."

Jacob makes his excuses and leaves.

"Gosh, that was an emergency." Ava says entering the lounge.

Looking around for Jacob, Florence explains to her that he needed to deal with some stuff.

"Ava. Why don't you come and sit down." Florence pats the seat next to her.

"Why do I feel like I'm about to be told off." Ava laughs.

"How's the counselling going? Are you having any more dreams?"

"It's going really well. I no longer feel emotionally connected to the dreams. So I guess the therapy is working," she nods.

"Okay, well perhaps that journey is coming to an end. Have you begun to date?" Florence asks cautiously, taking Ava's hand in hers.

Ava sighs. "There was someone last year. But he, ...I wasn't ready. He worked at my office." she pauses, "He moved back to his hometown in Albany." Ava swallows hard.

Florence stares at her daughter with love, knowing that Ava is opening up to her. She sits silently.

"I bumped into him at Thanksgiving," she says staring at her fingers twiddling in her own lap. "He, he was with his long-term girlfriend, and she had a stunning ring on her finger."

"So you... and this," Florence pauses, "man had an affair?" She gazes at Ava for eye contact.

"Good God, no. You know I would never do that. When he returned to the city they were back together. But when I was involved with him, he was single." Florence nods and wonders where to take this conversation next.

"Do you love this man, Ava?" she finally asks.

"It isn't a case of loving him, mum. He belongs to another woman. He has made his decision."

Florence turns to the flowers and back at Ava.

"Well, clearly not my darling, otherwise he wouldn't be sending you flowers."

Ava stands up and walks to the glass balcony doors.

She stops and looks at her mother, fully aware that Florence is watching her intensely.

"He has, I saw him today at the park and he told me the flowers were sent before he turned up here before Christmas."

"So he came here? What did he want? What did he say?"

"He," she pauses, "he told me that he couldn't marry her, and..." Ava pauses and her eyes begin to fill.

"Ava, darling. Did you turn him away? Did you purposely self-sabotage your own happiness?" Florence walks towards her daughter and embraces her tightly.

"Mum, I would never do that. After Richard had his affair, I would never be the other woman," she says through her heartbroken tears.

"But Ava. He isn't Richard. Not everyone is going to do to you what he did."

Ava sobs in her mother's arms while Florence strokes her hair and says nothing.

Olivia has organised a dinner for Michael's parents and her own. They are seated in the plush 'State' restaurant within The Empire State building. Michael rushes in, late again. Everyone is patiently waiting.

"Hey, sorry I'm late. I had a client ring at the last minute." He seats himself in the sectioned off booth.

"So." Olivia starts. "We have asked you here to let you know that we have a wedding date and we have also decided to go with The Plaza."

She smiles, taking Michael's hand and squeezes it.

As everyone else is congratulating them, Cora watches her son closely, says nothing and tries to gauge his reaction. He isn't maintaining eye contact with anyone at the table, staring back instead at her. He knows she knows that this isn't what he wants.

Finally, Cora asks, "When is the big day?" and forces a smile.

Olivia replies, "May 22nd. In four months."

Jennifer claps her hands in excitement. Michael's face looks shocked.

"Liv... I thought we said next year?" Moving his hand away from her. Only Cora notices.

"I know, but why wait? Neither of us are getting any younger Mike."

She smiles and looks at the rest of the table.

"Well that's a date then. We must start with the plans," Jennifer confirms.

Cora looks at her son and her heart sinks. She can feel George watching them both sensing that something is wrong, but says nothing.

Michael and Olivia enter their apartment, and Michael switches on the light. Olivia sits on the couch and starts taking off her shoes while Michael starts to pace about.

"Everything okay?" she says while still undoing her shoes.

"No, Olivia. It is not okay!"

"What's the matter?" She is wiggling her toes now that they have been released from her shoes.

"You decided that we're getting married this May, and you didn't think to tell me? I mean, come on. Are you kidding me? It's a pretty big decision and you could have run it by me first!"

"Oh Michael. Stop getting so stressed out. I can see how worried you have been, so I am taking control. Don't you wanna get married?" Standing from the couch, rubbing her hands up his chest sexually to his shoulders and looking at him with desire.

"Of course I do."

She slides her arms inside his suit jacket and slowly removes it, dropping it on the floor behind him.

"Good." She murmurs and places her lips on his. Michael grabs her by the waist, and pulls her closer. Olivia begins to unbutton his white shirt to reveal his hairless chest. She looks into his eyes and rubs his chest with her hands. He tilts his head back and sighs. Only it isn't just Olivia on his mind. Michael grabs her hands and looks at her.

"I'm exhausted and I need to shower." He leaves her standing there.

As he stands in the shower, Michael closes his eyes trying to relive a memory. Ava is wearing her red dress. He can feel her touch as the water trickles down his body. He looks down and his manhood is aroused by it, remembering the feeling of him sliding into her core. His breath shortens as he takes himself in his hand. He closes his eyes and pictures Ava's sweet spot and hears her moaning vividly with pleasure as he pounds her with passion and she pulses around his manhood calling out in gratification for what his body is doing to her. He works to please himself and groans as he comes at the thought of her. Panting under the steaming shower, his satisfaction has been released.

Ava's phone pings. It's from Jacob.

'What are you doing for New Year?'

Ava's sisters are sitting in their uncle's kitchen demolishing the lunch that Daniel has prepared.

"Do you guys want to go out for New Year with Jacob?"

The girls both clap with excitement.

"Oh most definitely." Katalyn agrees and Lydia wraps her arms around Ava's neck.

"Now that sounds like a fantastic idea."

Ava turns to her mother.

"I think I'll give it a miss and stay with you mum. I don't want you to celebrate New Year on your own."

Florence, Daniel and James, all stare at her. Lydia removes her arms from Ava's neck.

"Don't be so ridiculous Ava May!" Florence says "I'll be with James and Daniel."

James confirms "Yes, we are having a get together at the office actually, so you can come to that instead."

Lydia and Katelyn clap their hands and jump around in excitement at their own plans.

Ava replies to his text.

'I won't be coming but the girls are up for it.'

"So Mia." Olivia says, "Now we have you here with us, we have a question for you." Michael smiles broadly and Mia smiles back awaiting to be asked.

"Would you do us the honour of being our bridesmaid?"

Mia is shocked and looks to Michael relieved to see his happily pleading expression.

"Oh my God! Of course, I will. I thought you'd never ask!"

She wraps her arms around both of them.

"Have a great night tonight Mia," Michael says as they leave her apartment.

"You too, love you, Happy New Year, guys." she yells down the hall as they make their way down the stairs. Mia is spending New Year's Eve this year with her Mexican cousins who bought tickets to one of the busiest night clubs in New York. Michael and Olivia have been invited to an event with Donny, Olivia's brother. Michael is not happy but doesn't say anything.

Lydia, Katelyn and Jacob are dancing on the crowded dance floor. Jacob leaves them to make his way through the thick crowd of clubbers to go to the lit up circle bar. He spots Mia and taps her on the shoulder. She spins around.

"Well, well. Who do we have here?" She purrs and he winks back at her.

"Alright, hot Mexican?"

Lydia and Katelyn are dancing and singing to the words of a song.

James, Daniel, Florence and Ava are all on the top floor of TAC greeting guests as they arrive for the New Year's party. James and Daniel are slightly sloshed already and Ava loves to see her uncle relaxing unlike his usual clipped, stressed persona. The entire workforce, some clients and even the corporate owners are here. James makes the introductions. Daniel turns up the sound system they have hired and begins dancing with some of the women from the office. The atmosphere is light and cheerful when Donny makes an appearance, along with two guests. James goes to meet Donny and Florence follows behind, feeling awkward standing on her own.

"Donny, great to see you made it!"

"Ah, James. Thanks for the invite. You remember Michael Johnson," he gestures towards his guest, "and this is his future wife, my sister, Olivia."

James says "Hello" and introduces Florence. It doesn't take her long to realise that this is the Michael that her daughter has spoken about.

"How wonderful to meet you. I'm not in America for long. I just came to visit my daughter for the holidays." she says to Olivia, loud enough for Michael's ears to prick up.

"Sorry? Did you say you're Ava's mother?" he interrupts.

Florence eyes him cautiously.

"Yes that's right. You worked alongside her, didn't you?"

"Yes that's right, Ma'am. Would you excuse me a moment please."

He leaves them talking and wanders through the busy office floor. He can see Daniel singing and dancing with a crowd of people and laughs to himself. Daniel really is the life and soul of the New Year's get together. Michael needs five minutes of peace and walks to the quiet end of the office floor, towards Ava's office.

To his complete surprise there she is with her back turned to him. He slowly opens the door as she whirls around standing in complete shock.

"Michael! What on earth are you doing here?"

He walks in, shuts the door and stands there.

"Um, I'm here with Donny."

They stand silently for a moment. Michael slowly edges towards her. Ava watches and says nothing. She can feel her breath quickening and her heart beating faster as he comes closer.

Florence and Olivia continue to talk, and she finds Olivia opening up to her as they get a drink together. Olivia summarises her lengthy relationship with Michael and his current inconsistencies.

"It's really hard for Mike. He is always seeking approval from my family, you know? He struggles. He has been so stressed since he became a partner at his father's company and seems so distracted."

"Well you know what men are like," Florence agrees, "if they can't cope with too much at any one time." Thinking to herself *'From what Olivia has said, it is obvious that he has as much feeling for Ava as she does for him'*.

"Michael, you shouldn't be in here."

"Neither should you."

Ava and Michael are inches away from each other now and without any further hesitation Michael takes Ava in his arms and kisses her. Ava runs her hands through his hair and she is lifted onto the desk. The office is dark and the twinkling city lights glisten through the window. The music is beating in the distance. The passion grows between them and Michael runs his hands up Ava's bare thighs as she moans in appreciation. He kisses her neck and suddenly the music stops. Ava panics and withdraws from the kiss. Daniel is speaking on the microphone.

"I can't." Ava says as she slides off the desktop.

Michael's reluctance also surfaces.

"Ava, I need to tell you something," he says trying to rearrange himself.

Ava takes a step back and stares at him. She can't see his face very clearly but knows by his tone that what he is about to say is serious.

"I'm here with Olivia too."

Ava is quiet but quite shocked. Michael approaches her again. Without a thought she slaps him around the face.

"Holy shit. Ava, I… I deserved that!"

"How could you! Stay away from me Michael!"

She leaves with a tear rolling down her face which she wipes away, and takes a deep breath as she enters the busy party again.

Michael is left in the shadows of Ava's office, in complete disbelief of what he has done.

"Mum. I'm not feeling too great, I think I'll head back to my apartment."

"Ava, darling. Is everything okay?" Florence says looking at her daughter's pale shocked face.

"I'm just not feeling well."

"Do you want me to come with you?"

"No. I want to be alone. Thanks anyway, mum." She kisses Florence's cheek and disappears.

Florence scans the floor, watching and laughing at Daniel making his speech about how amazing James is and how well TAC is doing. She continues searching the crowd. Olivia and Donny are standing together but Michael isn't with them. Florence turns in the direction of the darkened offices and sees Michael sneaking from the shadows. She knows.

Watching Michael stride towards Olivia and Donny, his body language is cold. She watches as he runs his hands through his hair, and even at a good distance, she can see his withdrawn behaviour.

"Where have you been?" Olivia asks.

"Oh… I bumped into some of my old colleagues." he lies.

"Oh okay." she wraps her hand around Michael's waist while he stands stiff and clenches his fist.

Ava returns to her apartment, sits on the couch and throws her bag on the glass table in front. Her body has been awakened and she is still in complete awe of Michael's presence. Feeling breathless, she still yearns for him and his touch. Yet, she is both angry and frustrated, aroused and confused about what has just happened. Even so, she can feel her core is moist and wanting to be touched.

She begins to pace her apartment. *What has he done to her?* Back on her couch, she can feel that her cheeks are flushed, her body is burning and her chest is heaving with eagerness. She needs to end her arousal. Running her hands down her breasts to between her thighs, she knows that he has awakened her soul which is longing to be pleasured. She rubs her sweet spot through the lace of her lace knickers and throws back her head as she groans at her own pleasure. As her body releases she knows Michael has done this to her. He has lit her sexual fire that had gone out long ago.

Ava wakes to a text from Lydia and smiles as she reads it:

'Hey, how was your night? Mum has asked me to text and see if you are feeling any better?'

Several days have passed and it is time for Florence, Lydia and Katelyn to go home to England. They all stand outside James' house while his driver loads their bags into the boot of the car. Ava says her emotional goodbyes to her mother and sisters.

As she hugs her mother, Florence says, "Remember what I said, Ava." She kisses her daughter's cheek.

James wraps his arm around his niece as they watch the car pull away.

They go back into the house which seems silent. When the chauffeur returns, James says, "I need to get back to the office. Do you mind if I head off, Ava? Will you be okay?"

Ava, slumped on the couch, waves to indicate that she is fine. With that James leaves.

"You're hiding something, baby girl." Daniel says as soon as the coast is clear.

His gaze is intense and Ava knows she isn't going to be able to get out of the truth. She finds herself running her hands through own hair, fully aware of who this reminds her of.

"Oh god where do I even start, Daniel?"

Ava holds nothing back and tells him everything, withholding no details.

"So you love this guy?" Daniel questions.

Ava gets up and paces the lounge.

"I mean, of course I don't. It's lust, it's infatuation, it's everything but love. I thought it was love, but after seeing him on New Year's Eve, I realise that is all it was."

To Daniel, Ava seems to be erratic as she tries to decipher her feelings and her urges.

Mark is already in the building when Ava arrives for her swim. He is making his way to the changing rooms. She is surprised to see him going in as he usually passes her on the way out.

As she enters the cold water, Mark is already into his front crawl but stops to call out, "Hey Ava. Fancy seeing you here at this time."

Ava replies before she starts her lengths. "I know. I have been so busy over the holidays that swimming has been put a bit on the back burner."

They both swim their lengths and Ava finds she's really pushing herself. Coming out of the changing room, Mark is waiting for her.

"You fancy a coffee?"

"Of course. Why not?"

"Great there is a sweet little coffee house around the corner."

They arrive at a quaint cafe and Mark holds the door open for Ava. The owner shouts a "Hello" to Mark as they look for a table. There is one by the window and Mark waits for Ava to sit before sitting himself. The smell of freshly made coffee lingers and muffins lingers in the air.

"So, Ava. This is nice. How were the holidays for you?"

Instantly Ava is regretting this coffee. Mark is incredibly attractive with his blue eyes and blonde hair, but she gets the sense he is reading far too much into this coffee.

"Umm, yeah. It was fabulous, thank you. My family came to see me as a surprise."

"Where'd they come from?"

Ava can feel herself zoning out of this conversation.

"Sorry? I was distracted by the little girl out the window."

"Your family? Where'd they travel from? You know that little girl reminds me of my daughter."

"Oh you have a daughter? How old is she?" Ava asks, not really caring.

"Oh Nancy is four."

"Ah that must have been lovely over the holidays seeing her, and talking all about Santa."

After half an hour of meaningless small talk, Ava makes her excuses and announces she needs to leave.

"Well... it's been great! Perhaps we could go for dinner sometime?" Mark asks.

"Oh Mark... I," Ava pauses, racking her mind for an excuse. "I'm just not looking for someone to date right now. I'm really sorry."

She is shocked by her own admission.

"Hey... no need to apologise, Ava. It's cool. Thanks for the coffee. It was really nice talking to you."

"You too, Mark. Take care and I'll see you at the pool. I'm sure."

Ava darts out the door all too relieved to be out of that awkward situation. She left Mark at the table and she does not want to turn around just in case he is looking. She has realised that she is nowhere near ready to date and can't be bothered with the rigmarole of getting to know someone. Besides, Michael is continually on her mind.

"Joey! How are you?" Michael says as they make their way to the Knicks game in Madison Square Gardens.

"Yeah, I'm good. Super excited for the game!" he grins.

The venue is packed with fans waiting to see their favourite team play basketball. This has been a regular thing for Joey and Michael. They have watched the Knicks since being teenagers. When they were teenagers their father's used to take turns in taking them to the games. Joey was always the real Knicks fan and Michael used to go, just to spend time with his best pal. As Michael got older, he became more addicted to the game and he has really missed this quality time with his friend.

"You got the tickets Mikey boy?"

Michael digs about in his jacket pocket and withdraws the tickets and hands them over to the ticket desk.

"There you go."

They find their seats on row seven of the extremely busy basketball arena in Madison Square Garden.

"Now we know where our seats are Joe, you want a hotdog?"

"You know it. Extra onions and mustard."

Michael goes to the food counter and orders the hotdogs and soda. Handing over the cash, he juggles the hotdogs in one hand and two sodas in the other. It comes from plenty of practice.

Striding down the metal steps back to their seats, he finds Joey chatting away to another Knicks fan wearing a team shirt, baseball cap and foam finger. Michael weaves past the other supporters trying not to spill his soda.

"Sorry buddy.... Excuse me... pardon me." Finally reaching his seat.

The game starts. The fans stand and yell at every slam dunk.

The scoreboard hangs above the centre of the court.

"Oh come on. You gotta be kiddin' me man! That was so close!" Joey yells at the players.

"Crazy! We should have had that!" Michael adds.

They sit and watch the famously tall players running up and down the court dribbling the ball in an intense game. Michael turns to Joey and tries to get his attention.

"Joey!"

"Yeah?" he replies, flicking his eyes from the court to Michael trying not to miss any of the action.

Just then Randle makes a jump shot scoring two points.

"Get in there Randle!" Joey yells with excitement. "Sorry buddy. What was you gonna say?"

"So... Joe... me and Olivia are getting married."

Seconds later, the game halts at the end of the quarter and the players take a break. Michael now has Joey's full attention to ask the question.

"So, as I was saying. Olivia and I are getting married and I was wondering if you'd be my best man?"

Joey takes a few seconds to process what Michael has just asked.

"Are you kiddin' me? Of course I'll be your best man!" He grabs his oldest pal and gives him the biggest manliest hug and pats him on the back.

The two of them have been friends since kindergarten and growing up on the same block. Their mothers met on the first day of dropping their sons off. Both families hung out together, having barbecues and even Thanksgiving dinners in the past. It was only when Michael's parents divorced and the awkwardness between them that the families went their separate ways. It put a slight strain on Michael and Joey's friendship, but they saw it through. Joey's parents are still together and he cannot comprehend what Michael has gone through. The game resumes and the intensity returns. The crowds roar every time someone scores. Michael tries to remain excited, but reality hits him. He is marrying Olivia, in just a few months.

He gets his phone and scrolls to her name.

'Ava! It's Michael. I know you don't want to hear from me. But please spare me some of your time. Please meet me at the Whitney? Tomorrow? Say 6pm? Please Ava! M x'

Ava stands outside the Whitney Museum of American Art thinking to herself 'Why are you doing this?' She shakes off her thoughts, takes a deep breath and makes her way to the entrance. The building is another architectural wonder with a peculiar shape. It is a congregation of rectangles coming together with a triangular shape perched on the top. Ava pays for her ticket and makes her way through the gallery thinking 'Why here?' Never having visited this museum she finds herself drawn to the intricate details of each individual piece of art. The walls are painted white and the rooms are very well lit. She stands admiring one particular piece by Edward Hopper and can see all the individual brush marks on the painting. She can feel his presence behind her.

"Ava?" he says in a whisper.

She cautiously turns and is greeted with a man who looks broken.

"Michael?' she says coldly. "Why have you asked me here?"

Michael looks at her knowing that she is all he has ever wanted. *Why can't she just see that?*. In her presence, he feels whole and she makes him feel alive. Running his hand through his hair, Ava interrupts his thoughts.

"Well... I know you well enough to know that when you run your hand through your hair, it is either bad news or you're feeling awkward. So which one is it?"

He gulps. "Ava... I wanted you to hear it from me, I'm marrying Olivia."

"Well... yes! I already knew that! You got me here to tell me that? Is this some sort of joke? Insult to injury, Michael!"

"No! You're not understanding me! We're getting married this May." The air falls silent around them.

"Unless Ava," he pauses, "unless you give me a reason not to?"

"Is this a joke? So you meet me for a secret rendezvous in an art gallery, to get out of marrying your fiance? Michael I don't have time for this! I'm leaving!"

Turnin on her heels, she goes.

Michael is left alone at the gallery. But he has nowhere to turn or no one to turn to.

Ava runs through the doors of Pedro House in tears. Paying no attention she runs straight into Mr Truman.

"Oh gosh! I'm so sorry!" She tries to make her way to the elevator and he follows after her.

"Miss Turner. You seem a little upset?"

"No shit!" she fires back.

He stands for a moment. He holds the doors so they can't close. "Miss Turner. Come with me."

Ava cautiously follows him as he leads her behind the desk to a door that she had never noticed before.

As they enter, she can see the numerous security cameras and a young man watching over them.

"Julian. Could you give us a minute please?"

Removing his heels from the desk, Julian stands from his swivel chair and leaves.

"Watch over the reception!" Mr Truman demands.

"So... Miss Turner. What has happened for you to be so upset?"

Ava sits silently, the tears rolling down her cheeks.

"Well... can I at least get you a coffee? Or am I right in thinking that the Brits drink tea in an emergency?"

Ava bursts into laughter, and Mr Truman looks confused about what is funny.

"It isn't an emergency. So on this occasion, tea isn't required. It is a love triangle. So I think Vodka is required."

"Ah! Well... Good job I have some in this draw then!" and he gets out a half empty bottle.

Ava explains the whole situation to an unlikely ally and feels a whole lot better for doing so.

"Well... Miss Turner. Here is a secret. I was in love with someone once, and I let her slip through my fingers. I have never met anyone like her since. I understand your turmoil. But don't let it rule your life!"

Ava sits silently for a moment. She realises that her impression of Mr Truman has been all wrong. He is very much like her Harry in England.

"I'm sorry, Mr Truman."

"Call me Henry, Miss Turner."

"Call me Ava, Henry."

Chapter Twenty

April 12th

The wedding is only forty days away. Cora is at the florists with Olivia and her mother, finalising the arrangements. Her phone rings.

"Yeah. That foliage is perfect." As she rummages around in her bag trying to find where the sound is coming from. Finally, in her hands, she looks at the screen. 'George' is flashing on it.

"George. What can I do for you?" she asks distracted by the flowers standing in different metal buckets in front of her. Jennifer and Olivia are nearby looking at other displays.

"Can you talk?"

Cora pauses and watches Olivia excitedly picking single stem flowers.

"Hang on." she whispers to George and then yells.

"Olivia. It's Asha. I gotta take this. Do you mind?"

Olivia shakes her head and continues admiring the flowers.

Cora walks in the opposite direction of Olivia and Jennifer.

"Why do I feel like you are calling about our son?"

"Because that is exactly why I'm calling, Cora. Michael is turning up to work late and leaving early. He is being a real ass. The other day he lost it with Asha for no reason. And there's more."

Cora sighs and feels her stomach churn.

"Go on." She is preparing herself.

"I was going through the credit card statements from last year. Did you receive any flowers from our son at Christmas?" Cora thinks back.

"No, I didn't. Why?"

"Okay. Did you see any flowers in Michael's apartment on Christmas day?" Cora's eyes widen. She knows the answer already.

"No." She pauses, "No, I didn't." She is covering her mouth with her free hand.

"Well neither did I, Cora, neither did I."

Cora says that she will meet with Mia. They haven't had lunch together for a while and she can hopefully get some answers from her.

Cora is waiting outside Michael's apartment. She is there to have a private chat with Michael. Olivia is at a dress fitting with Mia and the other bridesmaids. Michael comes up the stairs and he stops when he sees his mother.

"I thought you'd be at the dress fitting with the rest of them." He comes to the door with his keys. Cora moves aside to let him unlock the door.

"I managed to get out of it."

Michael turns the key and pauses to look at his mother.

"Why would you need to get out of it?" he asks, looking puzzled.

"Let's go inside Michael and we can talk."

Cora follows Michael to the kitchen.

"Mom. What's this about?" They are by the coffee machine with his back to her.

Cora takes a deep breath.

"Michael. Who's Ava?"

Turning around to face her, his mother can see the pain slide across his face.

"Ava, is nobody. Alright?" he says in a raised voice.

Cora raises her eyebrows at his response.

"When you came home Michael, I asked you who you were running from. You lied to me. You were running from her, weren't you?"

Michael runs his hands through his hair and slams his hands on the kitchen worktop.

"Drop it mom. Just drop it!"

Cora moves closer to him, standing on the other side of the counter facing her son.

"How can I just drop it when you are ordering flowers for Ava at Christmas? And you are getting married to Olivia in just over a month?" she demands.

"Mia." he says looking at her, "She doesn't know when to leave it."

"No Michael. Don't deflect. This isn't Mia's fault. I went to her."

"How do you know about the flowers? Have you told Liv?" he asks her quietly.

"Your father rang me Michael. You were smart enough to order off the business credit card, but you forgot your father would check the statements."

"Michael do you love her?" she asks tenderly.

"She doesn't love me and that's all that matters." He opens up to his mother.

"I was talking about Olivia, Michael."

Michael stares at his mother.

"Of course, I love her." Then going back to get mugs for the coffee.

"Michael. You can't marry her if you are in love with someone else. You just can't."

"Mom, I said drop it!" Loudly but with anguish. Then he takes a slow deep breath.

"I love Olivia and I will be marrying her. Do not mention Ava again. You hear me?"

"Michael." she pauses, rubbing her face with both hands. "Does she love you?"

He puts his palms on the worktop opposite her.

"I told her how I felt before Christmas. I turned up at her apartment, and she sent me away. So that's it." he says, knowing that there is far more to the story.

Cora's eyes fill with tears.

"So, you gave up on her?" she whispers feeling her son's heartbreak.

"Ava doesn't want you. So you are going to marry Olivia instead? Is that it?"

Michael finds the signalling coffee machine as an excuse to think. Grabbing the mugs.

"You know what mom? That's exactly how it is. Eleven years I've wasted and..." he pauses, stirring milk into the coffees.

"Oh I see. Your biological clock is ticking. Is that it? So, you marry the next best thing. Because you want to settle down and have a family? What are you doing, Michael?"

He stares at the ceiling and sighs heavily.

"Is this your plan, Michael?" Cora demands.

"I'm not going to say it again, Mom. Drop it!" Slamming his hands on the worktop with force and temper. Cora, upset by the display of emotional anger, takes a step backwards.

"I just hope you know what you are doing, Michael."

Cora is leaving as Michael yells after her.

"Yeah. Because you and dad got it so right, huh?!"

After she shuts the door, he picks up his phone from the countertop.

'Mia, we gotta talk!! Meet me for a drink at Macy's!'

Michael clicks 'Send'.

Immediately, his phone pings.

"Okay, I'll message you when I leave the office. Is everything alright? Love you x x x '

He doesn't even have to think before he responds.

'No it isn't. Talk later!'

Ava and Jacob are out to dinner at Carmine's in Times Square. A personal favourite of Jacob's, it has become their Wednesday tradition since Christmas. The restaurant is bustling with knives and forks clattering on plates and the air is wafting with different delicious aromas. They are choosing their meals from the menu when Jacob blurts.

"So, I hooked up with the hot Mexican. We've been seeing each other on the down low for a while now." Ava looks up from her menu and smiles, and then confusion crosses her face.

"How come you are only telling me this now? If it has been going on for a while? I mean, I knew there was somebody floating around and assumed it wasn't serious, but why tell me now?" she lays her menu down.

Jacob does the same.

"You're absolutely right. There is a reason I'm telling you this now, Ava," he pauses, "Mia has asked me to be her plus one at Michael and Olivia's wedding. I wanted to run it by you first."

Ava's stomach turns, in the realisation that they really are getting married. She freezes.

"But if you're not happy with it, I'll make my excuses." He is shocked at the look on Ava's face.

She picks up her menu and continues to look at it. Then waves a waiter over and gives her order.

Jacob realises that she is ignoring what he has just told her and decides to leave it there.

Ava returns to her usual self for the rest of the evening as they enjoy their meal of juicy meatballs in a tomato sauce full of herbs, on a bed of spaghetti.

Back at her apartment, she shuts the door, lays on her bed and cries. Hugging a pillow with her arms, she sobs as mascara is smudging around her eyes. Each breath between her tears powers the next. She rocks herself hysterically. Her heart is truly breaking. Knowing that he is marrying Olivia, she realises like a tsunami, too late, that she wants him to choose her instead.

Mia arrives at Macy's and Michael is already up the bar with three empty glasses in front of him. She says nothing and sits next to him. He continues to stare in front of him but is aware of her presence.

"Why? Why did you tell my mom about Ava, Mia?" he asks, finally turning to her. Mia looks at him ready for an inevitable argument.

"Because Michael, you are marrying the wrong person. She came to me and told me about the flowers. I knew as soon as she told me that they were for Ava. Perhaps she will talk some sense into you?"

Michael looks at her, his face turning red with anger.

"Mia. How many times do you have to be told to keep out of it, when it comes to my mom! You don't fucking listen to me!"

Mia, shocked by the language, goes to leave.

He stops her and guides her to a booth.

"I leave work early, so I can get to 34th and just get a glimpse of her." He pauses.

Mia sits back down feeling sympathetic.

"I go to 'At the Deli' every day. Just in case she is there. I run in Central Park every day because I know she walks there." Pausing again. "I love her Mia. I am completely in love with her."

Mia throws her arms around him. Then she can feel him sobbing into her neck.

"Why didn't you tell me?" she asks. "Why have you kept this pain inside you?" She hugs him as tightly as she can.

"I haven't told anyone, Mia. I've been living with this alone." he says, wiping his face trying to hold it together.

"So, why are you marrying Olivia, Mike?"

She removes her arms from him, takes his hands and holds them tightly, staring at him with heartfelt love. They sit at the bar. Everyone around them is going about their business, ignorant of his despair that he wants a woman he can't have.

"Because I can't get out of it now. We are less than a month from the wedding, Mia!"

"So you are going to sacrifice your own happiness for Olivia. The woman who turned you down several times because you weren't good enough!" Mia is growing agitated by the very thought of Olivia.

"What am I going to do, Mimi?"

"Mike I can't answer that. Only you can. You have to do what is right for you. What you feel in your soul. If Ava is the one, then you have to go to her."

He begins to sob again. "She doesn't want me Mia. I already tried."

Time stands still in that very moment.

Mia holds him tightly knowing that he is truly broken by his confession that was buried deep inside. Mia can't fix this for her best friend. She doesn't know what to say, so rocks and hushes him. In all the years that they have known each other, she has never seen him as crushed as he is here and now.

Chapter Twenty One

Saturday May 22nd

Ava lays in bed, numb. Her phone rings and it's Jacob. Cutting him off, she clicks it on silent. She knows that today is the day. Her eyes fill with tears and one single tear tumbles down her cheek. She wipes her face and gets up. Today is a day to watch chick flicks and stay tucked away in her apartment. Making coffee, completely engulfed in her own thoughts, her phone rings again. It's her mother. She turns it off.

Michael and Joey are at his apartment. The lounge area has black suits and crisp freshly pressed white shirts ready to be used. Michael feels sick while Joey is bouncing about with excitement that his best friend is getting married. Joey did his duty as Best Man and stayed with the groom last night.

Mia arrives at the apartment and knocks on the door. Joey opens it.

"Mimi!!" He grabs her in his arms and swings her around. Mia tells him to go and get breakfast for them all. It will be the 'Last Supper' for the three friends before Michael ties the knot. Once Joey has gone, Mia goes to Michael who is sitting on the edge of his bed.

"Are you ready for this, Mike?"

She takes his hands. Michael stands and faces her.

"More than ever."

"You know there is still time to change your mind." she says quietly, looking into his eyes. He shrugs off what she has said and goes to shower.

The wedding is at 3 p.m. and they have plenty of time to relax.

Ava is dressed in a pyjama top and shorts to match and watching an appropriate film called 'My Best Friend's Wedding'. She is crying again. Julia Roberts is her favourite actress and this film signifies everything about how she is feeling today. Ava knows what a wedding day entails and the excitement it generates yet she feels so depressed. The actress declares her love in the movie and Ava cries with jealousy that she never had this courage. The apartment is a pigsty. Outside, the sun is shining brightly and dazzles her, so she walks over to shut out the light with the heavy curtains and returns to the couch and wraps the duvet tightly around her.

Mia, Michael and Joey, are eating their breakfast together, laughing and joking. They are enjoying bagels with soft cheese and bacon rashers. Mia notices the time and has to go to Olivia's parents to get ready. It's 1 p.m. She hugs Michael as he sees her to the door.

"Not long now. See you in a couple of hours."

Michael whispers in her ear.

"I love you Mia. Thank you for being there for me and holding my hand every step of the way." Finishing with a long meaningful kiss on her forehead.

It's 2:45 p.m. and Michael is standing at the front of the Terrace Room, in front of the guests. Joey is standing next to him. His brothers Asha and Andy are the ushers and they are indicating to arrivals which side of the aisle to sit. Every chair is dressed with a cream organza bow. Beautiful floral displays of seeded eucalyptus and white roses, lily grass, baby's breath and calla lilies surround the room.

Michael continuously runs his hands through his hair.

"Hey, Mike, don't panic. She'll show." Joey says patting his back, trying to calm his nerves.

The Terrace Room is rapidly filling with smartly dressed guests. Michael can feel beads of sweat on his forehead. He does not want to turn around to see the excited throng staring at him. He can feel the anxiety building within him. He tugs at his collar trying to create some room so he can swallow. He tugs again and again until Joey notices and takes a look.

"What, is your button done up to tight?"

Michael looks away from Joey's eyes, who straightens Michael's cream cravat. The music starts.

The Terrace Room decorated for the ceremony with lighting provided by the crystal chandelier glistening above looks spectacular as Olivia enters. Michael continues staring ahead. His heart beating faster by the second. He can feel Joey turning around to look at her. Olivia looks breathtaking. The long sleeved gown of white pleated satin has a sweetheart bodice, covered with a wide line lace. The veil trails over her elegantly tied hair, down her back. She strolls step by step with her father who finally leaves her to join Michael.

The music comes to a stop. Michael turns to his future wife. He cannot get over how beautiful she looks. The registrar addresses the guests.

"We gather here today to be a witness in the matrimony of Olivia Clarke and Michael Johnson." Olivia turns to Michael and mouths concerned.

"Michael."

He looks at her and a tear rolls down his cheek. She smiles while he licks his lips and swallows hard.

"I'm sorry." His brow is creasing and he runs both hands through his hair. Shaking his head, "I can't. I can't marry you, Liv."

Olivia stands completely shocked. Her eyes fill with tears. Michael leans to her and whispers in her ear.

"I'm sorry. I just can't." He kisses her cheek, he turns, makes his way down the aisle and then runs out of the room.

The guests all watch in complete disbelief. Olivia stands at the altar and slumps to the floor in her wedding dress. Her father and mother go to her. Joey stands completely confused, and Mia and Cora run for the exit. George stops Cora.

"Did you know about this?" he asks, holding her arm.

"Do you honestly think I'd let him go through with it, if I thought he'd run George. We need to find him."

"Okay, I'll go to the office!"

Joey comes over. "What the heck is going on?"

Mia tugs his arm and says in his ear, "We don't have time to explain. Come with me."

The main wedding party disburses in different directions.

Olivia's father calls out, "I knew that son of a bitch was never good enough for my Liv!"

Mia, Cora, Joey and Vanessa are standing outside the front of the Plaza Hotel. George has already gone. Michael's brothers and sister are going to their homes to see if he turns up. Cora calls a neighbour in Albany to see if he has gone there. Joey decides to go home just in case Michael turns up at his.

Cora turns to Mia.

"Where does Ava live?"

Mia, in her rustic pink silk spaghetti strap bridesmaid dress, flags a cab down.

"34th Pedro House."

Cora runs around to the other side and gets in.

"As fast as you can. Okay?"

Ava is asleep on the couch. A loud bang startles her and she can hear Mia shouting through the door.

"Ava! Open up!" she calls out, frantically knocking.

Ava opens the door.

"Mia. What on earth are you doing here?"

"Is he here?"

Ava looks at Cora, confused.

"Is who here?"

Cora stands in front of Ava who is half dressed and half asleep.

"So, you are the woman that my son has been running from?"

Ava's expressionless face begins to awaken.

"Mike left Olivia at the altar Ava. Is he here?" Mia asks.

Cora turns to Mia's worried face.

"You go back to your apartment. He may well go there. I'd like to talk to Ava. I'll then come to yours and we can carry on looking. Alright."

Ava stands completely dumbfounded at what she has just heard.

"Do you mind if I come in?"

Ava cautiously lets Cora enter.

"Do you mind?" Cora gestures to the closed curtains.

"No," she says, feeling embarrassed, and folding her arms trying to support her hanging loose breasts under her top.

Cora in her golden satin dress suit, turns back to Ava and takes a seat at the table. Ava sits at the other end. Linking her fingers, Cora starts.

"You know as a child Michael always worried his father and me. He was always so sensitive." She smiles fondly at the memory.

"He was never a deceitful child. If the twins misbehaved, he always told us, and when his sister suffered her attacks, he would look after her."

Her chest rising with a sigh, she looks at Ava.

"As a mother you always try to guide them in life and to make the right decisions. But eventually, they are too old for that advice." She swallows.

"My mother always says this." Ava replies and Cora nods in agreement.

"If he had married her today, it would have been a mistake, Ava. Now, my son seems to think that you don't love him?"

She tilts her head to one side and gazes as at Ava.

"But I'm not entirely sure that is the case. Do you?"

A tear rolls down Ava's face.

"Ah. Just as I suspected. He didn't fight hard enough for you." Cora has walked around to Ava and wipes the tear from her face.

Ava lets out a little sob. Cora cups her arms with her hands and gives them a little rub.

"Now on the very rare occasion Michael was naughty as a child, he would run and hide himself away. That is what he is doing now. Where would he hide Ava?"

Ava shrugs.

"I don't know." she says through her tears, shaking her head.

Cora nods and gives her arms a light squeeze of affection.

"Well Ava. It really was a pleasure to meet you at last. I'm going to find out if anyone has found where Michael is. If he calls, or turns up can you let me know he is safe, please?" She hands her a card.

"Of course I will. But I doubt he'll show up here."

Once Cora has left, Ava feels completely embarrassed at the state of her apartment. She washes up, tidies up, hoovers the floors and makes her bed.

Several hours pass.

She is standing under the shower washing away her filth and tears.

Cora's question *'Where would he hide?'* plays over and over in her mind.

Ava is sitting watching the news, still completely in shock from the revelation. Michael didn't marry Olivia, yet he hasn't turned up at her apartment. The sun is now setting.

Her phone pings. It's Jacob.

'Have you heard anything yet mate? Mia's really worried! X x'

Ava sighs, thinking everyone has got this so wrong. She replies,

'No! Nothing, I'll let you know if he does turn up. X x'

Trying to suppress her anxiety, she makes beans on toast which is quick and easy. Ava cuts through the toast with her knife and fork and takes a bite.

"He wouldn't come here!" She thinks to herself.

Finishing her snack, she begins to wash up. Then a realisation hits her. She plonks the sponge and plate in the water.

"He wouldn't, would he?" she mumbles to herself.

For some reason she just can't shake the feeling off.

What if she is right? What if that is where he is hiding?

The decision is made. Ava goes to the bedroom and uses a clip to tidy her curly hair up, her fingers shaking. She grabs a light jacket and slips on some shoes and heads for the elevator.It seems to take a lifetime to arrive. She steps in and presses the Ground Floor button. As it descends she starts laughing, feeling like she is crazy for doing this. Mr Truman watches her run across the lobby and out of the front door and smiles at her strange behaviour.

Ava sprints from one block to the next without stopping, occasionally accidentally bumping into other pedestrians. She stops to help an older lady who has dropped her shopping thanks to Ava barging into her.

"Gosh I'm so sorry. Let me help you."

"Oh it's alright." Picking up her rolling oranges.

Ava hands her the last orange and apologises again.

Breathlessly arriving at her destination, she runs up the steps and into the building to the front of the line.

"Hi, hello." Interrupting a man issuing tickets, "I need a ticket for one!"

"I appreciate that, Ma'am. But you can't jump the line. Can you please take your place at the end of it. Thank you.' Gesturing at the other sightseers. Ava does as she is told and waits, increasingly growing impatient. Finally, after twenty minutes of waiting she is back at the counter.

"So you'd like a ticket for one?"

"Yes please. I'm kind of in a hurry." Ava reminds him as he slowly issues one.

"So have you been to visit us before? Here is a brochure to help you get around."

Ava snatches it and runs to the elevators. Inside one she pressed the button labelled '84'.

It seems to take forever, but finally she sees 81, 82, 83 on the digital display and then the door opens on the 84th floor. Stepping out, she takes the deepest breath noticing that her whole body is shaking with fear. There, standing alone in the viewing room overlooking Manhattan with his back to Ava, is Michael. He has his wedding suit on with the top button undone and his cravat loosely hanging around his neck. He is leaning on his elbows on the metal railings. She pauses, not knowing what to do. Does she approach him? He starts to walk up and down the viewing platform punctuated by a hand running through his hair. She stands watching him. Turning in her direction, he catches the glimpse of her.

Michael looks down to the ground nervously. Ava slowly approaches him silently.

He shakes his head.

"I couldn't do it. I couldn't marry her, Ava." he says beginning to cry. "How could I marry her, Ava? How could I marry someone when my heart belongs to someone else?"

The tears roll down Ava's face.

"I love you Ava, and I have tried to fight it. My god, I tried. But, I can't. I love you with everything I have inside of me. You make me feel alive. I know how crazy that sounds, but I can't help how I feel. I'm infatuated with you."

Ava laughs through her tears. He sobs and Ava sobs with him. They embrace each other.

Michael holds her head in his hands and stares into her eyes.

"I love you Ava Turner. I should have fought harder. I should have told you how I felt a long time ago. I should have never run away."

Sightseers weave past the couple to gets views of Manhattan. No one notices them.

Ava stares passionately into his eyes, tears rolling down her face.

"I," she pauses while Michael wipes away her tears, "I love you too." Whispering as she finally admits the truth to Michael and herself. He embraces and lifts her in his arms.

Ava has fought against her feelings and stopped herself from loving the man of her dreams. Right here, right now however, it feels just perfect for her. This is where she belongs.

"You do realise that you have half of New York City looking for you."

He puts her down, pausing to gaze at the woman he really loves.

"Let's not worry about that right now."

Michael puts a hand behind Ava's head and brings her face to his. He drives his lips to hers and their tongues entwine, igniting their bodies as they become one. They kiss passionately, embracing each other ignoring the spectacular views around them.

Epilogue

They are standing back on the 84th floor of the Empire State Building.

"So Ava." Michael pauses as the saliva runs dry in his mouth.

"It's been the most incredible year."

She stares at him wondering what he is doing. He is making a real pig's ear of what he is trying to say.

"Oh, Michael. What are you doing?" Ava laughs as he kneels on the floor in front of her.

"Okay, here goes." he sighs heavily.

"Here goes what?"

"Ava. I love you with everything I have. You have brought me so much happiness."

Her chest tightens. *'Is he about to do what I think he is?'* Ava thinks to herself.

"I had no idea that this was going to be so hard!" he sighs again and runs his hand through his hair.

The man she loves is falling apart in front of her. She gets down on the floor with him.

"Michael, you don't have to do this."

The tears roll from his eyes with pure love and devotion he has for her.

"Ava May Turner. Will you do me the honour of becoming my wife?" He pauses to take a breath,

"Will you marry me?"

She looks at him bewildered thinking. *'Is he serious? Is Michael really asking me to marry him?'*

Michael grabs Ava's hands and looks into her eyes. She stares at him for a long moment before replying, "Michael, you don't have to do this."

"Ava, I do. I love you, and this is what I want."

Ava stares all around her and sees they have an audience of spectators.

"So. What d'you say, Ava?"

Staring all around them again, Ava looks at Michael with the same love.

"Yes. Yes of course I'll marry you Michael James Johnson." There is a massive burst of applause from onlookers who have realised what is going on.

Michael leans over and kisses the future Mrs Johnson and presents a beautiful unique platinum solitaire diamond ring in a box. He slides it on her ring finger and kisses her again.

Shock is now present on Ava's face.

There is an outburst of applause around them again as Michael lifts Ava and swirls her around on the spot.

"I love you Ava May."

"I love you too Michael."

They return to their apartment which was originally just Ava's.

Mia calls Ava on her mobile phone.

"Hey Mia. Are you okay?"

"Not really. Are you free? I need to see you. Like now!"

"That sounds serious. Is everything okay?"

"No. Not really. I can't say anything over the phone!"

"Okay. Not a problem. We'll be with you as quick as we can!"

"No! Don't! Come without him."

The phone goes dead. Michael walks up to her.

"Everything okay?"

Ava looks at Michael puzzled by the whole conversation she has just had.

"No! That was Mia. She wants me to go to her. Right now." she replies, concerned.

"Really? Okay so let's go. We can tell her our news."

"No... she asked me to come alone."

"Did she say why?"

"She couldn't say anything over the phone."

Michael looks surprised but accepts that Mia only wants to see Ava and not him. It is the first time Michael has ever felt that Mia is shutting him out.

An hour later, Ava arrives at Mia's apartment. She is still confused why she is there.

She knocks. "It's Ava, open up."

Mia opens the door and mascara is smudged around her eyes.

"Mia. Whatever has happened? You look terrible?" Mia hurries Ava through the door and shuts it promptly. As she turns in her friend's direction, Mia stands pale and in total shock.

"I've been feeling pretty ropey these last few days." She pauses and sits herself on the breakfast bar stool.

Ava senses the next sentence is going to be very important, she stands rigid.

"So... I decided to do a pregnancy test... and... well I'm pregnant Ava!"

Ava stands shocked starting to process the news. Her mind races, trying to evaluate the last few months, weeks and now seconds, that has brought her to ask this question.

"Who's the father?"

"Well, who do you think it is? Christ, Ava! It's Jacob of course." Mia fires back.

"What! You are joking? He has been gone for over six weeks now. He is travelling around Europe right now. It's not like we can even contact him Mia. Jacob doesn't even have a phone!"

Jacob had broken his phone on a group night out. Not being on social media makes him virtually impossible to find, to contact. He had vowed once he had settled he'd be in touch... only that hasn't happened yet.

Mia and Jacob had both dropped the 'L' word about six months ago, feeling content and comfy within their relationship. Jacob began to get itchy feet. Travelling is in his bones, it is a part of who he is. After the tears, the arguments Mia accepted that this is something he needed to do. Their relationship ended well and passionately, Jacob said he *'may well be back.'*

So what is Mia to do now? Can Ava help her dear friend? Will Mia turn to Michael, her dearest and oldest ally?

.